# TO TEMPT A TIGER

TIGER SHIFTERS 5

KAT SIMONS

T&D PUBLISHING

TO TEMPT A TIGER



Published 2015 by T&D Publishing
Cover art design © 2015 and 2019 The Killion Group
Interior book design © 2019 T&D Publishing
ISBN-13: 978-1-944600-16-7 (Trade Paperback Edition)



This is a work of fiction. All of the characters, places, organizations, and
events portrayed are either products of the author's imagination or are used
fictitiously. Any resemblance to actual persons, living or dead, business
establishments, events, or locales is entirely coincidental.

First printing: April 2019
For information, contact T&D Publishing www.TandDPublishing.com

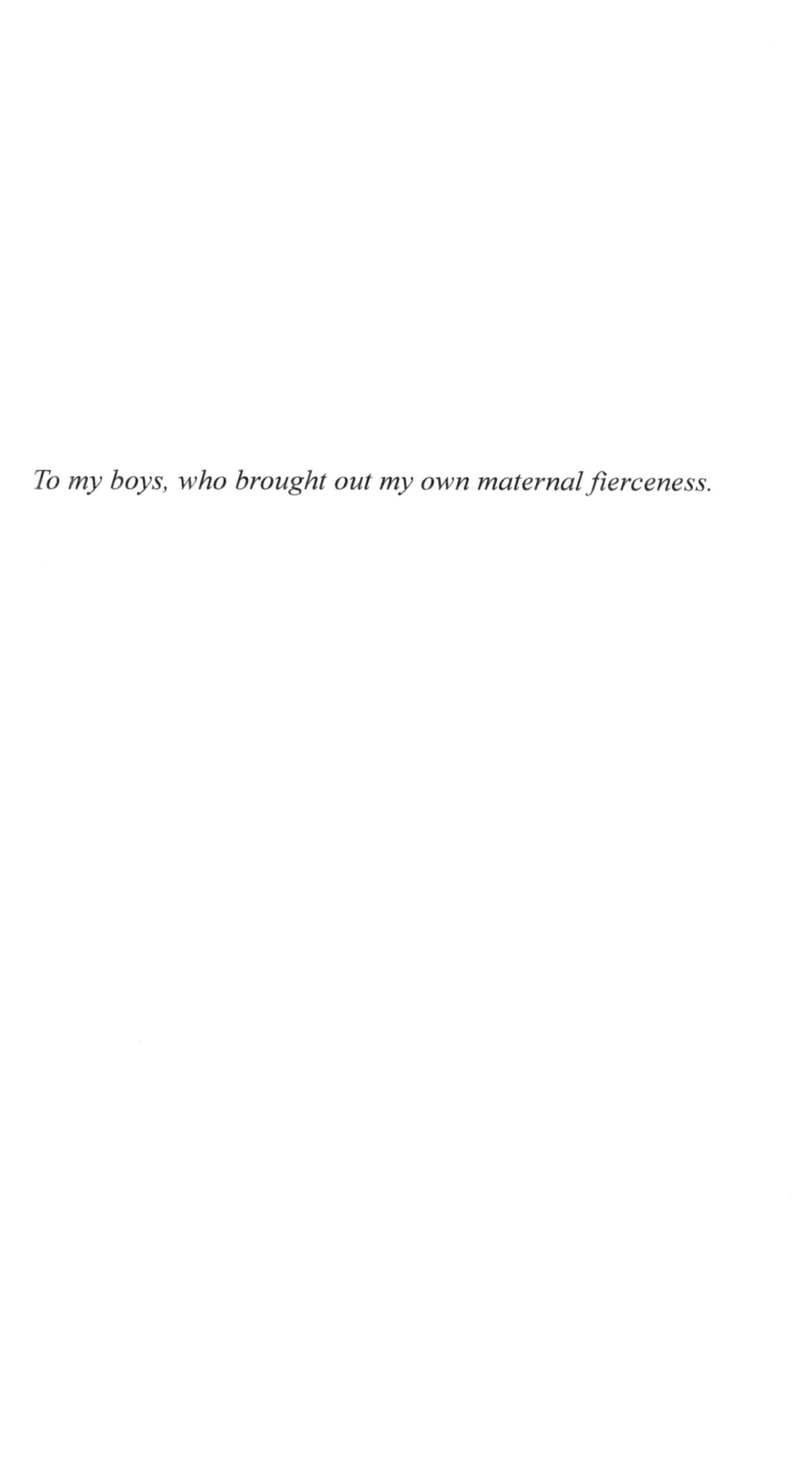

*To my boys, who brought out my own maternal fierceness.*

Rose Callaghan hugged her daughter, rocking her as another wave of pain wracked her little body. Panic and torment twisted in her gut, emotions she'd almost gotten used to over the last year. "I'm here, baby. It'll be okay."

"Hurts, Mommy."

"I know, I know. We'll fix it. We'll find a way."

The doorbell rang. Rose ignored it. Whoever it was could come back later. She rubbed the sweat-soaked hair from her daughter's brow, wondering if she should take her to the emergency room again. It never helped. Nothing helped. The doctors never uncovered the problem. No test had produced an explanation. No specialist had found an answer. No one knew why her daughter went through these episodes of extreme pain.

All her prayers to God, Mary, and all the saints she

could remember from mass didn't seem to be working either. But she had to do something.

Rose was desperate—she just didn't know where else to turn.

The doorbell rang again, followed by insistent knocking.

She growled then said, "Baby, I need to go get that. I'll be right back."

Zoe nodded, but as soon as Rose released her, she curled up into a ball on her bed, rocking as another wave of pain visibly shivered over her skin.

Rose ran to the front door, grumbling kid-safe curses, ready to take the hide off whoever was there. Why couldn't they take the hint and just go away?

The doorbell rang again, and Rose hissed a not-kid-friendly curse. She threw open the door, her mouth open to yell at whoever it was—until she saw the man on her front step. She froze, her brain momentarily too stunned to work.

Vladimir Dubrovsky. The love of her life. The man she'd planned to marry.

The man who'd accused her of cheating on him and left her when he found out she was pregnant.

Rose blinked as the reality of Vlad being on her doorstep sank in. He looked the same—dark hair, dark eyes, sharp, sexy features, the perfect mouth, and a body designed to make a woman's mouth water.

"Hello, Rose," he said. "I realize this is a little…unexpected."

His voice was still that deep rich octave that had always made her shiver. She released a loud huff.

"Unexpected?" She wanted to laugh. She grabbed his arm and jerked him inside. "Thank God. Get in here."

His wide-eyed shock might have given her some satisfaction, if she wasn't so worried.

"Your daughter is sick," she said, dragging him into her living room. "The doctors can't tell me what's wrong. She's in pain right now. What did you pass on to her? This isn't anything from my side—we've run tests and done the research. You need to tell me everything about your family medical history."

Vlad stood in her living room staring at her, his head angled down slightly, his brow furrowed. He looked at her like she was speaking a foreign language.

Her patience didn't stretch that far. "Damn it, Vlad, snap out of it. I need your help. What the hell is wrong with our daughter? While we're standing here wasting time, she's hurting, and I have to stop it. If you have any information that will help, you need to tell me. Now."

"This isn't the reception I was expecting."

"I don't have time for that right now. Can you help or not? If not, get out."

He shook his head like a dog shaking off water and straightened. "May I see her?"

She hesitated. This man had abandoned them. She hadn't seen or heard from him in four years. She wasn't sure she wanted him around her daughter—even if he was Zoe's father.

But if he could help with Zoe's pain...

The familiar panic and desperation churned in her

stomach and tightened her muscles. "Do you know what's wrong with her?" she asked.

"I might. Is the pain cyclical? Does it comes and go? Does she complain her muscles and bones feel like they're stretching and aching? Has she ever said her body feels like it's coming apart?"

"Yes! The doctors have tried a bunch of stuff and none of it works."

"None of it would. May I see her?" he asked again.

This time Rose didn't hesitate. "Come on."

If he could help with Zoe's pain, she might just be able to forgive him for breaking her heart. Maybe. She'd certainly stop wishing the torments of hell on him.

At the entrance to Zoe's bedroom, she spun to face him. The move brought them up close, and for an instant, her breath caught. He still smelled like the most delicious thing ever—spice and musk and male.

She pushed the thought aside and pointed a finger at him. "Don't scare her or hurt her. If you do anything that pisses me off, you're out of here. I'm too scared and worried about her to put up with nonsense. Also, no cursing." She turned and walked into her daughter's brightly decorated white and yellow room.

"Zoe. Someone's here to see you."

"No doctors." Zoe's frown was set, stubbornness in every cute, chubby little line of her face. Then her body jerked and she moaned.

Rose forgot about Vlad as she hurried to her daughter. "Baby, I'm here. I'm here. It's going to be okay. I promise." She pulled Zoe into her arms.

"Mommy, it hurts."

"I know, baby. We'll fix it." Rose hated that she said this every single time and hadn't been able to fulfill the promise. The words were like ash in her mouth.

"Zoe." Vlad's tone was soothing and soft.

Rose blinked. She'd almost forgotten him in those seconds of hearing Zoe's pain in her voice.

"My name is Vlad. I'm not a doctor, but I might be able to help you. Can I sit next to you?"

She glanced up at Rose, pain pinching the skin around her beautiful dark eyes—eyes that had always reminded Rose of Vlad's. Rose nodded her approval.

Zoe looked at him. "You got a funny name."

He smiled, then very gently sat next to her on the bed. "When the pain comes, does it feel like your skin is stretching?"

She nodded.

"Do you…see any images in your mind when the pain hits? Does anything pop up in your imagination?"

"Tigers."

He straightened and sucked in a sharp breath.

"What?" Rose asked. "What is it? Why are tigers significant?"

He ignored her questions and focused on Zoe. "I'm going to talk you through breathing and things to think about that should help ease the pain. Okay?"

Rose glared. Positive thinking wasn't going to help her baby.

"I want you to take a long, slow breath," Vlad coached.

"Can't. Hurts."

"I know. But this will help. I promise. One long deep breath, and imagine the way your arms feel when you feel good."

Zoe nodded as she tried to take a deep, stuttering breath.

"That's it. Good girl. Now close your eyes and concentrate on how your whole body feels when you feel good. How your two legs feel. What the shoes on your feet feel like. What it feels like to wiggle your toes against the inside of your shoes. Got it?" He looked up at Rose. "What's her favorite toy or game? Something that involves physical sensation."

Rose snatched up Zoe's special blanket and handed it to him.

"I want you to imagine feeling your blanket against your fingers," he continued, speaking to Zoe. "Do you remember what if feels like? Concentrate on the soft material against your skin."

"She sucks on the corner," Rose added.

Vlad nodded. "Remember what the corner feels like against your lips, on your tongue. How the blanket feels when it touches your cheek."

As he talked in slow, rhythmic, soothing tones, Zoe's breathing evened out and the tight lines around her eyes and mouth eased. Her little body relaxed and her shoulders slumped.

"Feeling better now?" Vlad asked.

She opened her eyes and smiled. "Better. I tired."

"You rest, baby," Rose said. Vlad stood and Rose tucked Zoe into her bed, making sure she had her favorite blanket in hand. "I'll be in the living room if you need me."

She nodded, then looked up at Vlad, her dark eyes narrowing toward sleep. "Thanks for stopping the pain."

"You're welcome."

Rose felt tears pricking her eyes and sniffed them back. She didn't like Zoe seeing her upset, not so soon after an episode. She motioned to Vlad, and they left Zoe to sleep.

In the living room, Rose stood for a long moment just staring at the pale carpet and breathing deeply. She felt so drained she wanted to sleep, too. And cry. She desperately needed to cry.

But she refused to do it in front of Vlad.

"Why are you here?" She kept her back to him until she was sure the tears pricking at her eyes wouldn't fall.

"I'm not sure how to start."

She finally faced him. "Let me start then…by saying thank you for helping Zoe. If you can tell me how to do that, I'd appreciate it. Then you can leave."

Vlad scowled. "I can't leave you."

"You did before."

"That's not what I meant. It's… This is a complicated story."

"I'm too tired for stories, Vlad." She crossed her arms and braced her legs to stave off the emotional exhaustion weighing on her. She wouldn't let him see her pain, only her anger. Even if he had just helped with her daughter.

"I was expecting a different reaction to my being here," he said.

"What?"

He shrugged. "I thought you might slap me."

"Maybe if Zoe hadn't been in the middle of an episode, I would have."

The corner of his mouth lifted, and Rose's heart thumped hard. Damn him, how did he do that to her with just a smile? She hated him. It didn't make sense that she could feel anything else for him, especially not this longing.

"Don't get cocky," she told him. "I still might slap you if you don't get to the point and then get out."

"I'll start with an apology then," he said.

She snorted. "Little late for that now."

"It's offered anyway."

"Why?"

He paused before saying, "I have reason to believe I was mistaken when I left."

She gave him a deadpan stare that would have shriveled a weaker man. "Really? What led you to this epiphany?"

"Discovering I had a half sister I didn't know about. Seeing the state Zoe was just in confirmed my suspicions."

"How does you having a sister have anything to do with our past?"

"I was telling you the truth when I said we couldn't have kids. At least, the truth as I knew it. You and I should not have been able to conceive a child. Because of that, I was left with no alternative but to think you'd been with another man."

"We did have a child. I didn't cheat on you. And if you'd truly loved me, you should have trusted me enough to believe me."

"I believe you now."

"Why now? Why were you so convinced back then that we couldn't have kids?"

All those years ago, he'd been very clear about the fact that they wouldn't be able to have children naturally. He'd always seemed sad when he talked about not having kids, and she'd really wanted them, too. But he'd been clear—if she wanted them, she either needed to find someone else, or they'd have to consider alternatives like adoption. She'd been prepared to adopt. So long as she and Vlad were together, it didn't matter how they built their family. At least not to her.

When she'd realized she was pregnant, she'd been thrilled, thinking whatever Vlad had been told about his inability to reproduce had been a mistake. She'd expected him to be as excited as she was, and she'd even deluded herself into thinking he'd propose the moment he heard the news.

But he hadn't proposed.

He fisted his hands against his thighs. "You're not going to believe what I'm about to tell you. But for Zoe's sake, you need to know the truth. Then we need to go somewhere safe for a few weeks."

"Whoa, whoa, whoa. What are you talking about? Why would we need a 'safe' place?"

"I'm pretty sure my brothers have figured out...about Zoe."

"Vlad, you are as clear as mud right now. What the hell?"

"Okay. The truth." He braced his feet a little farther

apart and met her gaze. "I'm a tiger shapeshifter. Tigers and humans aren't supposed to be able to have children. That's why I thought you'd cheated on me. Then I learned about my sister. Her father is human, but her mother—my mother—was a tiger. Turns out it is possible for me to have children with a human woman. And if my brothers learn Zoe is my child, they will try to kill her."

Rose pointed to the door. "Out. Now. I won't have a crazy man around my daughter. Out!"

"Rose…"

"No." She flexed her hands, making fists and releasing them in an attempt to keep her anger in check, but her entire body was stiff and ready for a fight. "No. This is nonsense. I can't believe I even let you in my home."

"I know this is scary and hard to understand."

"Not hard. You're insane. Have you always been insane? Is that what's wrong with Zoe?"

He held his hands at his sides, loose and open. "Rose, I'm pretty sure Zoe can shape shift, too. No, not pretty sure. I'm certain. That's what's causing her pain. Her body is trying to do something…well, something that's natural for my kind."

"That's even more ridiculous. Vlad, get out of my home now or I'm calling the cops. No, first I'm going to kick your ass. Then I'll call the cops."

"And then what? How will you help our daughter? How will you keep her alive if my brothers come after her? They'll kill you too, Rose. I can't let that happen."

"Why the hell would they want to kill us? No, this makes no logical sense."

But a small, ever-worried part of her thought, what if some of this was true? What if his brothers were insane, too, and they came after Zoe? Could she protect her daughter against a bunch of crazy people?

Her mind raced. Her dad had several guns he could loan her. She'd get those from him. Then she could get a security system installed. She wasn't sure where she'd get the money for that—taking care of Zoe, even with the excellent medical insurance she had through work, was expensive. But she'd figure it out. Her parents would help. Then she'd have to talk to the police and see if they could do something for her…

She was deep in thought, considering her options, when Vlad snapped his fingers in her face. He was standing in front of her, so suddenly she hadn't even realized he'd moved. She gasped and stepped back, but he grabbed her arms.

Panic pumped into her blood, and she moved on instincts that far outpaced her conscious thought. She grabbed his elbows, folded backward, and using her feet for extra leverage, flipped Vlad over her head, sending him careening into the opposite wall.

She rolled to her feet and spun to face him, taking a defensive stance, prepared to beat the ever-loving crap out of him if he came at her again. In fact, she almost hoped he did because kicking his ass would feel very, very good.

To her utter shock, he laughed. Laid out flat on his back, staring up at the ceiling, he laughed so hard tears leaked from the corners of his eyes.

She frowned and relaxed her stance—a little. He really was crazy. She had to get him out of her house.

He angled his head back to look at her. "I forgot about your black belts. That'll teach me."

She'd been training in aikido and jujitsu since she was Zoe's age. Before starting college, she'd spent a year in Japan studying under a top aikido sensei. All her training and practice meant a lot of her reactions were so instinctive she didn't have to think about them. She just flowed into motion with a speed that surprised most people who didn't know her well.

Her martial arts experience had been one of the things Vlad had said he loved about her.

That memory hurt more than it should, so she pushed it aside.

"Don't grab me again," she said, her voice raspy with emotion.

"I didn't mean to startle you. But you weren't listening to me—as usual—and I was just trying to get your attention."

"Figure out a better way of doing that next time. I take that back. There won't be a next time. You need to leave."

He rolled to his feet with a grace that made her scowl. No man should move that easily after being thrown on his ass. He seemed to have learned his lesson, though, because he kept his distance.

"Rose, I can't abandon you. Not again. Not when I know you're in danger."

"I'll take care of it. I've been taking care of things all on my own for years."

"Really?" He nodded to the bedroom. "That was 'taking care of things?'"

She crossed to him and slapped him hard enough to sting her hand. "Out. Now." The slap had felt too good. If he didn't leave now, she was afraid she might just hit him again.

He set fingers to his cheek and gave her a rueful half smile. "I deserved that. I'm sorry."

"You deserve worse."

"Yes. I do."

She crossed her arms to keep from pummeling him, and to hide the way her hands were shaking. Having him here, reminding her she was failing to help Zoe, when *he* was the one who'd left, it was all too much.

But worse was her physical reaction to him. Standing this close, staring into his dark eyes, her pulse pumped and her breath came in deep, sharp pants. Lust and need tightened low in her stomach. She wanted to lean into him, follow up that slap with a kiss that would scorch them both. Her fingers itched to take his face in her hands, to hold him in place while she kissed him until the desire she hadn't felt since he left was satisfied.

It was a terrible, embarrassing, stupid reaction. And it made her even angrier.

She dropped her chin and stared at him. If looks could kill, Vlad would be the one writhing in pain now.

"Okay, none of this is fair," he said. "I am truly sorry. And I'm here to help. You don't have to do this alone anymore."

She sighed, feeling so overwhelmingly tired she just wanted him gone. "Go away, Vlad."

"No."

"Damn it—"

"I am not leaving you to face my brothers alone. And I'm not leaving Zoe to the pain she's going through when it's not necessary."

That arrow hit home. She paused. Zoe's pain wasn't necessary? He knew how she could stop her daughter's agony? "What do I need to do for her?"

"You need to allow me to teach her how to shift so she can let her tiger out when it needs to get out."

She drove her fingers through her hair and pulled at the strands to ease some of the pressure on her skull. "There are no such things as shapeshifters."

Vlad's expression turned thoughtful. "My sister...she was pretty terrified when she saw me shift, but... Rose, I don't want to scare you, but I *need* you to believe me. For our daughter's sake. If you'll allow me, I'll shift for you so you can see I'm telling the truth."

# CHAPTER TWO

Vlad held his breath as he waited for her answer. This was a harsh way to introduce her to the tiger shifter world. If he had more time, he'd go slowly, ease her into the reality she had to face. Unfortunately, now that his brothers were on Rose's trail, he didn't have that kind of time.

He really, really hoped if she said yes, the shift didn't send her into hysterics. Rose had never been the hysterical type. She was an adrenaline junkie and usually thrilled at the strange and exciting. But this… This kind of thing could bring the most stable human to the brink of a breakdown.

He'd admired his half sister Nila's ability to stay standing after she'd seen him shift. Rose was going to need that kind of fortitude. The woman he loved, the woman he'd been in love with for years, was strong enough. But he hadn't seen Rose in so long, he wasn't sure he even knew her anymore.

The fact that she'd tossed him on his ass and then slapped him when he'd been a bastard assured him she was at least a little like the Rose he'd known.

She stared at him, and he held her gaze. A safer place to look than any other part of her. And even that wasn't exactly safe. But every time he let his gaze move lower than her face, he got distracted. He was here to protect her and Zoe, but he'd wanted Rose from the first moment they'd met and that desire hadn't gone away—not even when he'd thought she'd cheated on him.

Watching her, taking in her delicious scent—a mix of lavender and cardamom and her basic essence—left him a little breathless and a lot needy. His body buzzed with the desire to tug her close and feel every sexy inch of her pressed up against him, to taste her and savor the rasp of her tongue against his as he kissed her deeply enough to make them both forget the past. Just looking into her eyes sent his heartbeat racing. He wanted things he wasn't going to get right then. Maybe not ever if she couldn't forgive him. But that didn't seem to stop the wanting, or the rush of lusty fantasies dancing through his mind.

He reined in his wayward imagination. If he focused on her beautiful face and extremely angry expression, he could keep his mind—mostly—on the subject at hand.

Mostly.

Her eyes narrowed, and for a brief moment, he wondered if she realized what he was thinking. Could she tell he was having trouble keeping his hands to himself?

Then she shook her head, and he realized she wasn't going to allow him to shift. His heart sank. If she wouldn't face his tiger, he wasn't sure how he'd convince her of his story.

"I can't believe I'm going to agree to this," she said.

He blinked, not sure he'd heard her right.

"But when you attempt this 'shift' and fail, you will get out of my house and never return. Do you understand me? I will not have this crap around my daughter." She raised a hand when he opened his mouth. "I will make sure your equally crazy brothers get nowhere near us. Thanks for the warning."

"Rose—"

"Get on with it. And don't wake up Zoe." She waved her hand in an impatient gesture before crossing her arms again.

He had to force down a smile. So much fire. He'd always loved that about her. His heart thumped harder as memories of her bringing that passion and fire to their bed pushed to the front of his mind. "I'll have to take my clothes off first," he warned.

He watched something move through her beautiful blue eyes, and again he was tortured by images of having her under him, being inside her, swallowing her moans as he fucked her. Her scent was intoxicating. The flavors went right to his head, leaving him a lot warmer than the mild Arizona winter day warranted. Mixed with that scent was all her anger, but it wasn't nearly the distraction it should have been. He'd expected her anger. He hadn't expected to have so much trouble keeping his lust in check.

"I need to make sure Zoe is asleep," she said and hurried away.

But not before he caught the faintest hint of desire in her scent—a whisper of it, but it was there. Hope he hadn't dared feel before roared to life. He tamped it down with ruthless will. He couldn't afford those feelings or that hope now. First, he had to keep Rose and Zoe away from his brothers. He had to help Zoe. And he had to figure out how to keep them both safe.

Eventually, he'd have to bring them fully into his world. He wouldn't be able to hide Zoe from his people, not now that his brothers were sniffing around.

The implications… His gut hurt when he considered introducing that beautiful, vulnerable little girl to the tiger community. Maybe if she'd been a boy, things would be easier. A little. Because she was a girl and able to shift, she would be wrapped up in the same sort of trouble his sister had faced. But Nila was a grown woman. Zoe…

His first view of his daughter had broken something open in him. She was the most beautiful, perfect child he'd ever seen. Her dark eyes reminded him of his own mother. But her fiery red hair was all Rose. He smiled, remembering how he'd teased Rose about her name fitting her hair color. He'd gotten a not-too-gentle punch in the arm every time.

She walked back into the living room in that moment and caught him smiling.

"What?" she asked, though quietly.

"She's asleep?" He could hear Zoe's even breathing, the soft quiet snores, but he needed to change the subject.

Rose didn't need to know what he'd been reminiscing about.

"She was exhausted. The episodes always wear her out."

He took in the creases along Rose's brow and the little lines at the corners of her eyes and mouth, the deep circles under her eyes. "She's not the only one exhausted," he commented. "I wish I could let you rest before we do this. But it's important you believe me. Quickly."

She waved a hand in a vague circle. "It's better to get this nonsense over with while she's asleep. If you're gone before she wakes up, I'll have less explaining to do."

He narrowed his eyes, but decided they could argue about him leaving after she faced his tiger. "You understand what you're agreeing to?"

"Yes. I'm agreeing to let you strip and pretend you can turn into a tiger. When you can't, you will take your clothes and leave. If you refuse, I'll call the cops. Or worse, my parents."

He actually paused at that. Her parents were…well, they rivaled tiger parents in their fierce protectiveness of their only child. And they were both hunters. With a lot of guns. "After I shift, don't shoot me, okay? Give me a chance to get back to human and then we'll talk. And don't scream if you can help it. You'll wake Zoe."

Rose looked at him with her brows raised, her mouth a flat, disbelieving line. She showed no sign of fear or unease, just impatience to see him gone. He couldn't blame her for that, but this was too important.

He dropped the light jacket he wore, mostly for show,

across the back of a chair. Then pulled his long-sleeved t-shirt over his head. He heard her very faint inhale and his blood pumped faster. He met her gaze. Her expression hadn't changed, but her scent had. That hint of desire was stronger now, a delicious curl of spice he could actually taste. He smiled.

"I need you to watch me shift so you don't think I've pulled a trick. But if you'd be more comfortable, you can turn around while I'm undressing."

"Nothing I haven't seen before," she muttered. "Get on with it."

He nodded, trying not to let her stare affect him. He had to concentrate so he could shift as quickly as possible. He could change to his tiger form relatively fast for his kind, but it wasn't an instantaneous process. It took a few minutes. And he'd go a lot slower if he was distracted by lusty thoughts of the woman watching him. As it was, it was taking an act of will to keep from getting hard.

He toed off his boots as he unbuttoned his jeans, still too aware of her gaze on him. He wasn't shy or even remotely modest. Most tigers weren't. They spent a lot of time naked. But Rose wasn't just anyone. She was the woman who, four years ago, he'd been prepared to abandon his own kind for, the human woman he was so desperately in love with he'd been willing to face his father's fanatical anger and prejudice to stay with her.

Being naked with Rose was not the same as being naked with anyone else.

He slid his jeans and underwear off and draped them over the chair with his coat and shirt. When he faced Rose, she was making an effort to keep her gaze…up. That made him smile. She snarled.

He shook off his need to tease her and pulled his attention to the shift. After she witnessed that, there was the very real possibility it would kill any desire she still felt for him. He'd hate that, but the sacrifice would be worth it for Rose and Zoe's safety.

"This will take a few minutes," he explained. "I won't hurt you as the tiger. I'll still be myself. Just in a different body. Okay?"

She snorted her disbelief. "Get this over with, Vlad. I want you out of my house."

"Fine." He gave up trying to soften the blow and let his tiger out.

Rose's brain took almost thirty seconds to catch up to what she was seeing. For what felt like a long time, she simply couldn't compute the information her senses were sending to her. That delay probably saved her sanity.

By the time her brain caught up, Vlad's body had contorted into a form no human body could take on. His legs shortened and changed shape. His arms seemed to reposition and thicken. His hands widened and his fingers retracted, replaced by claws that came sprouting out from human skin now rippling with waves of russet, black and white fur.

The thing that had been Vlad folded forward, standing on all fours as his head and face contorted, moved and changed. Horror kept her still and mute. She couldn't have screamed if she'd wanted to. The part of her mind not curling into a ball of terror took note of her physical reaction to the shock—the sweat covering her even as she shivered with cold, the fine trembling in her muscles, the way she felt like she was floating and yet couldn't remember how to move her heavy limbs.

So this was what a mental breakdown felt like. She'd always wondered.

When the thing before her finally stopped contorting and shook out its fur, a massive Bengal tiger stood in the middle of her living room staring at her.

With Vlad's beautiful brown eyes.

Curses she'd never allow in the same house as her daughter piled up against her tongue, but she couldn't remember how to let those words out. In her mind, she screamed and denied, but beyond that, all she could do was stare.

There was a tiger in her living room, and she'd just seen the man she used to love do something that only happened in movies and fiction.

He'd said her daughter could do that. Zoe's pain was caused by her body *trying* to do that.

The thought brought her back fully into her body and gave her control of herself again.

"Sonofabitch," she hissed. "Vlad, you sonofabitch, why didn't you tell me about this? What have you done to our daughter?"

The tiger shook his huge head and sat, wrapping his long, thick tail around his legs just like a domestic cat. For some reason that struck her as odd, and in the next minute, she almost laughed that the tiger's position was what she focused on as being odd.

"Can you talk like that?"

He shook his head.

"But you understand? You can…think?"

He nodded, holding her gaze the entire time.

Her heart was pounding so hard she was afraid she might pass out. She could *see* Vlad in the big cat's eyes. And yet, it wasn't him. There was something both wild and contained in the depths of the tiger's gaze. Something powerful and dangerous.

To her utter astonishment, the danger drew her and helped tamp down some of her horror. She wasn't amazed at being drawn to danger and thrill—she and her parents made their living organizing and leading adventure travel. She was a danger junkie. Even after having Zoe, she still couldn't resist rock climbing or white water rafting occasionally, just enough to get her adrenaline pumping. She didn't take the kinds of risks she used to when she was with Vlad, but motherhood hadn't killed off her need for that rush of excitement.

And here she was, facing the most dangerous thing she could imagine. The part of her not screaming hysterical denials was suddenly…curious. And excited.

"Fuck me," she muttered. Then slapped a hand over her mouth and glanced back toward Zoe's door. The realization that she'd turned away from the dangerous predator in the room had her looking back quickly. She could swear the tiger was smirking.

She shook her head. "You need to change back."

He nodded and stood, his body starting to convulse again.

"I need a drink." She rushed into the kitchen, stunned that she'd actually chickened out and run away. But she wasn't ready to see the process reverse itself.

By the time she came back out again, Vlad was not only human but sitting fully dressed on the couch. The incongruity of it made her pause and blink. Had she imagined all that?

"You didn't imagine it," he said, as if reading her mind.

She scowled and continued to the chair across from the couch. She glanced at the yellow sunflower clock on the wall over the TV. Was it still so early in the day?

It felt like hours had passed, but he'd only just knocked on her door about forty-five minutes ago.

She sat on the edge of the chair across from him and stared. "So…tiger shapeshifters, huh?"

He nodded.

"Does it…hurt to change?"

"No. It's like stretching. There's a pull and tension, but not pain. This is what I'm born to do. There's nothing odd about it to my body. After, it's like a release of tension, and I feel really good and strong."

"Going human to tiger?"

"Either way."

"You think Zoe's body is trying to make her do that?"

"I know that's what's happening. It's trying to do something natural, but her little mind is getting in the way. Our young—"

"Wait, how many of you are there?"

"Not as many as there used to be. But that's a much longer story."

Curiosity sparked but she pushed it aside so she could focus on how this affected her daughter. "Can Zoe just *not* do that? Can you teach her how to do for herself what you did for her in there just now? Then she doesn't ever have to be…" She trailed off. She'd been on the verge of saying Zoe wouldn't have to be a freak. But she realized that would insult Vlad. "I just want her to have a normal life, be a normal kid," she finished.

"She isn't, and she'll never be a normal *human* child, Rose. But that doesn't mean she can't be normal for what she is."

"This just can't be real."

"If I'd thought this might happen, I would have…"

When he didn't finish, she narrowed her eyes, trying to see into his soul. "You would have what?"

"I would have prepared you, given you the choice of whether or not you could live in my world. And if you couldn't, I would have found a way to give you up before you got pregnant."

She remained silent for a long time as she worked her way through that admission.

Vlad was the first to break the silence. "We need to find someplace for you and Zoe to stay for a bit while I draw my brothers off."

"I'll take care of that. Why do you think they'll hurt us?"

He ran a hand through his hair and stared at the sunflower clock, his mouth flattened into a tight line. "It's complicated without giving you a lot of tiger shifter history —which we don't have time for now—but basically, they think any offspring from tigers and humans are…abominations that must be killed. They learned that lesson and attitude from my father."

"Your father?"

"He…" He swallowed visibly, then faced her, his expression impossible to read. "He tried to kill my half sister, Nila, because of what she is. My brothers hunted her down with him and would have happily helped kill her if they'd gotten the chance. They'll try to kill Zoe."

"They might try. They won't succeed. I'll rip them apart." Even as she said it, she flashed back to his shift and that huge tiger facing her with Vlad's intelligent eyes. She shook off the moment of fear and panic. Didn't matter what she was facing. This was her daughter's life. She'd tear apart all the demons of hell to protect Zoe.

A slight smile broke Vlad's expression. "You're as fierce as any tiger mom I've known. I'm glad. Our daughter obviously has a wonderful mother."

"How can I kill a tiger shifter? Can I just shoot them?" She ignored the little thump of her heart following his compliment. She didn't have time for it. But the fact that he thought she was a good mom pleased her a lot more than she wanted to admit. She couldn't trust the comment, though, not after he'd as much as called her a bad mother earlier for letting her daughter remain in pain. She grabbed on to the anger that thought produced and thrust it in front of her more complicated emotions like a shield.

"It takes some seriously heavy ammunition and more

than one shot," he said, "but yes, you can shoot a tiger shifter dead. Especially if you shoot them in the head."

"No special bullets needed?"

"We're not werewolves. But we do heal incredibly fast, so one bullet isn't likely to work—unless it's one of those military grade explosive things or you hit the shifter in the head in just the right spot. A broken neck, done just right, will work. But you'd have to practically rip a tiger's head off to make sure they're dead. It takes a lot of damage to overcome our healing speed."

"Can you kill another tiger? How would you do it?"

"I'd tear them to pieces while in tiger form."

She shivered a little, not sure if it was from fear or a rush of excitement, and not inclined to look too closely at what either might mean. "I don't have that option. I'll just have to get a few big guns." She started mentally scrolling through her father's inventory. She'd have to swing by their house.

On her way where?

"Vlad, I have a job. I can't just run off. And won't your brothers just track me down? What's the point? I'll be safer here with a lot of ammunition and the help and support of my parents."

"You're risking Zoe's life staying here. You don't know what my brothers are capable of." He wouldn't quite meet her gaze.

There was something he wasn't telling her. "Spill. What have you left out?"

He sighed. "My brothers aren't the only threat. They aren't the only ones who think like my father. There are a bunch of tigers as fanatical as my dad. Not all of them were killed when he was. Not even close."

The news surprised her. "Your dad is dead?" She knew Vlad and his father didn't get along—she'd learned that when she and Vlad were a couple—but losing his father had to hurt. She'd be devastated.

"He was killed by one of the tigers who rescued Nila from him. He would have been put to death by the elders anyway. He'd killed humans, which is an automatic death sentence."

"Elders?"

"Our governing body."

She was curious enough to ask more, but she didn't have time for it now. She needed him gone. Then she had to decide how best to protect Zoe. If she ran, she'd have no way of knowing when it was safe to return. She'd be in unfamiliar territory. And she'd be away from her parents if she needed their help.

"I'll tell you all about the shifter world later," he interrupted her thoughts, "when you and Zoe are safe."

"We're safe. I just need some guns." She went back to strategizing ways to protect Zoe. If Vlad's brothers were like him, she was facing some serious trouble. But it would be easier to defend from home. She couldn't tell Vlad that, though. He'd just keep coming back. She didn't want to see him anymore, and she certainly didn't want Zoe around him. She willfully ignored the fact that Zoe might be a shapeshifter and without Vlad her pain could continue. Rose would take care of that too…somehow.

"Rose." Vlad launched off the couch, circled it, and started pacing.

Back and forth, back and forth. To her astonishment, his movements reminded her of tigers in zoos. She sat up straighter in her seat.

"Rose, it's more than my brothers, though they're the reason I'm here now. Zoe needs to learn to shift. And she can't do that in your backyard. She shouldn't do it here, where anyone might see it. We need to keep her protected, and isolated, while she learns to control her other half."

He'd brought up the exact thing she was trying to pretend wasn't an issue. She was still hoping Zoe could just learn how to stop the pain without having to do…what Vlad had done. But what if he was right and she had to do that? "What will happen if Zoe doesn't learn to shift? What if she suppresses it? Will the pain get worse?"

"Likely. But beyond that, I'm not sure. She's unique. Even though Nila's also a hybrid, she can't shift, so she made it to adulthood without ever even knowing she was half tiger. Ordinary tiger shifters learn to do this when they're two years old. They're surrounded by it and don't consider suppressing it. So I honestly don't know what might happen to her if she does try to prevent the shift permanently. I'm not sure she can."

"There has to be—" she started, but Vlad cut her off with a raised hand when his cellphone rang.

He pulled the phone out of his pants pocket, checked the caller ID, and frowned as he answered. "Yes?"

She stood, readying to send him on his way as soon as he hung up. She had some planning to do and he was a distraction. The shifter thing… She'd worry about it once she was sure Zoe was safe.

He listened for a moment, then cursed. "Thanks." And he hung up. "All three of my brothers were just spotted at the airport. They'll be here soon. We have to go."

Before she could respond, she heard a sweet little voice from the hallway. "Mommy? What's going on?"

CHAPTER THREE

Rose rushed to her daughter, covering her panic with a smile. "Are you okay now, baby? Any more pain?"

She shook her head, glanced at Vlad, then back at Rose and whispered in that very loud kid whisper, "Who's he, Mommy?"

"This is Vlad. He's a…friend of mommy's from before you were born." God, with everything else, she hadn't even begun to think how she'd tell Zoe that Vlad was her father. *If* she'd tell her. She'd prefer he just disappear again and leave them alone. Then she wouldn't have to explain any of this to her daughter. A cowardly response, but there it was. Vlad complicated things. He'd brought trouble to her door. And while he'd helped Zoe, he'd also thrown Rose's world upside down with all the shapeshifter talk, with his very presence. She didn't want to deal with any of it, or him.

And for the moment, she had more immediate problems to deal with. If even part of what he said was true, she needed to get out of the house and get help now. "Are you up for a little trip to see Granny and Grandpa at work?"

"Yay!" Zoe bounced on her toes.

"Great. Let's go get your backpack ready."

"You'll need to pack enough for a week, maybe longer," Vlad said.

She glared back at him. "I'll take care of it."

"Are we going on a vacation, Mommy?"

She frowned. Zoe's little face had lit up. When they went on vacation, it was usually to some adventure, like bouldering, camping, hiking, or bodyboarding in the ocean. Zoe had inherited her mom's love of adventure.

"Okay," she relented. "You've been a very good girl. I think you've earned a vacation." She was stuck leaving now. Since she'd never been able to help with the pain, Rose worked hard never to lie to Zoe about anything else. And a plan was starting to form, a way to get Vlad off her back and still keep her daughter safe. "Go get your backpack ready."

Zoe giggled and spun on her heels, racing back to her room.

Vlad came up behind Rose. "She seems better now."

"When she's not in pain, she's really healthy and full of energy. Almost too much sometimes." She groaned and Vlad chuckled. The sound sent a little shiver down her spine and a tingling jolt of warmth to places lower.

She leaned back toward him against her will, drawn by his familiar scent, as heat pumped through her, making her skin tingle. She found herself imagining his hands on her arms, her waist, moving up to her breasts.

She straightened and snarled. She hated that she reacted to him in any way that wasn't anger. She might just have to go back to wishing the torments of hell on him—for both the trouble he brought with him and the way he made her feel.

"I'll go with you to the office, and then make sure you get away. After I know you're safe, I'll take care of my brothers."

She was curious enough to ask, "How?"

He paused, as if listening to something, then very quietly said, "I need to convince them Zoe isn't my daughter."

"That shouldn't be hard, since you never believed she was."

"Rose. You know why now. And I'm sorry I didn't believe you."

She closed her eyes briefly as the last four years of heartache washed over her. When she opened her eyes again, she kept her attention on the hallway so he couldn't see her emotions. "I've moved on. I don't have time to worry about it anymore."

"Where will you go on this 'vacation?'" he asked.

She'd been considering that. There was a cabin in Alpine her parents looked after for a family friend. It wasn't in any of their names, so it should be safe enough while she made more long-term plans to keep Zoe safe. But she wasn't about to tell Vlad any of that. "Don't worry about it."

"I still need to…" He paused.

She finally turned to face him, her brows raised.

"I need to teach Zoe how to deal with what's happening to her," he said.

She appreciated his vague reference to the shifter business. Zoe had outrageously good hearing. Rose couldn't even mutter a "damn" in the kitchen while her daughter was in the bedroom without Zoe scolding her for the "bad word." Come to think of it, he'd been quiet when mentioning Zoe was his daughter aloud. Did he realize she had acute hearing? Was it related to her being a shifter?

"Getting your brothers to leave us alone is your priority," she said. "Just tell me how to talk her through the pain."

"You need to get her thinking about what her—" he glanced down the hall, "—body feels like when everything is normal. Get her focusing on physical sensations that are distinctly human." He mouthed the word human rather than saying it out loud. "The way her blanket feels against her fingers and cheek is especially good because that's her favorite thing. Anything tactile will work. That will bring her back into her body."

"Will that work every time?"

"It should help for a little while longer."

Hopefully a lot longer because she didn't want her daughter to have any part of his world. "I can only stay away for a week. My parents can spare us that long, but my father is leading a white water rafting trip at the beginning of next month, and my mother needs me at the office."

He frowned. "That might not be long enough."

"How hard can it be? You just have to convince your brothers of what you've always believed. They'll leave, and Zoe and I can get back to our lives." With a few guns stored in her house. She hated having them around when Zoe was so young, but she didn't have much choice now. She didn't dare go without protection against things that could do what Vlad had done. She'd just have to get a good gun safe.

"It's not that simple," Vlad said. "I need to teach Zoe—"

He was interrupted by Zoe bouncing back down the hall. "Mommy, need help with blankie. It won't fit."

Rose narrowed her eyes. "How much did you pack?"

"What I needed."

"Uh huh." She gave her daughter a suspicious look and went down the hall to her room. She wasn't entirely surprised Vlad followed, but having him casually walk through her home, having him around her daughter, set her nerves on edge.

Suddenly this spontaneous vacation seemed like a really good idea. The farther she was from him while she figured out how to deal with the news he'd delivered, the better.

To her surprise, she wasn't turned off by watching him shift. It had been a pretty horrifying process. Something out of a nightmare. But for some reason, it did nothing to kill her ever-present desire for him, that edge of lust and love she'd only ever experienced with him. Which sucked. She didn't want to feel anything for him but anger. Damn the man. She should not still be thinking sexy thoughts about him after he'd just done…what he'd done. She should not be thinking sexy thoughts about him, period.

When she reached Zoe's door, she realized why her blanket wouldn't fit in her backpack. The little blue monkey pack was overflowing with toys. "Baby, you're gonna need clothes as well as toys. You know that."

"Don't," Zoe insisted. "I be naked!" She giggled and spun around.

Rose laughed. Shaking her head, she opened the backpack. "I'll pack your clothes with mine, but you have to leave some of these toys here. Or we can leave blankie behind?"

"Nooooo!"

"Okay, okay, no reason to yell. Here, why don't we leave these two dolls? And we can pick up a new pack of crayons and a coloring book along the way. As a treat."

"Yay!" Zoe threw out the offending "old" crayons, reluctantly put the dolls back on her bed, and then shoved her blanket into the backpack.

Rose marveled at her daughter. Not an hour ago, she'd been curled up in excruciating pain. Now she was all exclamation points and energy, not even a hint of the trauma she'd gone through earlier. Rose's heart ached with love as she watched her little girl. And her fierce protective instincts roared. If anyone thought they'd hurt her daughter, they were in for a rude and bloody awakening.

That went for Vlad, too.

She packed up a few necessities for herself and Zoe in her own well-worn travel backpack, tossed everything into her SUV, and buckled Zoe into her seat in the back while Vlad hovered over her shoulder.

He smiled when she straightened. "Still a light packer, I see."

"Habit. You can leave now. We're good."

"I'll go with you. I want to make sure you get out of town."

"Don't you need to take care of your brothers?" She could tell by the way his eyes narrowed she'd hit a soft spot. "Thanks for your help this morning and for the warning." When he still didn't move, she said, "You'd better go find your brothers. Or do you want them to find us first?"

She was playing dirty, but she didn't want him to follow her. She didn't want Vlad anywhere near her anymore. Her feelings for him, and about him, were too complicated. She needed space and time to consider the future and how she would keep her daughter safe.

When he frowned and glanced at the street, she knew she had him.

"Good luck," she said, then slipped into the driver's seat, buckled up, and backed out of the driveway, ignoring Vlad as he watched her go. Her brain was buzzing, so full of confused chatter and emotion she couldn't sort through it all. So she focused on driving, getting to her parents' office, taking the next steps to get her daughter safely out of town. She'd untangle all the chaos of the morning tonight, after Zoe was asleep and she was curled up in front of a fire with a glass of wine, or whiskey. This situation seemed to call for whiskey.

* * *

She'd left her parents' office with the keys to the Alpine cabin and was on her way to their house for one of her dad's rifles, when she started getting nervous for some unexplained reason. She kept checking traffic, looking for cars that might be following her.

Damn Vlad. He had her all paranoid.

Despite what he'd shown her, she had no real reason to believe anything he'd said beyond the fact that tiger shapeshifters were a real thing. Maybe he was the only one. Maybe what was happening with Zoe had nothing to do with the shifter stuff. Rose only had Vlad's word that his brothers might really try to hurt her daughter, and what good was his word to her after all these years?

She turned into the cul-de-sac and parked on the street in front of her parents' single story ranch. As she unbuckled Zoe from her seat, she kept a lookout for approaching cars. The neighborhood was extremely quiet that time of day— most of the residents were working people—and the empti- ness of the street left her much more nervous than she'd ever been in this area before.

She hurried Zoe inside, trying not to convey any of her own trepidation to her daughter. Zoe thought they were on some grand adventure to the mountains. Rose didn't want her to worry about anything but how big a snowman she'd be able to build.

Getting her dad's Weatherby out of the gun cabinet and collecting enough ammunition for it that Rose felt suffi- ciently armed didn't take long, but convincing Zoe she didn't need any of the toys she had stored at Granny and Grandpa's proved a little more difficult.

For reasons Rose couldn't precisely put her finger on, her nerves jumped and instinct was pushing her to get out of the house fast. She trusted those instincts even though she had no idea what was driving them. She hadn't been this panicked at her home when making plans to leave, even after Vlad had said his brothers were in town. But now, her every impulse screamed that she needed to get back to the car and get on the road now, before it was too late.

Unfortunately, Zoe picked that moment to remember she needed to use the bathroom and another excruciating few minutes passed as the anxiety crawling through Rose's stomach got worse.

"Come on, baby," she called through the bathroom door. "We want to get to the cabin before the sun sets."

Part of her wondered if the anxiety was because of the stories Vlad had fed her, or because she sensed Zoe was on the verge of another episode. Usually after a bad one like that morning, they didn't have to worry about the pain for days, sometimes more than a week. But after everything that had happened, Rose didn't trust anything anymore.

Finally, Zoe was ready to go. Rose ushered her outside, the rifle case in tow, more than ready to be on the road. She was locking the front door when she heard Zoe giggle. Rose looked up to see a strange man on the walkway behind them, not ten feet away.

She swallowed her shocked gasp and forced a polite, "May I help you?" This poor guy could just be a delivery man. No reason to panic or be rude. But her instincts told her otherwise.

In fact, as she stared at him, she realized he looked sort of familiar. He had dark brown hair, light eyes, and pale skin, but something in his features reminded her of…Vlad.

"Rose Callaghan?"

She edged Zoe behind her as she faced the stranger. His gaze dropped to her daughter and something Rose couldn't decipher, but didn't like, moved through his expression. She adjusted her stance, preparing to drop the gun case and fight if it became necessary.

Her every instinct screamed that this man was dangerous, a threat, and she was in serious trouble. "Do I know you?"

He took a single step closer and smiled—a forced expression that never reached his eyes.

"No," he said, almost pleasantly. "My name is Anton Dubrovsky. I believe you know my brother."

# CHAPTER FOUR

Rose forced herself to think around the unease clawing at her. If Vlad was right, this man wanted to kill her daughter because of what he thought she was. At all cost, she had to make him believe Zoe was *not* Vlad's child.

Rose cursed herself for not heeding her own instincts and having the gun out. It was useless to her in the case. Hitting a supernatural being who could turn into a tiger with it wasn't likely to slow him down. She'd thrown Vlad, so she knew her martial arts would work, but without the gun, there was only so long she could hold Anton off.

She adjusted her stance as subtly as she could, preparing to fight if she had to. For Zoe, she'd do whatever it took. Memories of Vlad's eyes in a tiger body moved through her mind and she forced back a rush of panic. Anton chose that moment to take another step closer and his smile flattened into a hard stare. At Zoe.

This was going to go bad fast if Rose didn't do something to distract him and throw him off. She tried bluffing. Maybe she could just get him to go away.

She forced a slight frown. "What do you want? I haven't seen Vlad in years."

"No point in lying to me, Rose. I can smell deception. And I can smell Vlad on you."

The way he said that made her stomach tighten. He glanced at her then turned his full attention back to her daughter. Rose moved to further block her. "I'm not sure what you're talking about."

"I know he's been to see you. What did he tell you?"

"I told her I wanted her back and she kicked me out."

The sound of Vlad's voice sent such a wave of relief through Rose she'd be embarrassed by it later. Right then, she was beyond grateful he'd ignored her wishes and followed her.

She looked around Anton at Vlad. His scowl was so dark, she shivered. "What are you doing here?" she asked, playing into the story he'd started. "I told you I needed time."

He looked at her long enough to say, "I was hoping to…talk more."

"Not now." She took Zoe's hand. "Come on, baby." To Vlad she said, "Later. Maybe. I'll…I'll let you know."

Keeping Zoe on the far side of her, she passed Anton. He stepped off the walkway to give her room, but he was still too close and her stomach tightened as she waited for him to attack. When she reached Vlad and Anton hadn't moved, she forced out a breath she hadn't realized she'd been holding. She glanced at Vlad, just a moment of eye contact, before moving quickly to her SUV. She tossed the gun case onto the front seat, strapped Zoe into her car seat, and climbed behind the wheel, all without looking directly at the brothers. But she kept her awareness focused on them and knew they were staring at her.

Her hands shook as she started the engine. She checked her rearview mirror as she headed out of the cul-de-sac. Anton was standing next to Vlad as they both watched her drive away.

Vlad waited until Rose had turned the corner before he faced his brother. "What in the ever loving hell are you doing here? Why were you talking with Rose?" He had to force down the panic that had shot through him when he'd sensed one of his brothers in the Callaghan's neighborhood.

Despite her insistence, Vlad had followed Rose from her house to the Callaghan Adventure Travel offices, then on to her parents' house. He'd kept a discreet distance, not wanting her to see him. Unfortunately, he'd gotten caught behind a fender bender and had to watch her drive off without him guarding her back.

He'd held his anxiety in check by reminding himself that his brothers couldn't get to this part of Phoenix from the airport in the time since they'd been spotted. He knew where her parents' house was. He could get there in time to ensure she got out of town safely.

He'd underestimated his brothers. The second time he'd made that mistake in the last month.

"Good to see you too, bro," Anton said dryly.

"Answer the damned question." His anger was strong enough to cover his other emotions, thankfully, because he was having a lot of trouble keeping his panic and fear buried. He was used to lying to his family, hiding his real feelings, but seeing Anton so close to Rose and Zoe…

He couldn't even consider what might have happened. He had to throw Anton off, make him believe the story he'd started about being here to get Rose back. For Zoe's sake, he had to make sure his younger brother didn't realize she was his daughter.

Fortunately, Anton couldn't have sensed Zoe the way their kind sensed each other. He should have been able to feel that she was a tiger shifter—a fact that would have made hiding her relationship to Vlad impossible. But Vlad's senses couldn't tell Zoe apart from a human, which meant Anton couldn't either. It had to have something to do with her being a hybrid. Vlad didn't understand it, and he had a lot of questions, but for the moment, he was just grateful Zoe's nature wasn't easy to discern.

Anton rocked from one foot to the other, not quite meeting Vlad's gaze when he said, "Just worrying about you."

"Worrying about *me*?" Vlad gave him a look.

Anton rolled his eyes and a hint of embarrassment, like the smell of overripe fruit, crept into his scent. "Yeah, well, a lot's happened in the last five months."

"So you thought you should come see my ex-girlfriend out of the blue?"

"You're here. You want to explain that?"

"No."

Anton was the younger of the twins, by about a minute, and the brother Vlad had managed to get along with, at least when they were younger. Andrey and Yuri were just too much like their father. But for some reason, Anton had been less inclined to hold Vlad's resemblance to their mother against him.

All three of his younger brothers bore a strong resemblance to their father—as was typical for tigers. Yuri was actually the spitting image of their father with pale blond hair and electric blue eyes. Both twins had darker hair, almost as dark brown as Vlad's, and Anton's blue eyes had a lot of gray in them, but his features invoked memories of their father. Both the twins were tall, taller than Vlad by a couple of inches, but Vlad had the advantage of age.

An advantage he used now. "What's going on?" He put his hands on his hips and glared at his brother, infusing as much annoyance into his tone as he could muster.

"What's going on with you and Rose?"

"None of your fucking business."

"Come on, man. You haven't seen her in what…four years? Now I find you at her parents' house."

"That's why you were talking to her? You were looking for me?" He waved his cell phone in Anton's face. "Use the fucking phone next time."

Anton's eyes narrowed and Vlad saw suspicion even

though his brother tried to hide it. None of his brothers could lie to him as well as he could lie to them.

"How *did* you find me here?" Vlad asked. "Where are Andrey and Yuri?"

Anton's eyes shifted slightly as he said, "Yuri went to the Callaghan's office and Andrey went to Rose's house."

"What the hell? Why?" Vlad let outrage and fury fill his voice and scent. They were strong emotions he had no trouble letting out. And they overrode the underlying terror he was desperately trying to suppress. What if he'd arrived a few minutes later? What if he'd never learned his brothers had booked flights to Phoenix? If one of his contacts hadn't tipped Vlad off to their plans, he might have stalled longer, trying to figure out how best to approach Rose.

He might have been too late.

"You still haven't explained why you're here?" Anton said defensively.

"I already told you it's none of your business. Besides, I have more right to be here than you. Rose is my ex. I'd like to know why the hell my brothers are hunting her down?"

"The little girl…she's got Mother's eyes. Your eyes."

Vlad used every ounce of self-control he had not to react to the implied threat. "She's got brown eyes," he said, evenly, with as much irritation as he could infuse in his tone. "Lots of people have brown eyes. The bastard Rose cheated on me with when she got pregnant? He had brown eyes. What's your point, Anton?"

"With what we know now, we thought, maybe…you were rethinking the 'cheating' part."

"Oh. Is that what you thought? And what? I'm here to kill the kid?"

Anton shrugged. But a hint of something pungent and sour crept into his scent, a flavor that spoke of suspicion and distrust, like rotting plant life.

"You here to help?" Vlad asked.

"We just wanted to check on you. We were worried."

Since his brothers had booked their flights before Vlad, he'd have known Anton was lying even if there wasn't a faint tinge of it in his scent. But Vlad hid his knowledge behind a resigned sigh.

"I'm not here because I think the kid is mine. She's not. Rose cheated on me. I almost killed the guy when I found him, except he's human."

"Then why *are* you here?"

Vlad ran a hand through his hair again and played up his part to the best of his acting ability—abilities he'd honed at the granite wheel of their father. "After all the shit with Mom's suicide and Dad's death, I guess I was feeling… I don't know. I missed Rose."

Anton's eyebrows rose sharply. "You really are trying to get back with her? I thought that was just some shit you told her."

The disbelief and surprise were the exact reactions Vlad had been hoping for. "Yeah, well, it wasn't," he snapped, putting on the defensiveness of a man caught doing something stupid.

"Vlad, man, she broke your heart. You haven't been the same since. And now you want her back? When she's got some other man's kid? What the fuck?"

His brother sounded sincere in his concern, but Vlad caught the continued suspicion in his scent if not his tone. Anton was playing a part, too.

"It's been four years," Vlad said. "I'm not getting a tiger mate. I want kids."

"Some other man's kid?"

"Same as if we'd adopted. Or if I'd met her after she had a child."

"No, it's not. She cheated on you with some *human*."

"She's human."

"Even worse."

"You sound like Dad now."

Anton sighed. "I just don't know how you can come back to a woman—a human woman—who cheated on you. How you could possibly want to get back with her. Aren't you disgusted by her?"

"Just because you don't like human women doesn't mean *I* want to be celibate for the rest of my life."

"You want to get laid, pick someone new."

"Why?"

"'Cause…this woman is no good."

Vlad watched a muscle in Anton's cheek twitch. A tell. Anton had managed to control his scent tells better over the course of their conversation, but the physical tell surprised Vlad. Anton only twitched when he was really angry.

"I disagree," Vlad said, sticking to his story as he watched his brother closely. "One mistake doesn't make her a bad person." He shrugged and admitted a truth he'd hardly admitted to himself. "I still love her. I just thought…

After we lost so much, it was stupid to ignore how I felt about Rose and waste more time."

That glint of suspicion returned to Anton's eyes. He could tell Vlad was being completely honest, and Vlad could tell that complicated his feelings about this conversation.

"What did she do when you told her you wanted back with her?" Anton asked.

Vlad snorted. "She slapped me." A completely honest statement. "Then she broke down and cried." He actually had to work not to laugh at that. Rose would *not* have cried in that circumstance. Kicked his ass, yes. Cried, never. But his brothers didn't know her, so they wouldn't realize crying was out of character for her.

"Guilt?" Anton asked.

"Some of it. Some of it was—" Vlad cut himself off and glared. "I'm not talking about this with you. It's personal."

"I'm your brother."

"Since when have we discussed *feelings*?"

His brother actually chuckled. "Fine. Is she going to take you back?"

"You heard her. She says she's too confused and can't think with me around."

"You gonna keep trying or take the hint?"

Vlad paused and looked into the distance, pretending to consider his options. "I still want her back."

"You're an idiot, you know."

"Yeah, well." Vlad gave his brother a look. "I don't see you having any better luck with women."

Anton snorted. Then his expression settled into serious lines and worry flavored his scent. "This is a bad idea, Vlad. You should stay away from Rose."

"None of your business, little brother. You can tell the others the same. If I want Rose back, it's my damned business. If she fucks me over again, it's my business. You three need to keep your noses out of my love life."

"Hey, I just don't want to see you hurt again." Anton shrugged.

"Still none of your business."

"Fine. Just don't come to me when she rips your beating heart out and smashes it into little pieces. Again."

Despite the outwardly caring words, Vlad knew it was an act—Anton playing the part of concerned brother. Vlad caught the subtle flavor of it in his scent. But anyone overhearing this exchange would just see one brother worrying for the other.

Vlad played his part in the exchange, pretending to believe Anton's concern was genuine. With a sigh, he said, "Go home. Take the other reprobates with you. All three of you have businesses to run. Or do you want to let all Dad built fall apart? Besides, with the elders keeping such a close eye on us, it's better if we aren't all in the same place."

That got a reaction Vlad hadn't been expecting. Anton's scent filled with a mix of pungent musk and a sharp acrid, chemical tinge. Vlad's tiger nose interpreted the combination as fear and resentment. All three of his brothers blamed the elders for their father's death—even though their father had put himself into the position which got him killed. Vlad had actually had to stop Yuri from talking about outright rebellion.

Even if some of the elders agreed with their father when it came to tiger-human interbreeding, they would not stand for rebellion. The elders were each individually powerful. As a collective, they were damn near omnipotent. At least that was the impression they gave the rest of the community. And they would band together, marshalling all that power against anyone who threatened them.

Vlad might not trust his brothers, or even like them very much at the moment. He might have to fight them to keep them from hurting Rose and Zoe. But he didn't want them utterly destroyed either. If he could get everyone out of this without anyone dying, he'd consider it a win.

He clapped Anton on the shoulder. "Thanks for worrying about me. But don't. I'll be fine."

Anton's lips thinned and Vlad could see him considering his next step.

Finally, he shrugged and shook his head. "I still think you're making a huge mistake, bro, but whatever. It's your life."

Vlad pushed his brother toward his rental car, parked at the curb in the spot just behind where Rose's SUV had been. "Go get the others and get out of here. I've got some strategizing to do."

His brother stood at the car, door open, staring at Vlad over the roof, his eyes narrowed. "You sure?"

"Go away, Anton."

"Fine. Your problem, then."

He dropped down into the car and slammed the door.

Vlad stood on the sidewalk, watching him drive away as he analyzed the information he'd gotten from his brother's scent.

His nose assured him Anton had been lying, putting on an act so Vlad would believe he'd given up.

This wasn't over yet.

* * *

Rose was shaking so hard she would have had to stop the car even if she hadn't needed to move the gun case into the back. She wove through the neighborhoods around her parents' place so she wouldn't be easy to find again, then she pulled up next to a quiet house and put the car in park.

She flexed her hands several times, trying to stop the quaking. She was used to adrenaline rushes—she'd spent most of her life craving them and going after them with enthusiasm. But this kind of fear… She didn't like it.

Knowing Zoe would be scared if she realized how terrified her mother was forced Rose to rein in her emotions and push them behind false bravery. Her daughter needed her to be strong and confident, not a blubbering mess. She studied her surroundings in the car mirrors, then turned to look at her daughter.

"I need to put the rifle in the back, okay, baby. We'll get on the road again in just a minute."

"What happening, Mommy? Why you scared? That man really Vlad's brother?"

Damn it. Rose should have known Zoe wouldn't miss

the tension. "Yes, he was Vlad's brother. And I'm not scared, just… It's difficult to explain, baby, but you don't need to worry." She hated lying to her daughter, but she couldn't tell her even a child-friendly version of this truth. Not yet.

"Gonna see Vlad again?"

"Sure," Rose said, trying to sound positive and upbeat, but knowing her hesitance still filtered into her voice. She wasn't sure she *should* see Vlad anymore, and she didn't want her daughter getting attached to him in case he took off again.

She didn't trust Vlad. She was grateful he'd shown up to help deflect his brother, but the fact that he'd been there meant he'd obviously disregarded her wishes that he leave her alone. The combination of relief and anger was too much to deal with so she pushed her emotions aside. For the moment, she just had to get Zoe somewhere safe. The rest could wait.

They had a drive ahead of them. And Rose couldn't get out of town fast enough.

# CHAPTER FIVE

Two days later, safely ensconced in the cabin in Alpine, Rose was still working to convince herself the whole incident with Vlad and his brother was a lot of fuss over nothing. Anton hadn't actually done anything particularly threatening, except stare at Zoe. Very intensely. But she only had Vlad's word that his brothers wanted to hurt Zoe, and she already knew she couldn't trust him.

Rose's instincts didn't buy this logic. There had been something in Anton's eyes that set off alarm bells and had warning claxons sounding in her head. Her every nerve ending screamed at her to keep Zoe as far from Vlad's brothers as she could get.

And then there was the tiger shifter part.

After two days happily hiking in the woods and playing in the snow with Zoe, Rose could almost believe she'd imagined that. Or that Vlad had somehow drugged her. That the real threat was Vlad's insanity.

Her instincts weren't buying this either.

She'd seen him change, watched with her own eyes as the man she used to love turned into a tiger. All the logic in the world wasn't enough to convince her deep down that it hadn't happened.

And what about Zoe's episodes? How else could she explain the pain her daughter went through, when no tests or exams had ever revealed a cause?

During lunch on that second day, while Zoe munched on her sandwich and told stories about squirrels, Rose tried to quiet her inner argument between logic and instinct so she could fully savor the peaceful moment. She loved seeing her daughter like this—feeling good and acting like a typical three-year-old. They were safe for this moment. Rose just had to decide what to do next.

Suddenly, Zoe raised her head and looked at the front door. "Vlad's here," she sang.

An instant later, there was a knock.

Frowning, Rose went to answer, more than a little surprised to see it really was Vlad. Her heartbeat sped up like it had three mornings ago when she'd opened the door to find him. A rush of warmth and lust curled in her belly, both surprising and irritating her. For an instant, time collapsed, and they were back in the heady days of their romance, before all the hurt and betrayal. She would have thrown herself into his arms and kissed him just for standing there looking so hot and adorable all at once. She could practically feel his mouth on hers, the firm pressure of his lips, and the dance of his tongue against hers as she tasted him.

When she realized she was staring at his mouth, she shook her head and met his gaze. His already dark eyes were darker still and she could swear he was standing closer than he'd been a moment earlier.

Would this reaction to him ever go away? When they'd been together all those years ago, she'd gotten excited every time she saw him, every time she heard his voice. Apparently, four years of pain and hurt hadn't lessened her feelings for him at all.

It had, however, broken her trust in him. "What are you doing here? How did you find us?" A light snow had started while they were eating lunch and Vlad's dark hair was flecked with white, but she didn't invite him in.

"I went to see your parents," he said.

"You faced Connor and Marta? That was ballsy." Her parents hated Vlad for what he'd done to her. And they were extremely protective of their only daughter—and now their only grandchild.

He grimaced. "Your mother did spend an hour scolding me in Spanish. There were a lot of very angry arm gestures involved."

She chuckled.

Her mother knew perfectly well Vlad didn't speak Spanish. When they'd first met, Vlad had wrongly assumed that because her huge husband was Irish and she had blonde hair and blue eyes, she must be Irish, too. Marta had not only assured him of her Mexican heritage, she'd gone on to lecture him on the mistake of assuming anything from someone's outward appearance. Most of the lecture was delivered in Spanish—a habit Marta wasn't inclined to stop because she knew it frustrated Vlad.

It used to make Rose laugh. She was sorry to have missed it this time. She imagined her mother had some choice words for the man who'd broken her daughter's heart.

"Did my father hit you?" she asked.

"No, but it was close. He did make a point of reminding me that he kept a gun in the back office."

"How on earth did you manage to convince them to tell you where we were?" She crossed her arms as the cold air seeped through her thermal t-shirt.

He took in the gesture. "May I come inside and talk? I don't want you standing here getting cold."

"I haven't decided yet. How did you convince my parents to talk to you?"

"My youngest brother, Yuri, went to see them. He got there about the same time Anton found you at their house. Yuri can be…intense." He lowered his voice to a very quiet murmur. "He doesn't hide his disgust with humans or his fanaticism well, though he thinks most humans are too stupid to notice. Your parents were extremely suspicious of his questions and put him off. I went to see them the next day—I wanted to make sure my brothers left town first—and they were nervous enough to let me in so they could grill me."

"Why didn't they tell me any of this?"

He frowned. "I don't know. Maybe they thought you already knew everything? I told them you did." He tilted his head, then winced. "I also made sure they knew my brothers had a lot of resources and they needed to be discreet on the phone."

"So, basically, you scared the hell out of them."

He winced again.

"Mommy, you coming in?" Zoe called.

"Just a minute, baby," she called back. "What did you tell them, exactly?" she asked Vlad.

"That my brothers wanted to hurt you and Zoe," he answered even more quietly, glancing past her toward the interior of the cabin—and Zoe with her bionic hearing.

"And they believed you?"

"Enough to tell me where you were. Eventually. I did have to do a lot of convincing first."

Rose trusted her parents implicitly. If they were worried about the danger enough to send Vlad here, she knew she should be worried, too.

"Come on in," she said, stepping out of the doorway to make room.

When he passed her, his scent reached out and enveloped her, going right to her head. She leaned toward him for an instant before she stopped herself. The urge to bury her face in his neck and breathe in all that yummy male scent was overwhelming. She'd almost forgotten she could feel this much heat and desire just from the way a man smelled. And if that man had been anyone other than Vlad, she might have given in to the urge.

She needed to focus on the situation, not the way Vlad made her feel. "You didn't tell them about…the other thing, did you?"

"The reason I can help Zoe with her episodes? Not specifics. Just that I could help."

"So you manipulated their concern for their grand-daughter?"

"Not manipulated. Told the truth. I can help her, and you. I just want to keep you both safe, Rose."

She nodded without actually commenting.

He shook out his coat before taking it off and hanging it on the coat rack in the entryway. She tried not to notice how snug his long-sleeved t-shirt was, or how wonderfully it showed off his upper body, but she failed miserably. Vlad had always been fit and nicely muscled. His shoulders and arms in particular were like chocolate to her—tempting and delicious. Images of him stripping in her living room, standing there in all his naked glory, sent a pulse of heat through her. She let her gaze wander over his beautiful physique for a moment before she remembered she was supposed to hate him.

The fact that she had trouble remembering that when-ever he stood too close was really starting to piss her off.

"My brothers bought my story about wanting you back, by the way," he said. "At least, they pretended to."

"Well, that's something anyway." She motioned him into the dining room.

When Zoe spotted him, she bounced in her seat. "Vlad! Knew you were here."

"She did actually." Rose faced him, frowning. "Before you knocked, she announced you'd arrived. Was she just guessing? Or maybe she heard you coming?"

His brows creased. "Zoe, can you…can you feel me when you can't see me?"

"Yup." She went back to eating her peanut butter and jelly, grinning around a mouthful of mushed up sandwich.

"Chew with your mouth closed," Rose said absently. To Vlad, she said, "What does that mean? She 'feels' you?"

He was still staring at Zoe. "My…family—" he met Rose's gaze, "—they can sense each other, even at a distance. I can always tell when another one of my people is around."

She appreciated his careful avoidance of words like tiger shifters in front of Zoe. "So you can feel Zoe like that?" she asked quietly, hoping Zoe wouldn't hear—an unrealistic hope. Fortunately, Zoe hadn't seemed to pick up the implications of the comment as she'd turned her attention to the chips on Rose's plate.

Vlad shook his head. "I can't sense her. Which is…odd."

"Good odd or bad odd?"

"Given my brothers…good odd." He paused and gave her a look.

Rose nodded her understanding. At least she thought she understood. If tiger shifters were real, and they could sense each other, the fact that they couldn't sense Zoe meant his brothers had less reason to believe she was Vlad's daughter. If she wasn't his, they had no reason to wish her harm.

"But what's stranger than that I can't feel her is that she *can* feel me," Vlad continued. "I wonder if Nila can do that?"

"You said your sister is…not like…" Rose blew out a breath. This conversation was impossible with Zoe sitting right there, listening to every word they said. And Rose knew her daughter would understand most of this—at least as much as her three-year-old brain could. What she didn't understand, she'd ask about.

"She's not," Vlad said, answering her unspoken question. "But in some ways she is, so there might be similarities."

"You want some?" Zoe asked Vlad, holding out a handful of crumbled potato chips.

Vlad grinned and shook his head. "Thank you. I had lunch already."

"Your tummy grumbled," Zoe said.

"Did it? Well, maybe I didn't eat enough. May I sit down with you?"

Zoe nodded and scooted across the bench, leaving Vlad plenty of room. Rose watched in awe. Her daughter wasn't exactly shy, but she did tend to be leery of new people. She held back, waiting to see if she could trust them not to be doctors. She wasn't that way around other kids, but she needed time to get used to grownups.

Yet she was already as comfortable with Vlad as she was with her grandparents. Could she tell he was family? Or was it because he'd helped ease her pain without poking and prodding at her like a doctor would?

So many questions and there was no way to ask them without explaining things to her. As Rose watched her set some chips and a part of her sandwich in front of Vlad, she accepted that she was going to have to tell her Vlad was her father, sooner rather than later. Especially if he kept showing up like this. But how could she explain his absence all these years?

Admitting the truth to Zoe would mean allowing Vlad into their lives. Once her daughter knew, Rose wouldn't be able to deny her access to her father if she wanted to see him. She was completely prepared to send Vlad packing and never let him near them again—for her own peace of mind. But if Zoe wanted her father in her life, Rose couldn't say no to that.

Vlad glanced at her, his smile soft. "You're worrying," he said. "I could always tell when you got that crease between your eyebrows. You're thinking too hard."

"Lots to think about," she said. Then she sighed and sat across the table from them. "Do you want anything more to eat?" She nodded at the bits of a meal Zoe was leaving for him.

"Don't go to any trouble. I'm fine."

"Where are you staying?" She hadn't intended to bring that up yet, but once it had popped out, she realized she'd been worrying about it since seeing him on the front stoop. She didn't trust herself around him. All her anger and resentment weren't keeping her more lusty thoughts in check, nor were they preventing all those long ago feelings from rising up to taunt her. What they could have had, could have been, if only he'd believed in her…

She couldn't trust her heart, she certainly couldn't trust her body, and she didn't trust him. They couldn't afford to be in the same house together, not now, when so much hung in the balance.

"Don't worry about me," he said.

"You managed to get a room in one of the motels last minute?"

"I said don't worry."

She frowned. "You're not thinking of sleeping in your car or something like that, are you? It's freezing out there. I can't allow that."

"I wasn't going to sleep in the car. But I don't want to rent a room and give my credit card out, in case my brothers trace it. And paying in cash draws too much curiosity."

"Your brothers could…find you that way?"

"Yes. I don't think they can trace your cell, despite what I said to your parents—they don't have nearly the same connections as my dad did—but you might be careful about using your phone too much."

Great. One more thing to worry about. She shook it off to ask, "If you're not sleeping in your car or at a motel, where will you sleep? Not outside? This is not great camping weather."

"Won't be a big deal. I have a…fur coat to keep me warm."

She blinked as his comment sank in and she realized what he was saying. He intended to shift and sleep in the open as a tiger? "Is that…safe? What if someone sees you? Can you take the cold?"

"No one will see me. Yes, I can take the cold. Yes, it's safe. Maybe safer than staying anywhere else."

He met her gaze and she knew he was thinking of them staying under the same roof. Her pulse thumped as she got caught in his dark gaze. Yes, staying in the same house was definitely *not* safe. Tempting. Shockingly tempting. But not safe.

"If you're sure." There was a spare room, but she resisted saying that out loud until she could think through the repercussions.

She watched his gaze move over her face, dipping briefly to her breasts. That quick, discreet look warmed her cheeks. She was definitely safer without him in the house. How the hell could she still be this vulnerable to him? She tried to call up the anger she'd harbored for the last four years, but it was all mixed up with confusion now. Not nearly strong enough.

He'd helped pull Zoe out of an episode. Despite everything else, that single fact muted all her resentment, tangling it up with gratitude for easing her daughter's pain.

She didn't know how to feel about his explanation for leaving. She supposed she had to accept that he couldn't have known the truth about Zoe being his. But part of her still thought he should have known, he should have trusted her. How could she ever get over the fact that in that most important moment, he hadn't believed in her?

Though she still wanted to, she couldn't quite hate him anymore. Beyond that, she didn't know exactly how she felt. With Zoe, everything was so much more complicated. What if Zoe came to accept Vlad, and he left them again? Rose couldn't risk that. Yet, could she really deny Zoe a chance to have a relationship with her dad if Vlad did stay?

She pulled her still-warm tea mug close and hid her confusion in a deep drink.

"We need to discuss Zoe's…lessons," Vlad said, breaking into her thoughts.

She blinked and looked up at him. "I haven't decided…"

"It's not a decision, Rose. She needs to learn how to do everything she can. It will help her."

"Help me what?" Zoe asked as she moved some of the crumbs of chips in front of Vlad back to her paper plate.

Vlad faced her. "I want to help you get rid of your pain."

Her eyes widened. "You do that?" Then her eyes narrowed. "Thought you said you not a doctor?"

"I'm not."

"What are you?"

He chuckled. "Among other things, I'm an inventor."

"What you invent?"

"I develop sports equipment. Things like better safety equipment for rock climbing, gear for rafting and parasailing, that kind of thing."

"Like stuff Granny and Grandpa and Mommy do?"

He nodded. "That's how I met your mother. I was testing a new cam my company was working on, and she happened to be climbing in the same area." He glanced at Rose, his expression mischievous. "Testing out a new site for a future expedition, if I remember correctly."

Zoe glanced between them, then looked at Vlad. "Where'd you go?"

"Utah."

"I like climbing," Zoe announced. "Mommy takes me."

Vlad raised his brows, and Rose shrugged.

"She's good at it. We use the gym by the offices, and she scurries up like a goat. She does the same thing in trees if I let her."

"Climbing fun," Zoe confirmed.

"I agree," Vlad said, his expression soft.

Zoe yawned then bounced off the bench as if she wasn't getting tired. She didn't take a lot of naps anymore, outside of the sleep she needed after an episode, but since arriving in Alpine, she was often tired after lunch and napped for an hour or so. Whether it was the altitude or all the time spent outside in the cold, Rose wasn't sure, but she knew Zoe was happier if she took that hour.

"Nap time?" Rose asked.

"No. Don't wanna. Talking with Vlad."

"I know, baby, but you'll feel better if you nap. Vlad will still be here when you wake up." She glanced at him for confirmation.

"I'm not going anywhere."

"Not tired," Zoe insisted, stamping her foot.

"Fine," Rose said, "but if you get grumpy, we won't be able to play in the snow this afternoon."

Zoe paused to consider that. It rarely snowed in Phoenix, and hadn't once in Zoe's short lifetime, so the opportunity to play in the snow wasn't taken lightly.

"Won't get grumpy," Zoe announced with a confident chin jut.

"Okay. Your choice." As Rose cleaned up the remains of their lunch, she caught Zoe yawning again.

Vlad followed Rose into the kitchen, bringing the cups Rose hadn't had hands for. For a strange, disorienting minute, Rose could *feel* what their lives would be if he hadn't left—this moment as a family vacation they'd decided to take for fun, rather than to avoid danger. The sensory impression shocked a depth of emotion from her. It was so vivid and real. Like stepping into an alternate time-line. Hurt and longing, love and satisfaction all tangled into a complex mix she couldn't sort out.

She shook off the thoughts and focused on putting the remains of lunch away, trying to ignore how right it felt having Vlad in the kitchen with her, helping her do the little domestic things.

To Zoe, she said, "Why don't you go into the living room and color for a bit? I need to talk with Vlad."

Zoe flounced off, but not before reminding her mother, "We go out into the snow soon."

"Soon," Rose confirmed with a smile.

Even with Zoe in the living room, Rose knew she'd hear everything they said. "This would be an easier conversation if she'd just nap," she murmured as quietly as she could.

"Not tired," Zoe yelled from the living room.

Vlad laughed.

"You want a cup of tea?"

"That would be nice. Thank you."

Rose concentrated on putting on the kettle as she asked, "What else has she inherited?"

"Probably an excellent sense of smell and good night vision."

"Never asked her about the night vision, but her sense of smell is very good." Rose thought about it. "She's never asked for a night light. I suppose that could mean good night vision."

"Or she's just fearless, like her mom."

Vlad settled against the kitchen counter, his arms crossed. The position emphasized the bulge of muscles in his arms and shoulders through the tight fit of his shirt. She was a complete sucker for his arms. That first meeting, climbing in Utah, she'd had a hard time not staring as he pulled himself up the rock face. Unfortunately for her distracted mind, she was soloing and couldn't afford to lose her focus. She'd nearly gotten into trouble twice.

Being distracted by him now was going to get her into trouble, too. And she didn't have any ropes to catch her if she slipped this time.

"So your brothers really believed you were trying to get back together with me?" It was probably the wrong topic, but she was curious and the question had just popped out.

He shrugged. "They knew some of what had happened between us. It's a believable story."

She blinked at the admission. "Before you knew about your sister, you wouldn't have considered it, would you?"

He didn't quite meet her gaze when he answered. "I never stopped thinking about you, Rose." His voice was quiet and deep. "I...I don't know if I would have tried to get you back before, but I never stopped thinking about you."

She had to swallow hard around the lump in her throat. She sucked in a shaky breath and tried to ignore the rush of her pulse. "They think I cheated on you, right? Why would you want me back? Why *wouldn't* I want you?"

His entire body stilled as she asked her last question and she realized she'd revealed something she hadn't meant to.

"Could you consider taking me back?" he asked, so quietly she barely heard him.

"That's not why you're here." Hedging and avoidance. She was embarrassed by her own cowardice, but she couldn't help it. She had no idea how to answer his question. She still wanted to take him to bed, a lot more than she cared to admit. And those glimpses of the life they might have had kept haunting her. But she couldn't get past four years of pain in a few days.

And that didn't even take into account the fact that he wasn't human. That his brothers supposedly wanted her daughter dead. That her daughter's entire future hung in the balance.

She turned to make his tea. "Are you sure you can't just teach Zoe how to do that thing you did with her the first day? You're positive she needs to learn about the other stuff?" She kept her back to him as she asked, but her spine tingled with awareness of him.

"I can't hide her from my people forever," he said. "She'll be safer if she understands everything."

"I'm not sure how to tell her any of this," Rose admitted. "She's still so young."

"It's better that way. The young are adaptable. Chances are good she won't even remember anything before this by the time she grows up."

Rose wasn't sure if that was good or bad. "There's a lot I don't understand. You have a lot of explaining to do."

"I know. I will. I think we should start by showing Zoe my other form."

Rose spun to face him. "Oh no, you can't show her that. She'll be terrified."

"Rose. I'm not going to change in front of her, not yet, but she'll have to watch me change eventually so she knows it's possible."

Everything about that rubbed Rose the wrong way, even as her logical side recognized that he was probably right. "You had to…" She glanced toward the living room, then lowered her voice so much she wasn't sure even Vlad could hear her. "You had to take your clothes off. That's not appropriate in front of her."

"I keep forgetting…" Vlad frowned. "With my people, nudity isn't really a thing. We barely notice it, especially around family, because we need to be nude to change—unless we want to keep replacing damaged clothing."

"You didn't take nudity so lightly with me," she murmured.

His expression changed again, his eyes darkening as his gaze moved over her body. With just a look, her pulse started pounding and the tingling excitement of lust tightened in her belly.

"With you, no," he said, his voice rough and even deeper. "That wasn't something I could take lightly."

She swallowed hard. "We need to change the subject."

"Yes." He pushed away from the counter and edged closer.

The closer he got, the faster her breathing came, until she was practically panting. The part of her brain still functioning reminded her that her daughter was just in the other room. That didn't seem to slow her pulse or prevent her from staring at his mouth. She watched him lean toward her, lowering his mouth to hers, and was helpless to move away. She didn't want to stop him. She didn't want to say no.

She'd never wanted a man to kiss her so much in her life.

His breath was hot against her cheek. She closed her eyes, anticipation making her muscles tighten. She felt the soft brush of his lips, once, twice, and then cold air.

She blinked her eyes open, confusion sparking a hint of anger. Until she heard Zoe's little voice a split second before she wandered into the kitchen.

"Can I have juice, please?" she asked.

It took Rose several moments to recover her senses. "Of course, baby," she said, trying to ignore how breathless she sounded. "Give me just a sec then I'll get you a juice box."

Zoe grinned and spun around, dancing back toward the living room.

Rose let out a long, shaky breath and leaned against the counter, her eyes closed. What was she thinking? What was she doing? How the hell would she have explained that to her daughter?

"Okay, that can't happen again," she said aloud to Vlad, finally opening her eyes to look at him. "Not…not now. I want to explain things to Zoe without what's between us complicating it. She's the one that matters. Do you understand?"

He nodded.

She couldn't tell what he was thinking, but in that moment, she decided it was probably for the best because if his imagination was wandering through the same fields of naughty lusty thoughts as hers, they were both in a lot of trouble.

Vlad leaned against the counter again and kept his hands on the countertop, holding tight to avoid reaching for Rose. His body pulsed with the need to finish that kiss, to do more than just take a brief sip. He wanted to take, savor, glut himself on her taste. Hell, he hadn't even put his hands on her yet and it was all he could do not to pull her into his arms. His palms actually tingled with the need to feel her skin.

It was probably better he hadn't put his hands on her. The faint sound of Zoe's footsteps had jerked him back to reality just in time. If he'd had Rose's body pressed against his, he wouldn't have been able to react so quickly.

He squeezed the counter as tight as he dared and tried to force his mind away from visions of Rose naked. Before his imagination and body had run amuck, she'd brought up a valid complication in him teaching Zoe how to shift.

Zoe had been raised by humans who were much more sensitive to nudity than his own people. The casual nudity among tigers could be disturbing to a child not used to it—especially with a male who was essentially a stranger. He hadn't even considered that, until Rose mentioned it. Taking his clothes off to shift was simply a pragmatic necessity, not something he'd ever given much thought to.

But she was right. He couldn't just strip down in front of Zoe to show her the shift.

So how could he show her how the process worked? How could he explain it and teach her without actually showing her?

Damn. He was going to need help, female help.

Deep in thought, considering his options, he was surprised when Rose put a mug of tea under his nose. He took it automatically. "Thanks."

"You're thinking really hard. What about?"

"How to show Zoe what I need to show her, without shocking and offending you both."

Rose's expression softened. "Thank you for taking my discomfort seriously."

"What did you think I'd do?"

"I don't know. Try to convince me it was natural and no big deal."

"Rose, I don't take your worries about any of this lightly. This is a huge thing for you both. It's complicated and scary. I understand that. It's necessary. She has to know and learn. But I won't diminish the difficulty of that either."

Her smile robbed him of sense for a moment. She used to look at him like that all the time. And every single time it had shaken him to his soul. Until that moment, he hadn't realized how much he'd missed that expression, the way her face glowed with warmth, giving him a smile meant for him and him alone.

He'd do anything to have her smile at him that way for the rest of his life.

She turned away, ending the moment. And he hid his disappointment by sipping his tea. They would have time for their relationship, he promised himself. He hadn't been lying to his brother about wanting Rose back. He just had to prove to her that she could trust him.

To do that, he had to make sure Zoe was safe.

"If I can find a female to help us, someone I can trust with knowledge of Zoe, would that be easier?" he asked.

"Do you know someone? Wouldn't that alert your brothers?"

"The person I'm considering wouldn't go to my brothers."

"But?"

He sighed. He should have known Rose would hear his unspoken worry. "But she doesn't necessarily like me. It'll take some convincing to get her here."

"If she doesn't like you, how can you trust her?"

"I trust her to consider Zoe special and to be protective of her."

"Who is this person?"

"She's a close friend of my sister's fiancé."

"The sister you just met?"

"Yes."

"Are you friends with her fiancé?"

"No."

"Then why would his friend help you?"

He still had so much to explain to Rose, about his people and the tiger community that Zoe would have to learn to navigate. Explaining Nila's relationship, explaining who Alexis Tarasova was and how he could trust her with Zoe, were difficult things to do without Rose knowing more.

"There's a lot I need to tell you first, things better discussed after Zoe goes to bed tonight. I won't do anything without your permission, though. I want Zoe safe as much as you do."

He watched her swallow visibly, but she nodded.

"Part of me wishes you were just…ordinary," she murmured. "Just another guy. And Zoe didn't have to deal with all this other stuff."

"And the other part of you?"

"I still wish Zoe didn't have to deal with all this. I certainly don't want her in pain anymore. But…" She cringed. "But I kind of find the danger…sexy." She rolled her eyes. "I know. I know. That sounds weird and wrong. I don't want my daughter in danger, don't think that. But if she weren't in harm's way…"

She trailed off as a beautiful pink blush brightened her cheeks. Vlad gripped his mug tightly to keep his hands to himself. When he heard the ceramic crack, he set it down with a clunk and moved to put more space between them.

"Maybe we should go out to the living room," he said. He had to clear his throat to get rid of the husky sound. "I think we need a chaperone."

"Good idea." She hurried past him.

The move washed him with her scent. The delicious

flavor of lavender and cardamom melding with the added spice of her desire made his head spin. He shook off the effect and followed her, working hard to keep his need in check.

Damn, but this was going to be a hard few weeks.

CHAPTER SIX

They spent the afternoon playing with Zoe, building more snowmen, and hiking through the pine trees at the back of the cabin. Zoe, true to her word, didn't take a nap but also didn't get grumpy. In fact, she glowed with energy, bouncing around, telling stories, building snow people and their homes with the determination only a three-year-old could muster.

Vlad was a little surprised she could stay in the cold for so long, but every time Rose asked if she needed to go in and get warm, Zoe shook her head and went right back to building things out of snow.

"She just doesn't get cold easy," Rose murmured as they watched Zoe throw a clump of snow at a tree then double over giggling. "So long as she's moving, she's comfortable."

"She got my metabolism, too, then," he said very quietly.

"Lucky girl," she said. "I always envied you that."

"You did?"

"Of course. You never had to worry about what you ate. If I wanted to keep doing all the things I loved, I had to work at staying in shape and eating right. You just seemed to come by it naturally. Used to piss me off."

He laughed. "I like your shape just the way it is."

"Don't start that now. We'll get into trouble again."

Too late, he thought, as his imagination taunted him with memories of her naked, pressed against him, with only an open sleeping bag between them and the ground on a cool spring night. He shook off the memory. She was right. He needed to stop thinking about her body.

By the time Zoe admitted defeat and agreed to come in, the sun had set and darkness had filled in the space between the trees. While Rose readied dinner, Vlad stayed in the living room with Zoe, stretched out on the rug in front of the fire, coloring in books filled with ponies and race cars as she explained to him which colors were the right ones to use.

Vlad was utterly charmed by his daughter. The thought that he'd sacrificed those first few years of her precious life because of his hurt pride poked at him. He'd had a lot of logical reasons to believe Rose had cheated on him. But her scent hadn't carried deception and she'd been glowing when she told him she was pregnant.

He should have known. He should have *realized*. Rose wasn't the kind of woman to cheat or lie. It was one of the things he'd loved about her—that straightforward, honest attitude. If she'd wanted to sleep with another man, she would have just dumped him and gone off with the other man.

"You not watching," Zoe scolded, nudging his hand. "See. You need green now."

"Of course." He smiled and pushed aside his dark thoughts. He could berate himself later.

Over dinner, Vlad had another hit of regret. Sitting down with Rose and Zoe felt so right. They were his family. *His* family. And he'd tossed them both aside because he'd believed what he thought was fact over what he'd *known* to be the truth.

How was he going to make that up to Rose? Would she ever be able to forgive him and trust him again?

He savored helping her put Zoe to bed, his chest tight with emotions too powerful to name as they tucked her in with her favorite blankie in hand and kissed her goodnight. When Rose said, "I love you, Zoe," and Zoe answered, "I love you, Mommy," Vlad thought his heart would break completely.

He followed Rose to the living room after, and then… waited. He wasn't sure what he was waiting for. Her to kick him out. Her to ask him to stay.

When she motioned to the couch, he sat, a little jump of his pulse betraying his hope. If she were a tiger, she'd scent a lot of his emotions in that moment, probably be able to detect the desire and longing easily enough. He could hide his feelings from his family. But with Rose, he was an open book. He was lucky her human senses weren't strong enough to read him. He'd be in real trouble then.

She settled on the opposite side of the couch from him and

faced the fire, her expression pensive. He opened his mouth to start the conversation then thought better of it. He was treading a very delicate line here. He needed to let her take the lead.

"Zoe can still hear us," she said quietly, her voice soft against the gentle crackling of the fire.

"She's almost asleep," he assured. "We can wait to talk until she's drifted off."

Rose faced him. "How can you tell?"

"I can hear her breathing when I concentrate."

"Your hearing is that sensitive? Doesn't that make being in cities difficult? All the noise doesn't hurt?"

"Since my hearing has always been like this, I've spent my life learning how to…adjust what I take in. I'm used to it. Does living in the city bother Zoe?"

"Doesn't seem to. Sudden loud noises make her cover her ears. But I've seen other kids her age do that. It's possible with all the other pain episodes, she's never noticed her hearing as causing her discomfort."

"She likely won't. To her, hearing well is normal and she'll naturally learn how to adjust to her surroundings."

"You said the other thing is natural to her, too. Why hasn't she just…done what you do?"

"She doesn't know it's possible. She's never seen it. Our children grow up with that all around them. It's normal."

"When do your kids start this part?"

"It varies, depending on the child, but sometime around two they start…flipping shapes."

"Flipping?"

He chuckled. "Once they start, it can be hard to keep them in one form for very long. They hop back and forth for fun. Usually with lots of kid giggles. It's both cute and frustrating for parents—so I'm told."

She smiled, but a furrow formed between her brows. "Doesn't that hurt them? Can they just keep changing without, I don't know, wearing out?"

"It's like anything kids do. Eventually, they do get tired and have to stop, but they've got a lot more energy at two than you and I do at our ages."

"True. When she's not in pain, Zoe can play well past the point when I wear out."

"She's a really good kid, Rose. You've done a good job with her." He swallowed back his guilt and said, "I'm sorry I wasn't there for you two. I should have been."

She shook her head. "How could you have believed me when you thought it was impossible?"

But he heard the hesitance and distrust in her voice. "I still should have known. I can…scent a lot. Emotions have different signatures, flavors I guess you could say. My senses told me you weren't lying, that you were excited about being pregnant. I should have realized you didn't cheat."

"Yeah, you should have," she said, the comment barely audible, even to him.

He watched her swallow visibly as she focused on the fire, not meeting his gaze.

"What's done is done, Vlad. We can't change the past. All I care about now is making sure Zoe is okay." She glanced behind her, toward the hallway and the bedrooms beyond. "Is she asleep yet?"

He paused to listen. "Even breathing, little snores. She's out."

Rose faced forward and pressed her lips together before saying, "This shifting business scares me."

Vlad forced himself to drop the subject of their relationship. He couldn't fix that without first helping Zoe, and to help Zoe, Rose needed to understand what being a shapeshifter meant for their daughter. "What specifically scares you? Outside of everything."

She flashed him a half smile before turning serious again. "At the moment, the thing that freaks me out the most is the idea that she might start to change shapes and then get stuck."

She faced him finally, her beautiful blue eyes wide and glistening. The fear in her scent broke him.

"Can that happen?" she asked. "Can the shifting hurt her more than not shifting has?"

"No. Not for a tiger shifter anyway. Once the process starts, it finishes. Even if a tiger wanted to, they couldn't stop the shift once it really gets going. We don't do half shifts or get stuck."

"You said not for tiger shifters. Does that mean there are other shifters?"

"Oh, yeah. Lots of species."

"What? How is that possible and *no one* knows?"

"Centuries and centuries of hiding in plain sight. I don't know for sure with other species, but for tigers, we have enough problems at the moment. We don't need the complication of fending off human hunters. So we are very careful to keep our natures secret. That's the whole reason killing a human is a death sentence crime."

"I didn't think it was possible to keep anything secret anymore."

"It might not be for much longer. But for now, we're careful."

Rose blew out a breath that lifted the tendrils of red hair curling on her forehead. "This is a lot to take in."

"I know. And there's a lot more. Maybe we should focus on what Zoe needs for now and I'll explain the other stuff as you feel able to face it?"

"Probably a good idea. But I want two questions answered first."

"Okay."

"One, other species can do half shifts or get stuck mid-shift?"

"Getting stuck *is* a problem for a couple of shifter species—mostly the ones that can 'convert' humans. Were-wolves, for example. The humans turned wolf are the ones that get stuck. If it's not natural to the individual, it's complicated and potentially dangerous. Dragons are one of the species that can do half shifts. Elephant and bear shifters can, too."

Vlad watched her eyes grow bigger with every sentence and was afraid she'd just shut down. He shouldn't have gone into so much detail so quickly. "This is too much, isn't it?"

"Yes. Dragons? There are shapeshifting *dragons* in the world?"

"Most legends have some basis in reality."

"Yeah, but the reality behind dragons is supposed to be dinosaur bones. Not *real* dragons."

"Little bit of both contributed to the various legends."

"*Dios*," she breathed. Then shook her head. "I need a drink. I'm gonna get a glass of wine. You want anything?"

"Tea would be nice."

She smiled and some of the shock eased from her features. "Teetotaler," she teased.

That had been an ongoing joke between them. He'd never really developed a taste for alcohol but couldn't get enough tea. For some reason, Rose found that quirk both charming and amusing. He didn't understand why, but since he liked her smile so much, he wasn't going to argue with her.

"Be right back." She disappeared into the kitchen.

Leaving him to consider everything he'd just said to her. They'd gone off topic a bit, but there was a lot she'd need to know once Zoe entered the shifter world. And though his people were insular and didn't interact much with other shifters—or any other species of otherworldly creatures for that matter—knowing the world held such beings would be important for Zoe's survival.

When Rose returned with his tea and her wine, she echoed his thoughts. "We should probably get back to the stuff that will immediately affect Zoe. The rest...I know I need to understand all this, but for now, it's too much."

"We'll have time for the rest later."

"So back to my two questions. Getting stuck won't be a

problem for her. You're sure? Even though she's half human?"

"I'm sure, because she was born to it." He put as much confidence in his voice as he could, but in truth, he wasn't positive. There were no cases in modern times of a shapeshifter born from a human parent and a tiger parent. Nila was the only case of a hybrid that anyone knew about, and she couldn't shift.

But from what he understood, getting stuck halfway through a shift in other species was the result of fear and lack of confidence. So no matter what, he had to ensure that both Rose and Zoe were confident and unafraid when Zoe started her first shift. Because of her age, and because she was born to it, he hoped Zoe's body would just do what it was meant to do.

"Okay," Rose said, "then my second question. You said tigers were in enough trouble. What did you mean by that?"

Ah, the part that really would freak her out because this would directly affect Zoe's future among the tigers. If Zoe had been born a boy instead of a girl, this would be a lot less complicated. He debated how much to tell her and decided to stick with the basics, enough to satisfy her curiosity, but not so much as to terrify her and send her running away from the tigers.

"Tiger shifters are facing extinction. Female birthrates have dropped so dramatically it's left the sex ratio really skewed."

"How skewed?"

"Roughly 90 percent males to 10 percent females worldwide."

"Wow. That sounds bad."

"And it's not getting better."

"What are you doing to prevent extinction?"

Her eyes narrowed, and he could see the wariness and suspicion in her expression. He knew she'd catch on quickly. But he didn't want to tell her how bad things had gotten when the dwindling female numbers were finally noticed. The truth about how violent tiger males could be might just send her into hiding. So he skimmed over that part of their history. "The elders set up the Mate Run. It's essentially a way for males to compete for females."

"How does it work?"

"During a female's estrous cycle, she goes into one of the areas we have set up in an isolated forest, and she runs from a group of males. Whichever male she allows to catch her, gets to be with her for the three days of her cycle. If they get pregnant, they're allowed to mate permanently— get married if they like. Or she can run again for a new mate once her cycles start again. There's a lot of flexibility for the female, and the choice of mates is entirely up to her."

"And if the couple doesn't get pregnant?"

"The female keeps running until she does. She can stay with the same male cycle to cycle, or she can choose a new male with each Run. Entirely up to her."

He was making a point to emphasize how much control the females had during the Run to keep Rose from panicking, but as he watched her, he realized she hadn't yet made the connection that this would be something expected of Zoe. She frowned and took the information seriously, but there was nothing in her scent or expression to hint at worry for her own child.

"How did the Run solve the skewed sex ration?"

"It didn't. It's just helped stave off extinction."

"What's being done about the low female numbers, then?"

"A lot of research." He took a breath. "Some of that research involved the possibility of humans and tigers mating."

Her eyes narrowed. "So you knew before your sister that it was possible?"

The bite in her voice made him flinch. "No. Most tigers think it's just the stuff of myths and legends. We have a story of an ancient couple—human woman, male tiger—who had children together, but most tigers assumed the story had no basis in reality."

"Then why is there research being done?"

"One of the elders believes it might be the key to tiger survival. Until my half sister, though, there was no evidence of half breeds."

He winced at the term. His father had imbued that phrase with a great deal of disgust and hatred whenever he discussed tiger-human offspring.

Rose didn't seem to notice his reaction. "And now Zoe." She pulled in a breath. "What does all this mean for our daughter?"

He set his tea down and leaned forward, resting his arms on his knees and staring at the fire. He didn't want to tell her this part. But she had to know some of it. Again, he settled on giving her the basics. "Some of my people think those like Nila and Zoe are…saviors. They represent hope of other breeding options. Then there are those like my brothers, my father…who think tiger-human offspring will dilute our bloodlines and lead us to extinction faster. They argue that successful matings between humans and tigers—if they could even happen—would result in only humans, like my sister."

He fisted his hands when they started to shake, a combination of anger and betrayal swamping him. He pushed thoughts of his family aside and turned to face Rose. "Zoe proves tiger offspring can come from mixed matings."

"And that means?"

"It means we'll have to eventually introduce her to the elders and get her protected under our laws."

"I don't see why?"

"Because without that protection, my brothers will just keep coming for her."

"You said they bought your story about wanting me back and Zoe not being yours."

He ran his hands through his hair. "They did. I think. But I can't guarantee they won't figure it out eventually. Rose, she has my eyes. Anton saw that."

She sighed and dropped her head back against the couch. "If she's a shifter, though, why would they still want to hurt her?"

"They're convinced hybrids will dilute our bloodlines no matter what kind of offspring is produced."

She rolled her head to look at him. "What good will the protection of the elders do?"

"It'll mean severe punishments for anyone who tries to hurt Zoe. She'll be safe."

"So why aren't we heading to the elders now?"

"I don't want to introduce Zoe to the tiger world before she can control her own tiger."

Rose nodded and looked away again. "Okay, I guess that's fair enough." She sipped her wine and sighed. "I don't want any of this to be real."

"But it is."

"Yeah, well, that doesn't mean I have to like it. I just want Zoe safe and healthy."

He did, too. "I'll make sure she's safe, Rose. I promise. We have time for all this stuff."

They stayed silent for long moments, the only sound the quiet crackling of wood and flames. He turned his attention to Zoe, assuring himself she was breathing peacefully, sound asleep.

Finally, he said, "Thanks for the tea and for dinner." He stood. He'd given her enough to think about for one night. "I'll come back in the morning and we can consider how to tell Zoe about all this."

Rose patted the couch. "I'm not letting you sleep in the snow, Vlad. This place has enough bedrooms for all three of us. You can stay here."

He swallowed hard as he stared down at her, caught in her eyes. He didn't trust himself to be in this house with her overnight, not when her scent filled it and drifted around him like temptation. He was pretty sure the only way he'd stay out of her bed was to spend the night in the freezing temperatures in his tiger form.

"I don't think it's a good idea," he forced out.

She blinked but didn't turn away. "I'm not going to lie and say I'm not still attracted to you. Especially after that almost kiss earlier in the kitchen. But I'm also not ready for anything to happen between us. I'm still…hurt and leery and confused. And frankly, I still don't trust you. So while you're invited to sleep in the spare room, you are not invited into my bed. Not tonight. Probably not for a while."

The fact that he might be invited sometime in the future was enough to make his pulse pound. Still, could he stay here, dizzy with her scent, and not try to change her mind? For the last four years, he'd essentially been a monk because he couldn't get over her. The temptation to seduce her and make her forget all the hurt and betrayal between them was hard to resist.

She shook her head. "Vlad, I can tell you're debating being noble and leaving. Don't. I'll just stay up all night worrying that you're freezing to death."

"I'll be in tiger form. I won't freeze."

She tilted her head to one side, a slight furrow between her brows. "It is so odd trying to remember that you're… different like that." She motioned him to the couch again. "I'm not finished talking with you, so you're going to sleep here tonight."

He eased back onto the couch. If she still had questions, he was obligated to answer them. He wasn't using her curiosity as an excuse, he assured himself. He owed her the time. That was the only reason he was going to stay.

She smiled a little at him, and his heart thumped hard.

This was going to be a long night.

# CHAPTER SEVEN

They talked well into the night, mostly about the tiger world. Rose had more questions than she could even remember to ask. She was fascinated, appalled, and scared in equal measure. The fear was for her daughter. The complications of having to navigate this alien world, of the things Zoe was going to have to deal with, overwhelmed her a few times. She had moments where she wanted all of it to go away.

But it wouldn't. She had to face it and learn how to deal with it so she could help Zoe.

"I don't want to let her try to shift," Rose admitted. "I've watched her in pain so much, I'm not sure I can take any more."

"The change won't hurt her. It's what her body is trying to do."

"So you keep saying. I have no reference for this, Vlad.

It's…it's myth and fiction. It's impossible. And, no offense, but it wasn't pretty either."

He grimaced. "I know. To humans the process is difficult to see. But from my perspective, from any tiger shifter's perspective, it's normal."

She let out a breath and leaned back into the couch. He had his arm across the back, his hand near her shoulder. She tried to ignore how close they were to touching, but her skin actually tingled with awareness of his strong fingers just inches from her. She knew insisting he stay was the right thing to do. And she had been telling the truth when she told him he wasn't invited into her bed. But temptation still lingered, despite logic.

She rolled her head to look at him. He was staring at her with those fabulous brown eyes. She'd always loved his eyes. And his voice, God, she loved listening to him. The longer they talked, the deeper his voice seemed to get, to the point that now, every time he said something, the sound caressed her and sent little tingles of excitement through her stomach.

The clock over the mantle dinged quietly, three in the morning. She sighed. She needed to sleep. She got so little as it was, she really shouldn't have stayed up this late. When a yawn popped out, she covered her mouth and grimaced. "Sorry. Guess we'll have to wait on the rest till tomorrow night."

"We have time," he said.

"A few days. Then I have to get home, where your brothers will be able to find us if they still want to."

His silence spoke volumes.

"Wouldn't it just be better to…pretend she's exactly what you thought all those years ago?"

"Rose, you know she has to learn to shift."

"Yes, yes. I'm not talking about that. Once she learns, she can control it, she won't be in pain, and she can get on with being a little girl. Why do we have to tell the tigers about her at all? If no one knows about her, she won't need the protection of tiger laws."

He frowned a little. "We can't hide her nature forever."

"Why not? You said you can't sense her the way other tigers can sense each other. She *can* sense you, so we teach her to avoid people who 'feel' like you. And even if she encounters tiger shifters, they won't be able to tell she's one. She can just go on with her life as if she were human."

"What if she wants to meet other tigers? What if she goes looking for that community, but because we've kept her hidden, she has no protection from it? What if, despite all our efforts, they find her anyway?"

Rose wanted to throw something. It wasn't fair. And yes, yes, life wasn't fair. But for Zoe it should be.

"Rose."

He leaned closer and gripped her hand. The contact sent a little tremor through her. She stared at their linked fingers rather than meet his gaze.

"Rose, I'd love to keep her safe from my world. To keep her hidden and protected and never let anything bad anywhere near her. Ever. But someone will eventually figure it out. If not my brothers, then someone else. It's better if we control her introduction to the tiger world and ensure, through protection from the elders, that she's safe there." He touched her face with gentle fingers, forcing her chin up so she had to look him in the eyes. "I promise I will do everything in my power to keep her safe."

His sincerity shined with a fierceness that surprised her. His jaw was firm, his lips set in a hard line. She could practically feel his determination through his fingers on her chin and the hand holding hers.

He meant what he was saying. At least in this moment, he meant every word.

Before she thought better of it, she leaned in and kissed him. Whether out of gratitude, relief, or simply because she loved the taste of him, she wasn't sure. A little of all of that. Plus a bit of desperation for something normal amidst the upheaval. They'd always been good at lust. The way his lips felt so right against hers was something she could grab onto as solid and real.

She edged closer, angling her head to better the contact, and he opened to her. The instant her tongue brushed against his, her body flamed to life with a passion she'd been afraid she'd never feel again. Lust as strong and intoxicating as it had been before all the hurt and anger and betrayal.

It felt so good. So right.

She tunneled her fingers through his thick hair, savoring the feeling and texture, melting against him when he wrapped his arms around her waist. She wanted to climb onto his lap and take and remember and give. The thrill of the moment, the rush of adrenaline was like a drug to her— it always had been—and she was beyond desperate for that simple, uncomplicated sensation that washed away everything else.

He changed positions and before she knew it, she found herself sitting on his lap, just as she'd wanted, their kiss turning into something serious fast. The feel of his erection against her hip heightened her need. Everything about this felt so damned familiar, as if four years didn't separate this moment from the last time they'd been together. She wiggled closer and swallowed his groan with so much satisfaction it was like a mini-orgasm all by itself.

She hadn't been with a man since Vlad, so the feel of strong hands stroking along her spine and over her hip left her weak with wanting. Familiar, but new. She remembered what it felt like to just be a woman in the arms of a man she wanted. She hadn't felt this release and freedom in so long. And it would be so, so easy to forget the real world and just wallow in his heat. Her body felt heavy and lush, ready for the sensation of his warm palms on her bare skin. Even the thought of it made her thighs clench.

"Rose." His voice was harsh and deep, sexy as all hell, and he sounded as desperate as she felt.

She remembered that sound, that tone. The power and satisfaction of knowing he wanted her as badly as she wanted him had always made her feel strong and feminine. She gave herself permission to explore the hard muscles of his shoulders and back, running her fingers up his neck, triumphing in his hard shiver. When he moved a hand to her breast, cupping her through her clothes, she arched into him. He squeezed gently, then ran his thumb over her nipple and all she could think was that there was too much material between her skin and his fingers.

She dropped her head back as he moved from her mouth to her throat, kissing and sucking, nibbling at the sensitive spots he knew made her crazy. The tension in her core built. She'd been alone for so long, she was pretty sure he'd only have to brush her clit through her jeans and she'd come. Her hips bucked at the thought.

She gripped his wrist, intending to move his hand lower, to give her that longed-for orgasm, when the little voice of reason that had gotten stronger since she became a mother warned her to stop. She wasn't ready for it. Too much history and emotion still remained between them. Too much distrust. Sex might have been simple and uncomplicated at one time, but not anymore. Not with him.

That irritating voice poked a hole in the lovely sensual world she'd lost herself in and forced her to face reality. Instead of moving his hand to her jeans, she linked her fingers with his and then pulled back so she could see his face. His eyes were dark and hot and for just an instant she forgot her resolve. Then she blinked and straightened.

"I'm sorry. I know I started this, but I have to stop it, too. I'm not ready yet."

He nodded, but she watched him swallow visibly and the tension in his body didn't ease. "This is why I offered to leave."

"I know, and I appreciate that."

"I can still go. If you want me to."

"No. Just because I have trouble controlling myself

around you isn't any reason to force you to sleep in the snow."

"I don't know. I could use a hit of cold air about now."

She laughed. Then sighed. "I've missed this." She spoke so quietly, she wasn't sure he'd hear her, though she should have known better.

"I've missed you," he said.

She traced her fingers along his jaw, rubbing her thumb against the prickly texture of his unshaven cheek. Her heart thumped hard with the continued kick of need running through her blood and a sharp thrust of emotions too complicated to tease out just yet.

When she felt herself leaning toward him again and realized she was staring at his mouth, she jerked away and stood. "Come on. I'll show you the spare room."

He followed without a word. She was both relieved and disappointed that he didn't try to touch her as she led him down the hall, past hers and Zoe's rooms to the third bedroom. This was the smallest room, with only a single bed and a small closet. But it was better than freezing outside, she was sure.

Away from the fire, the only light was the faint glow of moonlight on snow that snuck in through the windows. She stared up at his shadowed features, memories of times past colliding with the here and now. If she let herself, if she gave up all the pain and resentment, she realized she could easily love him again. She wasn't entirely sure she'd ever stopped loving him, even when she'd hated him with every ounce of her being. She suspected she wouldn't have hated him so much if she hadn't still loved him, too.

"So complicated," she murmured. "Too complicated."

"Worth it," he said quietly. He cupped her cheek. "We have time, as much as you need."

"Do we? And to what end? I can't afford to take anything lightly anymore, Vlad. Not with Zoe to consider."

"I know. I don't take what's between us lightly, and I never have. It's never just been about sex with us, Rose."

"Well. Maybe it was in the beginning. Just a little."

He dipped his chin to look her in the eyes. "Are you telling me when we first met, you were only interested in me for sex?"

"Well, yeah. You're sexy as all hell. I couldn't wait to get you naked."

He scowled, but the expression turned rueful a moment later. "I'm trying to be offended by that, and I can't seem to manage it."

"That's because you're vain. You like that I want you and think you're hot."

"True." He smiled. "We have always been good at sex."

"Don't remind me or I won't sleep."

He leaned in close, as if he would kiss her again, and she felt herself falling toward him. Then she shook her head, not a denial as much as a way to clear the fog of desire from her brain.

"Goodnight, Vlad." She stepped out of the doorway, moving away from his touch.

"Goodnight, Rose. Sleep well."

She stayed in the hall as he closed his bedroom door, then she rolled her eyes. "Sleep well," she muttered. "Yeah, right."

His answering chuckle followed her to her room.

Rose came to, groggy and out of balance, when Zoe shook her awake not long after the sun had come up. Her daughter climbed up next to her in bed and snuggled against her as Rose forced herself to some semblance of wakefulness.

"Are you hungry, baby?" she murmured, savoring the warm sweetness of her daughter cuddling with her, healthy and not in pain. She lived for these quiet, peaceful moments.

"Thirsty," Zoe said. "Can I have chocolate milk?"

"Yes, you can because we're on vacation."

"Love vacations."

Rose chuckled. "Me, too."

Though she was loath to disrupt the cuddling time, nature called. She patted Zoe's back, then sat up, rubbing her hand over her face as she worked to shake off the slightly nauseous feeling of having gotten too little sleep. "Head out to the kitchen," she said. "I'll be there in a minute after I use the bathroom."

Zoe danced out of the room, singing the alphabet song as she went. Rose smiled, then grimaced. Zoe wasn't exactly quiet. That singing would probably wake Vlad.

Ah well. He wanted to be in their lives again, he'd better learn now that sleeping in was a thing of the past.

Though, as she recalled, he'd never slept in as much as she had.

By the time she got to the kitchen, she was only a little

surprised to see Vlad awake and putting the kettle on for tea. Zoe was sitting at the small kitchen table, her legs swinging as she told Vlad some story about a squirrel. He smiled and nodded at all the appropriate places.

Rose watched them from the doorway for a moment. The scene left her feeling a complex mixture of joy and sadness, melancholy and worry. She shook off the confusion as she cleared her throat and walked in to join them.

"Mommy! Vlad drinks tea like you. He said coffee was yucky." Zoe giggled into her hand.

Rose smiled. "Don't tell Granny."

By the time they finished breakfast and Zoe nagged them into going outside to play again, Rose's already confused emotions were a tangled mess. Having Vlad with them felt too damned right. He *belonged* with them. He was Zoe's father.

And she deserved to know. Rose just didn't want to cross that bridge yet. Despite what had happened, or almost happened, between her and Vlad last night, she really had no idea what his intentions were going forward. He still wanted her. And he wanted to protect Zoe. As far as Rose could tell, he intended to stay in their lives.

But what did staying in their lives mean? Marriage? Co-parenting with the occasional tumble in bed on the side for Mommy and Daddy? So many years had passed, she wasn't even sure what *she* wanted anymore. Before he'd left, she was positive he was the only man for her.

Unfortunately, the intervening years hadn't actually changed her mind about that. As she watched Vlad help Zoe build an even bigger snowman, she admitted—if only to herself—that she couldn't imagine bringing another man into her life. Ever.

He was the only one for her.

If her daughter hadn't been around, Rose would have cursed, long and colorfully, with language that would have had her mother sending her to confession.

Whatever the future held for her, though, she had to protect Zoe. For the moment, that meant keeping the fact that Vlad was her father a secret. She didn't have any idea how to tell her anyway.

"Look, Mommy!" Zoe pointed at the lopsided stack of snowballs. "It's as tall as a giant!"

"Sure is, baby."

Vlad looked up and smiled at her over the top of the snowman. She smiled back, despite the worry gnawing at her gut. They had time, she assured herself. She'd figure this out. She just needed some time.

After lunch, Vlad excused himself to make some phone calls. "I'll go for a walk," he said, "and let you guys rest for a bit."

"No naps," Zoe announced before plopping down in front of the cold fireplace to color.

Rose shook her head. "Shame," she muttered. "I could use one."

The sound of Vlad's chuckle as he headed out the door made her stomach flip-flop with pleasure.

She settled on the couch next to Zoe, content to flip through a travel magazine while her daughter amused herself. She had no idea how long Vlad would be away, but the house felt very quiet without him. Anticipation kept her checking the clock on the mantle, excited for his return.

That she was waiting for him, even though he'd only been gone a half hour, was irritating and embarrassing all at once.

She'd been happier hating him.

Okay, well, maybe not. But she felt silly mooning over him like a teenager. She should have outgrown that nonsense years ago.

She was about to toss the magazine aside and find something else to read when she heard a sound she dreaded with every ounce of her being.

A soft little moan. And then, "Mommy, I hurt."

Vlad paced in a circle, his cell to his ear, listening to the ringing. He'd made a few calls to associates keeping tabs on his brothers. All three had shown up to their respective offices on the east coast over the last two days, which meant even if they were still looking for Rose and Zoe, they hadn't found them yet. Then he called in to his own office in Saint Paul to make sure his business wasn't falling apart and manufacturing of their latest climbing ropes was well underway. Everything was functioning as it should. He'd hired excellent people—one of the few lessons his father had taught him that he'd found useful.

Finally, he faced the call he was exceedingly nervous about because it mattered so damned much.

She wouldn't recognize his number. Would she let it go to voicemail? And if she did, what kind of message could he leave to get her to return the call?

He was debating his options when Nila finally answered.

"Hello, this is Dr. De Luca."

"Nila. It's Vlad. Please don't hang up."

Silence.

"I need your help with something. Please."

More silence.

He glanced at the phone to make sure it hadn't disconnected or she hadn't hung up on him. The seconds were still ticking by on a connected call.

"Why are you calling me for help?" she asked.

He put the phone back to his ear. "You're the only one I can talk to who will understand."

"Your brothers still want me dead, Vlad. Why should I trust you?"

"I helped save your life?"

"Hmm. I haven't decided about that yet."

"It concerns my daughter," he said bluntly. Whatever else Nila might think of him, he knew from his research she was a compassionate woman. As a vet, she was known for her skill and empathy with the big cats she looked after. A woman who liked animals so much couldn't refuse helping a little girl, could she?

"You have a daughter?" Confusion and curiosity lilted her voice.

That was good. She wouldn't hang up on him yet. "She's a little over three years old." He paused, reminded himself his own phone was secure and no one was listening in on this call. His father might have managed that, but his brothers didn't have the skills or connections to trace and tap cellphones. He let out a very quiet breath and leapt. "Her mother is human."

Another ringing silence followed the admission. He could hear Nila breathing, but for long moments, she didn't say a word.

Vlad was about to say more when she finally spoke. "You're positive the girl is yours?"

"I am now."

"Is this why you didn't want me dead?"

"One of the main reasons."

She snorted. "Well, that makes a lot more sense now. So you have a hybrid daughter. What kind of help do you need from me?"

"She's…she's not entirely like you. She can shift."

"What?"

"She was born a shifter. At least… Well, that's what I need help with."

"I can't shift. How can I help?"

"I need a woman to help me teach Zoe. She's been raised by humans. I can't just strip off my clothes and change in front of her the way I might a tiger child."

"You changed in front of me without any worries."

"You're an adult. She's three years old."

"Watching you shift was still a fucking shock. I still have nightmares, you know?"

"I'm sorry about that, but it was necessary at the time. And if it scared a grown woman, how much worse will it be for a preschooler?"

"Yeah, okay. I get your point."

"I'm actually more worried about the nudity than the shift itself."

"Ah." She paused, then, "Does your daughter know she's different yet?"

"No. But she's going through periods of severe pain because her body is trying to shift and she doesn't even know it's possible. I need to help her, soon, or the pain will only get worse. But teaching her myself is…complicated."

"Fine. I still don't see why you're calling me?"

"I want you to ask Alexis to help me."

"Alexis? Why?"

"She's had three cubs herself, one of them female. And because of her relationship with your fiancé, she'll do a favor for you where she wouldn't necessarily help me." He paused before adding, "I know she doesn't share my brothers' opinion of hybrids either. She's the only female tiger I can be sure will treat Zoe with respect and not want her dead."

"Elizaveta won't want her dead."

No. The powerful elder would probably want to study Zoe, just as she'd coerced Nila into allowing medical tests. "I can't trust any elder yet," Vlad said aloud. "You know why."

One of them had helped his father hunt Nila.

Vlad had been quietly investigating, but he still hadn't uncovered which one his father had been working with—

both his father and the elder were too clever to leave evidence of their connection.

There were three elders on the council who shared his father's opinions of half breeds—Adarsh Deosthali, Chen Yuditsky and Zhang Lei. There were four others with varying opinions on the matter, most of which involved a more wait-and-see approach that didn't necessarily represent their true feelings about hybrids. And there was one elder besides Elizaveta, Kamal Ghosh, who had become very pro-hybrid since Nila's introduction to the community.

Elizaveta Chernikova was the only one who, from the start, *wanted* to find hybrids. She was the one elder who would support Zoe's entry into tiger society without qualms. But he couldn't contact her without raising suspicions and getting his brothers' attention.

Until he was ready to introduce his daughter to the community, the fewer tigers who knew about Zoe, the better.

He was risking a lot just calling Nila.

"Well," he said when more silence followed his comment. "Will you help me? Will you contact Alexis for me?"

"Of course, because we're talking about a three-year-old baby. You knew I'd help the minute you told me how old she was."

He smiled but tried to keep his tone neutral. "I hoped." He gave Nila directions to the Alpine cabin to pass on to Alexis. "The sooner she can get here, the better. Zoe needs to learn to shift soon. It's the only way to keep her pain away." And to keep her safe.

At least, he hoped it would help keep her safe. Unlike Nila, Zoe didn't have to enter the shifter world with only a vulnerable human form to call on. If his daughter could learn to embrace her tiger side, she'd have an advantage.

He exchanged a few more details with Nila then hung up and hoped. If Alexis didn't get here in the next day or two, Vlad would have to start teaching Zoe himself. Rose wouldn't stay up here, away from work and her parents, indefinitely. They had to start Zoe's lessons now.

He headed back to the cabin, taking his time as he considered what he had to do over the next few days. When he reached the front door, he started to knock to announce his entrance but paused when he heard a strange, discordant sound. He focused on the noise. When he realized what he was hearing, fear and adrenaline shot into his blood.

Zoe was whimpering in pain.

# CHAPTER EIGHT

Vlad flung open the cabin door and hurried to the living room. Rose was on the floor, holding Zoe, rocking her as the little girl's body seemed to seize, her limbs going stiff and trembling, before she relaxed and started to cry.

Rose looked up. "I can't get through to her. She's hurting too much to listen to the sensory thing you taught her."

Vlad knelt beside them. As he watched, Zoe's limbs jerked, a spasm that looked like a human seizure, but was actually her body trying to shift. Rose gasped as colorless fur sprouted from Zoe's arm and disappeared the next instant.

"Zoe," Vlad said near her ear, "can you hear me? Nod if you can hear me."

No reaction. Her jaw was tightly clenched, her eyes squeezed shut, and a fine tremor coursed across her skin.

Patches of white fur sprouted along her cheeks and didn't immediately disappear. Zoe's ears seemed to shift on her head, moving higher and lengthening, before snapping back into place.

Vlad's heart thumped hard. She was fighting the shift and it was fighting back. Her tiger wanted out. Panic robbed him of thought for a split second. If she would just let go, she'd be fine. But she wasn't ready yet.

"Vlad, do something. Oh, God. Help. Please." Rose started praying, quietly under her breath, a Catholic recitation he wasn't familiar with.

The terror and panic in Rose's voice forced him beyond his own fear. He took Zoe's stiff, trembling body from her. "Go find a needle, something really sharp."

"She's in enough pain. What the hell?"

"Rose, just do it."

She scrambled to her feet and disappeared. While she was gone, Vlad murmured against Zoe's ear. "It's okay, sweetie. This is perfectly normal. Just relax. I have you. Stay with me. Do you hear me? I've got you. Nothing bad will happen."

Rose dropped down next to him and handed him a sharp paring knife. "This was all I could find. What are you going to do? Don't hurt her any more, Vlad, please."

He met her gaze. "Trust me. I'm going to shock her out of this. It will require I hurt her just a little, but the pain will be different and enough to refocus her brain. I can't pull her back without it."

Tears dripped down Rose's cheeks, but she nodded and gripped Zoe's hand.

He set the knife down and took Zoe's other hand. He pinched hard into the soft webbing between her thumb and first finger. The pressure point worked good on headaches in humans. In tigers, it had the added benefit of pulling their full focus. Zoe's head twitched. He pushed harder and her eyes fluttered, not quite opening, but no longer clenched so tightly.

"I'm here, Zoe. I've got you. Are you listening? Concentrate on the feel of my hand on yours. Focus on the way your fingers feel. Flex them if you can hear me."

Her fingers twitched, barely, but they moved.

"Good girl. Keep concentrating on your hand. Keep thinking about your fingers."

He released his hold on the pressure point, picked up the knife and poked the tip quick and hard into Zoe's first finger. Her hand fisted and relaxed in a quick jerk. A small drop of blood appeared. Her eyes fluttered, opened, and then closed again. Vlad poked the knife tip into her middle finger, just enough to draw a drop of blood.

"Ouch," Zoe said through clenched teeth.

Rose sucked in a breath.

"Ah, there's my girl. Good job, sweetie. Come on back to us." He set the knife down and pinched the pressure point again, keeping her brain focused on that hand, on her fingers.

Slowly, her breathing eased and her body relaxed. Her jaw loosened enough for her to say. "Mommy?"

"I'm here, baby. I'm right here." Rose met his gaze and he handed Zoe over to her mother. She scooped her up into a tight hug, holding her close and running a hand through her hair. "How are you doing, baby?"

"That hurt, Mommy."

"I know. I know it did. How do your fingers feel?"

She was quiet a minute, then, "Like when stupid doctor pokes me."

Rose chuckled, a shaky sound that went a long way toward easing Vlad's worry.

"We don't use the word stupid, baby, remember?" Rose said.

"Don't like doctors."

"I know. Are you feeling better now?"

"Yeah. Tired."

"Okay, baby. You take a nap. I'll be right here when you wake up."

"Love you, Mommy."

Tears fell fast down Rose's cheeks now. "Love you too, Zoe."

They sat on the floor, Rose cuddling Zoe, until Zoe's body relaxed fully and her breathing grew deep and even.

"Do you want to take her to the bedroom?" he asked.

"No. But help me get her onto the couch where she'll be comfortable."

He stood and lifted Zoe so Rose could get to her feet. Then he settled the little girl on the couch, and Rose gently tucked a blanket around her. She stared down at her daughter for a moment before turning into his arms and bursting into such heavy, sobbing, silent tears, she broke his heart.

He didn't have words. He just held her, tucking her head against his shoulder, and let her cry out her fear.

Her breath stuttered out as the tears eased. Finally, she pushed away from him. Keeping her head down, her hair curtaining her face, she said, "Keep an eye on her. I'll be right back."

She disappeared down the hall and he heard the bathroom door shut.

Seeing Rose cry had torn him apart like nothing else he could have imagined. The ache of that was second only to the fear he'd felt for Zoe in those moments before he remembered how to help her.

Rose never cried. At least not in front of him. He'd been with her on a hike when she fell and twisted her ankle so badly he'd worried it was broken. And she'd never once cried, despite the pain. Her tears now were like bullets punching into his chest, and his guilt nearly choked him.

He watched his daughter breathing easily now, her body lax in sleep, and knew he wouldn't be able to wait for Alexis. They had to tell Zoe everything. They had to teach her what to do. Fending off the shift like this, he wasn't sure her little body could survive much longer.

They'd run out of time.

R ose splashed cold water on her face, washing away the tears as best she could, though a few continued to leak out. Then she hung her head and focused on breathing steady and slow. The adrenaline of her panic was fading now, leaving her limp and exhausted. Her chest ached, tight with anxiety and terror for her daughter.

Finally, she sucked in a breath, splashed more water on her face, and dried off. When she glanced in the mirror, she grimaced. Her pale skin turned mottled red when she cried, patchy and not attractive. She hated crying, but she hated crying in front of people more.

Though, the relief of actually having someone to cry on had been overwhelming. He'd helped her daughter, pulled her back from a brink Rose couldn't even quite comprehend, and then he'd held Rose without saying a word, just giving comfort.

She loved him. Despite everything that had happened between them, she still loved him. And she was only just realizing how much she needed that love and support. If he left them now, he'd take a part of her soul with him. She'd go on. She'd be strong for her daughter, and she'd learn to enjoy her life. But she'd be missing something.

She glared at her reflection. "Well, that sucks." With a groan, she left the bathroom and went to stand next to him where he was still watching over their daughter.

"Thank you," she said, her gaze on Zoe, as she carefully avoided touching him. "I didn't know what to do."

"I'm sorry I wasn't here when it started, to keep it from getting that far."

"We can't delay teaching her anymore, can we?"

"No."

She'd been afraid of that. Seeing the fur sprout out of her daughter's skin, the way her body moved and shifted in ways that shouldn't have been physically possible, had driven home the reality of Zoe's situation. A part of Rose was still trying to deny the shifter thing, secretly believing Vlad was wrong and this was something else. Even after seeing him change, knowing tiger shifters were a reality, she hadn't been able to dismiss the quiet little voice in the back of her mind whispering that Zoe couldn't be a shifter and all this was bullshit.

She couldn't afford to fool herself any more.

"How will you start?" She dropped into a chair near the side of the couch where Zoe was curled up, near enough that she could reach her quickly.

"I left a message for Alexis, through my sister, but I don't know how long it will take her to get here."

She heard his unspoken comment. "Or if she'll come?"

He made a face. "I'm hopeful. I made a point of telling Nila how old Zoe is. Alexis won't refuse to help such a young child."

Rose nodded. She didn't have the energy to argue. "What do we do until this Alexis woman shows up?"

"That episode will have drained Zoe. She's so strong." He murmured the last, with awe in his tone. "I can't believe she's been able to prevent her tiger from getting out. How long have the episodes been happening?"

"Since around the time she turned two. Like you said happens for ordinary shifters." She rubbed her neck as tears prickled her eyes again. "Other parents worry about the 'terrible twos.' They have no idea what terrible really is. I'd have taken months of tantrums over watching my baby in such pain."

"I wish I could change things. I wish I'd been there to help."

"If wishes were dimes… No point in considering all the what-ifs. You're here now."

He looked away. "Because this episode was so exhausting, I doubt her tiger will try to get out for at least another few days, which gives us some time. For the most part, the shifts don't wear us out—we can go back and forth between shapes indefinitely unless we're injured or there's some other reason we're worn out. But Zoe's fighting hers and that's taking a toll. Once she's able to let go and allow the change, and control it, she won't get so tired after."

"And the pain?"

"The pain is from fighting the shift. It'll go away, too."

Rose took a shaky breath. She was making him repeat things he'd already told her. But after the last hour, she needed all the reassurances she could get. "How will you start to introduce the concept to her? It's not like anything she'd have ever encountered. I don't read her scary stories or let her watch scary movies with things changing into other things. She's much too young for that."

"Until Alexis gets here, we have to let Zoe see that tiger shifters actually exist. I'll change for her, but not in front of her. She'll be able to see me as a tiger, and that I'm safe and aware. I hope that'll help her get used to the idea before Alexis shows her a shift."

"When?"

He looked at Zoe, his gaze thoughtful. "I think we should start as soon as she's recovered. Maybe after dinner? We need to let her get her strength back. I'll let you tell me when you think she's ready to handle it. But we should start tonight. We can't afford to delay even until morning."

Rose nodded. "Yeah." She stared at the cold fireplace, wanting this moment to last longer than it would. Her daughter blissfully ignorant and resting peacefully. The new reality still out there somewhere in the future. For this one instant, everything was okay and her daughter was fine.

It was an illusion, she knew, but it was a nice one.

"It'll be okay, Rose. I promise."

She forced a smile and kept her doubts to herself. "Okay" wasn't something she was overly familiar with anymore.

After dinner, Zoe was her usual self again, bouncing around as if nothing had happened. It never ceased to amaze Rose how quickly she rebounded from the episodes, like she was a perfectly healthy, perfectly normal little girl.

Because she knew they were in for a difficult few hours, she let Zoe have two cookies after dinner instead of just one. Zoe was clever enough to realize this meant something bad was coming, but her suspicion didn't keep her from scarfing down both treats.

"No doctors," she said around a mouth full of chocolate chips, her expression pinched into a stubborn pout.

"No doctors," Rose agreed. "But we do have something…interesting to show you tonight."

Her eyes widened. "What?"

Rose exchanged a glance with Vlad, then ushered Zoe

to the couch. "Okay, this is going to sound very strange, baby, but we know what's been causing your pain. And Vlad is going to help it go away. Forever."

"He is? How that?"

"First, there are some things you need to…learn. Is that okay?"

She nodded.

"One of those things is that you are special. You're a lot like Vlad."

"I am?"

"You are," he said, coming into the conversation. "Which is why I can help you. Do you want to see what makes me special?"

"Yeah! Is it same thing makes me special?"

"It is."

Rose took her daughter's hands. "Baby, this might be a little scary, but everything is okay. You remember the tigers we saw at the zoo? You liked them, right?"

"Love tigers. Soooo pretty!"

Rose smiled. "Yes, they are. Do they scare you?"

She shook her head.

"Good. Okay, well, the thing is…" She looked at her daughter's wide dark eyes and plunged in. "The thing is, Vlad can change into a tiger."

Zoe's eyes got even wider and she looked at him. "You can?"

"I can."

"Really?"

"Really."

For a long moment, Zoe stared at him. Then she grinned. "Cool! Show me."

Rose blinked. "That doesn't scare you, baby?"

"No. Why? Is cool!"

Rose puffed up her cheeks then released the breath. "Okay." She was saying that a lot. "Vlad is going to go into his bedroom and when he comes out, he'll be a tiger."

"Why he go away to change?"

"I have to take off my clothes first," Vlad answered.

Zoe giggled into her hand. "Silly."

"Yes, I suppose it is. I'll be right back. But when I come out, I'll be a big tiger."

"Yay!"

Vlad shook his head and flashed Rose a befuddled expression that reflected her own mood perfectly. He disappeared into the back, leaving Rose to wonder at her daughter.

Several minutes passed as they waited for him to return. Rose continued to hold Zoe's hands as her daughter swung her legs against the couch, bumping them off it loudly. Rose glanced back down the hall when she caught a very slight sound. A moment later a huge Bengal tiger walked slowly out of the shadows.

She sucked in a breath. She still saw Vlad in the tiger's dark eyes. And yet, the beast was so…primal, so terrifyingly beautiful, it was hard to reconcile the fact that it was Vlad. The jump of her pulse at the sight of a wild animal in the cabin held a little too much excitement and not nearly enough fear.

She squeezed Zoe's hands and nodded to the tiger. "Here he is."

Zoe turned to stare and her mouth dropped open. "Tiger," she breathed. "Wow."

The tiger came around to stand in front of them, sitting a few feet away, looking as innocuous as a six hundred pound cat could look. He stared at Zoe, calm and casual—not the intense focus of a predator looking at food. Though as Rose took in Zoe's rapt expression, she wasn't sure her daughter recognized the potential danger in this situation. She seemed fascinated and not even remotely worried.

After staring for a long minute, she frowned a little and looked at the tiger askance. "You really Vlad?"

The tiger nodded.

Zoe grinned, her mouth open, and looked at Rose. "Mommy! That Vlad. He cool."

"Yes, I suppose he is. Do you like talking to a tiger?"

"Yeah. Can I pet?"

Rose glanced at Vlad and he nodded again. "Just be gentle. No pulling."

Zoe eased off the couch and approach the big cat slowly, reaching out a hand toward the thick white ruff around his neck. Rose's heart thumped hard as she watched. The scene seemed so wrong—allowing her little girl to approach a huge predator was not normal. Yet it also seemed so…natural.

The dichotomy made the moment surreal.

Zoe buried her fingers in the tiger's ruff and sighed. "Soft, Mommy." She proceeded to pet him on his head and along his neck, as gently as a three-year-old was capable.

Vlad remained passive, giving every sign of being harmless. He even released a rumbling sound that would have been a purr from a domestic cat.

"Can I ride him?"

"No," Rose said as she choked back a sudden laugh. "He's not a pony, baby."

"He big enough."

"Well, yes, he is. But you still can't ride him without his permission."

"Can I ride you?" she asked the tiger directly.

The tiger nodded and lay down, his side presented to Zoe.

Rose hadn't thought her daughter's expression could glow any brighter. When she scooted up to him, she gave him a sweet little pat first, then she grabbed his ruff and threw herself sideways across his back. It took a great deal of scooting and wiggling to get around so she sat astride the tiger, during which Vlad remained motionless and passive, though Rose heard him grunt once when Zoe's knee bounced against his side.

She grimaced. "Easy, baby. Don't hurt him."

"Not hurting." As soon as she was settled, she sat up a little, still gripping Vlad's fur, and grinned at her mom. "This is cool."

Rose smiled, both pleased and baffled by her daughter's reaction to all this. Did she *get* that the tiger was Vlad? Or did she just think he was a pet tiger? It was hard to tell.

Vlad gently eased upward, hind legs first, then lifting the front of his body. Zoe tottered around, slipped gently sideways, and dropped onto the rug.

"His skin slides," she exclaimed, giggling. "So silly. Up. Up again!"

Vlad settled in a squat again and Zoe scrambled onto his back, with a little less difficulty and kicking. This time, Rose went to help her keep her balance. As Vlad stood, Zoe rolled around on his back again, but with Rose's help she managed not to fall off this time. They walked one circuit around the living room, Zoe grinning the entire time.

Vlad eased back down in the same place as they'd started and Rose lifted Zoe off.

"Was that fun?" she asked.

"Very fun. Again?"

"No. It's time for Vlad to be in his human shape again."

"Ah." Zoe actually pouted. "Love tiger. He so soft."

"I'm sure you'll be able to play with him as a tiger again soon."

Rose met the tiger's eyes. He stood and ambled back to the bedroom.

While he was gone, Rose sat Zoe on the couch. "That didn't scare you?"

"No. Was very cool."

"You do know that was Vlad, right?"

"Was." She bobbed her head in a very definitive nod.

Rose hugged her close. "Well, that went better than I thought it would."

A few minutes later, Vlad came out in his human shape, fully dressed and looking none the worse for wear.

"Did she kick you too hard?" Rose asked as he settled into a chair next to the couch.

"I can take a little three-year-old kicking. Don't worry, I'm fine." To Zoe he said, "You liked the tiger?"

"Yeah. Was fun. Can I ride again?"

"Yes, later. When your mother says it's okay."

"Yay! Your skin all slippy."

"It is when I'm a tiger." Vlad flicked a glance up at Rose before focusing on Zoe again.

Rose read a lot in that look, including his pleasure that Zoe was taking this so well.

"You skin slip when you a boy?" Zoe asked.

"No. My skin is just like yours when I'm like this." He frowned a little, before saying, "Would you like to turn into a tiger, too?"

"Yeah!" She jumped up and down. Then her little face fell into a sad frown. "But I cannot."

"Why do you think that?" Vlad asked.

"People cannot be tigers."

"But you said you knew that tiger was Vlad?" Rose put in, frowning at her daughter. "He turned into a tiger."

"He not people. He a boy." She spoke with the tone of someone stating something so obvious that to even ask about it was ridiculous.

Rose had to suppress a chuckle. She glanced at Vlad.

His brows were raised. "What are you teaching her?"

"I have no idea where she got that idea." She faced Zoe again. "Honey, Grandpa is a boy and he's people."

She frowned and considered that. "You change to a tiger, Mommy? Why you never show me?"

"No, I can't do it, but Vlad and I think you can."

"Why me and not you?"

Rose pursed her lips. That was a much more complicated question to answer. "You're special, baby," she finally said. "You're like Vlad."

Zoe eyes got very wide. "Cool." She said the single word as an awed exhale.

Once again, her reaction both baffled and pleased Rose. She looked at Vlad.

He shrugged. "Three-year-olds."

"How can I be a tiger?" Zoe asked.

"Well," Vlad took over, "I've got a friend coming who is going to help teach you. Would you like that?"

Zoe actually paused to consider, her face screwed up in a frown. After all her enthusiasm, her taking a moment to really think about if she wanted to learn or not was another surprise to Rose.

After swinging her legs and considering her options, Zoe finally said, "Yes. I wanna be tiger."

"Okay," Rose said. "Then we'll start your lessons as soon as we can."

"It hurted?" she asked Vlad.

"Nope. Feels like stretching."

"Will my 'sodes be bad for it?"

Rose pulled Zoe into a hug. "Actually, baby, we think if you learn to be a tiger you won't get any more episodes."

"Really?" She blinked large eyes up at Rose.

"We hope."

"You gonna learn to be tiger, Mommy?"

Rose smiled. "Wish I could. But I'm not special like you."

"You still special, Mommy."

"Thank you, baby."

They spent the rest of the evening talking about tigers. By the time Zoe went to bed, she'd peppered Vlad with so many questions, Rose couldn't remember half of them.

One thing was for sure, though. Her baby wasn't afraid of the tigers, at least not yet. That went a huge way toward alleviating Rose's worry.

Now they just had to teach her to shift—and hope she didn't get hurt.

* * *

"Well that went better than I expected it to," Vlad said as he walked into the kitchen.

Rose stood at the sink, rinsing dishes from dinner and putting them into the dishwasher. "I can't believe she thought that was fun. I've been so worried she'd be terrified."

"Three-year-olds," he said.

She smiled over her shoulder at him then went back to the dishes. "She's asleep?"

"Finally. I think having a pet tiger to play with gave her a second wind."

"That and her two-hour nap this afternoon. I'm surprised we got her to sleep before midnight."

Vlad tried his best to stay near the door, but Rose's scent drew him. She smelled delicious. He went as far as the counter near the sink, then forced himself to stop with several feet still between them. After all the worry over Zoe through the afternoon, he'd let his guard drop with Rose and now all he could think about was burying his face against her neck and breathing her in.

She paused when he got close, then went back to cleaning.

"You need any help?" He had no real excuse to be here. He just didn't want to go to bed yet. At least, not without her.

*Don't push*, he warned himself. She was in enough turmoil with what was happening to Zoe. He knew that. He knew their relationship should wait. But his tiger thought waiting was a terrible idea.

"No thanks. You don't have to stay up with me," she said. "I'm going to sleep as soon as these are done."

"Not really tired yet." He edged closer. He couldn't help it. He wanted to feel her heat. The scent of her desire eased into the air and he closed his eyes a moment to savor it.

"Any word on your brothers?" she asked.

The change in topic should have dampened his amorous feelings. It didn't. All it did was spark protective instincts that urged him to hold her close and keep her safe. "They aren't heading this way. That's good."

"Have they given up?"

He wanted to say yes. He wanted to assure her she was safe now. He didn't think she'd appreciate the lie though. "No. Yuri's been running searches into Zoe's medical history." He just got that bit of news tonight after putting his daughter to bed.

Rose faced him. "Those are supposed to be private. How can he get at them?"

"He's rich and has his ways. Just like all the Dubrovsky brothers."

"Nuts." She stared at the floor, hand on the counter. "He'll figure it out then, won't he? Undiagnosed pain since turning two. He'll know she's not…normal."

"Unfortunately, he's smart. He'll put the pieces together." And any hope of keeping his daughter's secret indefinitely went out the window. He'd known he couldn't keep her from the tiger community, but part of him wanted to.

"How much time do we have?"

"It'll take a while for them to find this cabin."

"Didn't take you long." She held his gaze.

"My brothers won't get the location from your parents, like I did." Without thinking about what he was doing, he edged closer. "They have a lot of places they'll have to search. That'll take time."

She didn't move away, despite the fact that he was now invading her space. She tilted her head back a little to meet his gaze, almost defiantly. He'd always loved that about her. So damned fearless. He'd never known anyone quite like her.

"How long?" she said again. But this time her voice was husky, deeper.

The sound went right to his cock. He inched as close to her as he dared, close enough that a deep breath would brush his chest against hers. He kept one hand on the counter and one hand at his side, not touching her despite the temptation, but the anticipation of touch was over-whelming.

"A week. Maybe more. Long enough to make sure Zoe can control her tiger."

"If Alexis gets here soon."

"Either way. If I have to, I'll start teaching her. I can afford new clothes."

She smiled a little and all his attention zeroed in on her mouth. She wet her lips, leaving them glistening and ripe for kissing. He dipped his head closer, just a little, still not touching her, but he was oh so tempted.

When she didn't back down or tell him to stop, he came closer. Her breath was warm on his face and her scent washed through him, leaving his head spinning with need.

"Vlad…"

Too much. The sound of her sexy voice, his name almost a plea…it was too much. He couldn't resist her anymore. He closed the last breath of space and kissed her.

He'd intended the kiss to be just a gentle brush of lips, nothing too serious, and nothing too hard to pull back from. He failed miserably. The instant he tasted her, he needed more. He took hold of her shoulders, pulled her tight to him, and deepened the contact. To his overwhelming satisfaction, she returned his kiss, open and bold.

This had always been one of his favorite things with her. Not his only favorite thing, but the feel of her generous lips, the dance of her tongue against his, the taste of her… He could kiss her for hours and never get tired of it.

He wrapped his arms around her back so he could feel the press of her breasts against his chest, and she moved into him, leaving no distance between them, her hands coming up to his waist, clenching at his shirt. He considered stepping back to rid himself of the offending garment, but he wasn't ready to let her go yet.

Then she moved her hands up under his shirt, her palms hot against his skin, and destroyed any rational thoughts he had left in his head. He slid one hand up to hold her head in place, tunneling his fingers through her thick hair. He stroked his other hand down to her ass and squeezed, irritated with the material keeping him from her soft, luscious skin. He caressed her butt and hip over the area where her sugar skull tattoo used to be and wondered if it was still there.

He was so focused on the idea of finding out, he didn't feel her pushing him at first. Then she shoved him hard and the message finally got through the foggy haze of lust swamping his brain. He instantly dropped his hold, moving away as fast as if she'd burned him.

She blinked and had to hunt for him at the opposite side of the kitchen because he'd retreated faster than her human eyes could register. "*Dios*, you can move. Or did my brain break?"

He shook his head, trying to laugh, but he was breathing so hard, his voice came out huskier than he intended. "Your brain is just fine. Shifters move very fast."

She nodded. "Vlad, I…" She shook her head and let loose a chuckle that sounded more pained than amused. "I want you a little too much."

How the hell was he supposed to resist that admission? "I can't help the way I feel about you either. I can't stop wanting you."

"I should send you to sleep somewhere else. I'm not going to. But this is getting…more difficult."

He couldn't agree more.

She turned back to the sink and her hand brushed against a tea cup sitting too close to the edge of the counter, knocking it off. He rushed to save the falling mug but she beat him to it, catching the cup up so quickly and instinctively, the speed gave him pause. She put the cup into the dishwasher as if she hadn't just moved fast enough to beat his shifter speed.

"Some reflexes there," he commented, carefully putting distance between them again. The moment he got too close, all he could think about was pulling her back into his arms.

She looked up and blinked at him, then glanced back at the cup. She flashed him a half smile. "Yeah, having Zoe has really sped them up, even faster than they were from all the martial arts. You wouldn't believe how fast a three-year-old can get into trouble."

He chuckled. "That's going to get worse, you know."

"I know," she groaned. "And then before I know it, she'll be a teenager."

She infused the word with such dread, he laughed again. His tension eased, though his skin still hummed from having her hands on him and he was still hard. He needed to get away from her now, while he could still force his tiger to obey logic.

"Goodnight, Rose."

Her soft goodnight followed him down the hall, and the taste of her went with him into his dreams.

CHAPTER NINE

The sound of feet shuffling over the wooden floors brought Rose out of a deep sleep. She sat up, looking immediately to her bedroom doorway for Zoe. When she didn't see anyone, she got up and made her way in the dark to Zoe's room. She was still sound asleep, breathing easily, no sign of another episode coming on.

Releasing a sigh, Rose went back into the hall and glanced toward the living room. She stood listening, wondering if she'd dreamt the sound of footsteps. Then she heard the front door open. Vlad was leaving? She jogged to the living room, glancing at the mantle clock to check the time. Four in the morning. Where would he be going so early?

Thoughts of his brothers and the danger they posed had her moving faster. She heard voices just outside and froze. As she listened, it crossed her mind she should go back and get her father's rifle. Then she realized one of the voices was female. Before she could fully process that, the door opened and Vlad walked in with a tall, dark-haired woman.

Without any lights on, all Rose could make out of the woman was that she had shoulder length hair, pale skin, and moved like a trained fighter. Rose recognized that confident gait easily after years of her own training.

"Rose, this is the woman I told you about. Alexis Tarasova. Rose Callaghan."

Alexis crossed to her and took her hand. "It's a pleasure to meet you. You must be so worried. I understand. But we'll make sure your little girl is just fine."

Rose blinked at the woman, forcing down a fast and unexpected rush of tears. "Thank you for coming," she said around the lump in her throat. She'd thought her worry had eased after this evening, but apparently all it took was a kind word to set her off again. "You got here very fast."

"I was in Colorado when Nila called me, and I took the first flight I could get. I didn't want to delay. Vlad tells me your daughter had a really bad episode yesterday afternoon?"

Rose's cheeks puffed up with her breath. "Yeah, that was terrifying. But she took to Vlad showing up as a tiger pretty well, so we're hopeful."

"Good. Good. Okay. I think after breakfast and introductions, we should start her lessons. There's no time to wait, not if you want to prevent any more episodes." She glanced at Vlad. "You should know, your brothers booked flights back to Phoenix for today."

"What? How do you know?" He looked more annoyed

than worried. He pulled his phone out and checked his messages as Alexis answered his questions.

"The Trackers have had them under surveillance since early September. Are you surprised?"

"No. We all knew as much. I'm just surprised you knew about their flights before I did. You're not even a Tracker anymore."

"I keep informed because Nila's about to be my… sister-in-law, I guess. Maybe niece?" She shrugged and looked at Rose. "Vlad's sister is engaged to one of the boys I consider a brother. Technically, I'm the adopted daughter of their grandmother so really I'm their aunt, but we've always interacted more like siblings."

"That's…nice?" She had no idea what to say to all that, especially at four a.m. when she was still dopey from sleep.

Alexis chuckled. "Too much information? Okay, let's just say I consider Nila a member of the family now. Which sort of makes Vlad family, too." She narrowed her eyes at him. "Sort of."

Vlad didn't say anything, but there was clearly an undercurrent of tension between them.

"Anyway," Alexis said, "with your brothers coming back to Phoenix, we need to make sure your daughter can control her tiger. Then…" She faced Rose. "Then, I'm sorry to say, I think you need to bring her to the elders. For her own safety."

"We're not ready for that yet," Vlad said. "You know why."

"I know why you're hesitant. But Elizaveta will make

sure everyone behaves. She's going to want to meet your daughter."

"Wait, wait, wait," Rose said. She rubbed her eyes. "I'm not entirely sure what you two are talking about. But I'm not taking my daughter anywhere she might be in danger."

"Believe me, I understand," Alexis said. "I have a daughter. I'd kill to protect her."

"Then we understand one another."

Alexis smiled. "Perfectly. That said, there's no way to keep her hidden from the tigers now that Vlad's brothers are suspicious. They'll keep coming around, trying to figure out if she's his or not."

"We tried to throw them off the scent, but Yuri's dug up Zoe's medical records," Vlad put in. "They're probably convinced she is mine by now. I'm sure that's why they're coming back to Phoenix."

"There you go. You're out of time." Alexis frowned and half to herself said, "We're going to have to make her medical history disappear. Don't want blood samples floating around in the human world."

Vlad cursed and settled his hands on his hips, hanging his head. "Dammit. I forgot all about that. I've been so worried about her shifting and my brothers finding her…"

Alexis waved him off. "Don't, Vlad. The Trackers will take care of it."

"They can do that?" Rose asked, frowning at them both.

"Not the first time they've had to," Alexis said.

"But the doctors have run all kinds of tests on Zoe. Do I have to worry about human scientists now, too?" It was much too early in the morning for this. Rose wanted to scream.

"I'll make sure it's taken care of, Rose," Vlad said.

Alexis echoed his assurances. "There won't be any samples or records of those samples left that might lead humans to her." She took a deep breath. "But this is just one more reason you need to bring her forward, present her to the elders, and make her an official part of our community. It will mean our enforcers and the power of the elders can be brought in to protect her. She'll be much safer that way. Especially because she's a girl. And she can shift."

"Vlad's told me she needs to be covered under your laws for her own protection. I was just hoping we wouldn't have to introduce her to that world yet."

Alexis exchanged a look with Vlad before saying, "You know about the Mate Run?"

Vlad glared. Rose frowned. What hadn't he told her about it? "He told me it was how the tigers were staving off extinction. What don't I know?"

Vlad and Alexis stared hard at each other for a few minutes, then Alexis said, "Nothing you'll have to worry about for years." To Vlad, she said, "She'll need to know all of it before you go to the elders."

"What don't I know?" Rose demanded.

Vlad glanced at her then looked away, not meeting her gaze when he said, "The tigers will expect Zoe to take part in the Run because she's a shifter."

"No." Rose didn't even think about her answer, it was so automatic.

"Rose…" He held his hands out to the side, palms open, and shrugged as if he didn't know what to say to that.

She didn't care what reasonable excuses he might offer. She would not allow the tigers to force her daughter into being a breeder for them. Zoe would grow up knowing she had choices, choices Rose intended to protect fiercely if need be.

The fact that Vlad had kept this little bit of information to himself hurt, and she wondered what else he hadn't told her.

Alexis looked at both of them as the silence drew out, then said, "That's a long way off. Nothing you need to even think about yet. The first thing we have to do is make sure Zoe is safe and protected."

"Which means taking her to the elders now?" Rose asked Alexis.

"Yes. It does."

She turned to Vlad, her eyes narrowed. "You wanted to wait until Zoe could shift. Is that the only reason you wanted to wait?" Now that she knew he'd kept one important nugget of information from her, she was questioning everything he'd said.

He glanced at Alexis, then back to her. "There are a few of the elders who…more or less agreed with my father's stance on interbreeding between humans and tigers. They assumed all offspring would be human, and defective, driving tigers to extinction faster. Zoe isn't human, but…"

"But like your brothers, it might only make things worse because it means the 'defective' human gene can hide in a shifter."

Alexis scowled. "Stupid. That supposed human gene is already part of our DNA, since recent revelations prove the myth is true. Those ancient shifters from the mythical couple had to have mated with other shifters. Which is why you and your mother could have babies with humans."

"And you think that logic will do anything to change their minds?" Vlad asked. "You know it won't."

Rose raised a hand to get their attention. "What does this mean for Zoe?"

"It means I wanted to have a plan in place before going to the elders," Vlad said. "Some leverage. I wanted to have an arrangement with the ones who aren't opposed to human-tiger matings to make sure you and Zoe were protected before I got you anywhere near their compound —where you'd be surrounded by tigers."

"I can speak for Elizaveta," Alexis said. "You'll have her support. And all by herself, she's a force to be reckoned with."

"I want it in writing," Vlad said. "I want guarantees they'll be protected while we're there. I'm not taking chances with their lives."

"Keeping them away now is riskier. After Nila, the elders have set a precedent for protecting hybrids. You don't have any of those protections out here, not without their official backing."

"I have my own resources and ways of keeping them hidden."

"I'm not going into hiding," Rose said, stepping closer to Vlad. "I have a family and responsibilities and a life."

"Your parents will understand."

"Yes, they will. In fact, they might even encourage it once I have a chance to tell them everything that's going on. That doesn't mean I'm going to do it."

"You sure you want them to know…everything?"

"Yes. This is their precious granddaughter. They need to know. Besides, she's three. It's not like she's going to keep the ability to turn into a tiger to herself around them. I might, and I mean might, be able to convince her to keep the secret around most people, but with her grandparents, no chance. Even if she tries, it'll pop out. They're very close."

Vlad ran a hand through his sleep-mussed hair, making him look even sexier. She was already having a hard time ignoring the fact that his flannel shirt was hanging open, giving her a lovely view of his chest and six-pack abs. She'd always loved his body, but in the middle of discussing their daughter's future, it seemed wrong to be admiring his physique—especially after discovering he'd been keeping information from her.

The little voice that encouraged her to take risks and go after the adrenaline rushes she loved so much whispered, *You know you still want him. After the last few days, there's no doubt he wants you. If you seduce him, he's yours.*

That voice was going to get her into trouble. Again. How the hell could she still want him this much, have this much trouble resisting him, when she still couldn't trust him? She pushed the lust and confusion to the side and tried to focus. "How much longer can we delay taking Zoe to your elders?"

"Not long," Alexis said before Vlad could answer. "Not

if you want to stop your brothers. I wouldn't even go back to Phoenix. You should head straight to West Virginia."

Rose squeezed her eyes shut, a hint of an exhaustion headache building in her temples. "Are my parents in danger?"

"Not until they know the truth," Vlad said. "And only then if we tell them before Zoe has the elders' protection. After, they'll be included in the arrangement we make with the elders. I'll make sure of it."

She opened her eyes. "Fine. To keep Zoe safe, we'll do what you think is best. I'll tell my parents we're getting specialized help for her. They won't be happy that they can't come with us, but for Zoe they'll curb their suspicions." She looked at Alexis. "How long will it take to teach her what she needs to learn?"

"To get started and go through her first few shifts, a couple of days maybe. Depends on her, really."

"Fine. That gives you enough time to arrange things?" she asked Vlad.

"I'll get it worked out. You better warn your parents my brothers are coming again."

"They'll put them off and cover our backs. They're so protective, they wouldn't give anything away even if they knew all the details."

He smiled a little. "I used to worry they were so protective of you they were going to try chasing me off before I could marry you."

She snorted. "They're more likely to chase you off now than they would have been back then."

She stared at him for a long, silent moment as memories of better times mixed with the years of pain in between. Alexis cleared her throat, bringing them back to their surroundings.

"I don't want to put you out or worry Zoe if she gets up early and spots a stranger on the couch, so I'll head out. I'll come back at a more reasonable hour and you can introduce us."

"Don't be ridiculous." Rose waved off her offer. "You sound like Vlad. I'll crawl into bed with Zoe. You can take my bed. You must be exhausted."

"I'm okay. Are you sure?"

"Yeah, I'm probably not going to sleep much more tonight anyway."

"Try," Vlad said, putting a hand on her shoulder and squeezing lightly. "It's going to be a big day."

She stared up at him, worry clutching her stomach, overriding her reaction to his touch. "She'll be all right?"

"She'll be fine. I promise."

She nodded, but his promise didn't ease her worries at all. Not now. She motioned them all down the hallway to the bedrooms. After she'd seen Alexis into her room, she crawled into bed next to Zoe, snuggling up with her daughter. This wasn't the first time she'd done this. Anytime Zoe had an episode, or Rose worried about an episode coming on, she shared a bed with her. It was worth the kicks and occasional punches from her restless daughter to know she was breathing through the night.

Despite her prediction, having the warm, sweet-smelling comfort of Zoe with her allowed Rose to drift back into sleep. All the worries and fear would wait until morning.

"I'm more nervous than she is," Rose whispered to Vlad as they gathered in the living room after breakfast, readying for Zoe's first lesson.

"Why you nervous, Mommy?"

Rose sighed. This little girl and her hearing. "I'm nervous to see your first lesson, baby. Just like I was nervous the first time you went to daycare, even though I knew you'd have fun. That was fun, right?"

"Yes." She nodded with her entire upper body.

"This will be fun, too. I'm just excited for you."

"Me, too. Wanna be a tiger."

Alexis met Rose's gaze and smiled. "This is a good start."

Hopefully, Rose thought.

Alexis motioned everyone to sit, then settled on the floor, resting on her knees so her face was level with Zoe's where she sat on the couch. "Okay, I'm going to show you how to turn into a tiger, but it's going to take some time. So no rushing. This is very serious and important stuff." She gave the little girl a level look and Zoe nodded solemnly.

Rose pressed her lips together so she wouldn't grin.

"I need to show you how I turn into a tiger first. We call this shifting. Can you say that?"

"Ssshhhhifing."

"Close enough. In order to shift, I have to take off my clothes."

Zoe nodded, not even blinking at that. Yet another surprise reaction. Rose was starting to feel like she didn't know her daughter at all.

"You are just going to watch at first. I'll show you how I shift and then how I get back into a people body. This takes a little time and it can look pretty gross. How do you feel about gross things like frogs and slimy worms?"

"Yay, worms!"

Alexis laughed. "That's what I thought." She glanced at Rose. "This is a great age for her to learn, because everything is fun."

Rose was still processing how easily Zoe had taken to Alexis. She just accepted her as one of Vlad's friends and another person who could turn into a tiger. Rose was having a harder time with this new reality than her daughter.

In some ways, she was grateful for that. Especially since Zoe was the one who had to learn to become a tiger.

Alexis gave Zoe a few more details about the way her body would move and parts would look weird and fur would sprout up. Then she went into detail on how she triggered the shift.

"I picture my body feeling like a tiger. I feel my big, heavy paws. I feel the fur on my skin, the way my ears can twitch, the swish of my tail. I relax and…let my tiger out. Now, once my tiger starts to come out, I don't resist or try to stop it. Okay? That just hurts. When I relax and let go, it doesn't hurt. Does that make sense?"

Zoe nodded, frowning a little.

"It's like if you hold your breath too long. That hurts. But if you just relax and breathe, you don't hurt."

This time Zoe nodded with more enthusiasm. "I can hold my breath for long time before it hurts."

"That's very good. Are you ready to watch me change? If you get scared, you can close your eyes, and we'll work on this more when you're comfortable, okay?"

"Yes. I won't get scared. Mommy says I very brave."

"You are, baby. You're the bravest girl I know."

"See," Zoe told Alexis proudly, her little chin tilting up.

"Perfect. But it's okay if you do get scared. Don't worry. We have lots of time to learn this."

"'Kay."

Alexis stood and pulled her loose sweater over her head. "Rose, I know the whole nudity thing can be… uncomfortable for humans. Are you okay with this? Do you want to stay?"

"I'm not going anywhere."

Alexis grinned. "Didn't really think you would."

She stripped, laying her clothes across the back of the couch, completely unconcerned with being naked in front of virtual strangers. Rose glanced at Vlad. He looked on impassively, showing no sign that having a naked woman in the room even fazed him. Alexis had a beautiful, lean, fit body. How could he not react to that?

He glanced at her and squeezed her hand. "You okay?" he mouthed so Zoe wouldn't hear.

"Yes," she mouthed back. "No." She frowned. This was all so overwhelming and surreal, she didn't know how she felt about it. But as she turned back to watch Alexis, she gripped his hand tighter, only a little surprised by the comfort his presence gave her.

"Here I go," Alexis said to Zoe. "See the way the fur sprouts? Isn't that funny?"

Zoe nodded, her eyes wide. When Alexis giggled and claimed something tickled, Zoe giggled, too. Alexis talked through the change until her face started to move and show the tiger, making speech impossible.

Rose tried not to react to the sounds of snapping tendons and breaking bones. She worked hard to only show interest and amazement so that was all Zoe would see. Inside, she was as horrified as she'd been when Vlad had shifted for her. The thought of her little baby doing this, going through this, was almost too much to bear.

*If she doesn't learn, she'll continue to have episodes of severe pain,* she reminded herself. *This is for her own good.*

She chanted that phrase to herself like a mantra and when Zoe turned big eyes on her and exclaimed how "cool" it was, Rose nodded and agreed with more enthusiasm than she felt. The entire time, Vlad held her hand, a strong and comforting body next to her.

When the change was done, a giant Siberian tiger stood in the living room. She had beautiful orange and white fur, gleaming black stripes, and a gentle neck ruff that wasn't as big as Vlad's. Zoe clapped her hands and bounced on the couch. The tiger swept one of her front legs under her belly, dipped her head, and dropped into a bow. The gesture surprised a chuckle from Rose and another round of cheering from Zoe.

"She changed slowly so Zoe could watch," Vlad said

against Rose's ear. "Her shifts are usually faster, like mine."

Rose hadn't actually realized how long the process took. She couldn't have timed Vlad's either. Shock tended to warp her senses.

"Will Zoe have to make a slow shift?"

"Not sure what will happen the first time. Depends on Zoe. Some kids flip back and forth really fast when they first get started and then have to slow down as they get older. Only really, really strong shifters can change quickly, and no tigers can change instantly."

"You were specific about tigers there. Why?"

"Other shifter species have individuals that can shift in an eye-blink. With leopards, for instance, strength and power depend on birth order and the birth order of the parents. So the first born of two first-born parents will be exceptionally strong. Some of them can shift instantly. Tiger biology follows different rules."

Rose dipped her head to one side. "This is a very strange new reality." She watched her daughter playing with the giant tiger, who was extremely gentle, and knew she'd never look at the world in quite the same way again.

Zoe plucked and poked at Alexis, showing no signs of fear or disturbance that a human had just turned into a tiger before her eyes. Rose supposed to a child, those kinds of things were entirely possible. It was only after growing up that most people lost their belief in the mythical.

"I'm glad we're doing this now," she said to Vlad. "While she's so young."

"Me, too." He released a breath. "It would have been

easier when the urge to shift first came on, but at least she didn't suffer too long."

She heard the guilt in his voice. Part of her wanted to comfort him, assure him it was okay. Another part wanted him to feel that guilt, to suffer for leaving them and feel just a little of what she'd been going through for the last year. That part of her made her feel petty, but the other voice, the one that wanted to comfort, made her feel like a gullible idiot. So she kept her mouth shut, because she didn't want to be an idiot or a petty bitch.

After a few more minutes of Zoe poking at Alexis' various tiger parts, including gently pulling her thick tail, Alexis nudged her to the couch and backed up. The shift to human form went a little quicker than the change to tiger, but because she was watching for it, Rose realized the change still happened slower than Vlad's had. Zoe paid close attention, as if studying the process.

When Alexis was human again, she said, "So, Zoe, what do you think? Do you want to try changing? Or do you want to watch me shift some more? You don't have to try until you're ready."

"Wanna be a tiger." Her face bunched up in a frown. "But don't think I can."

"Why not?" Alexis kneeled on the floor in front of her again. She hadn't bothered to dress, but Zoe didn't seem to notice.

"Tried last night after saw Vlad. Didn't work."

Rose felt her mouth drop open and had to snap it shut. That was news to her.

"What did you do to try?" Alexis asked, calm and reasonable.

"Closed my eyes and imagined being tiger. Nothing happened."

"Did you picture the tiger?"

Zoe nodded.

"Did you feel the tiger paws like they were your own?"

Zoe's frown deepened, then she shook her head. "No. Just saw the tiger."

"Well, there you go. You have to feel your tiger for her to get out. Easy peasy. Do you want to try now? So I can help?"

Zoe paused, then looked at Rose and Vlad. "I gotta take my clothes off?"

"If you don't want to, you don't have to," Alexis said.

"Changing while you're dressed will tear your clothes," Vlad said. "But we can buy you more. Would you feel better if I left?"

Zoe's mouth pursed as she considered. Then she said, "Yes."

Vlad smiled. "You got it." He squeezed Rose's hand and said, "I'll go make some phone calls, start setting things up so we can make our trip safely."

Rose still wasn't sure about facing the ruling body of the tiger shifters yet, but since both Vlad and Alexis thought it would keep Zoe safe, she accepted the trip as necessary. She just wished she knew more about what they were getting into.

After he'd left the cabin, Zoe said, "What trip?"

"I have to talk to Granny and Grandpa first, but I think

we're going to be on vacation a little longer. Is that okay? We're going to go to West Virginia."

"What we do there? Is there snow?"

"I don't know about the snow. We'll see. We're going to meet some people. People like Alexis and Vlad."

"More tigers? Wow."

"Are you good with that?"

She nodded. "Wanna be tiger first. So I can play with other tigers."

"Fair enough."

Zoe stood and pulled off her sweater, then pushed her leggings down and reached for Rose's hand to keep her balance as she stepped out. She shuffled out of her underwear next, then giggled and shivered.

"You too cold like that, baby?"

"Nope." She spun in a circle and plopped back onto the couch, facing Alexis.

Alexis said, "Do you remember how my paws felt? The way the fur covered them and the hard bottoms?"

Zoe nodded.

"Think about that now, only with your hands and feet. Imagine your hands feeling like a tigers, how it feels to have fur and paws instead of hands. Go ahead and close your eyes. Good." In a quiet, calm cadence, Alexis talked Zoe through the way a tiger body felt.

As Rose watched, her daughter's little hands twitched. Her brow crinkled and the twitching stopped.

"Good, Zoe, you almost had it," Alexis said. "Did it hurt?"

"Felt weird."

"It does the first time. Can you try again? Just focus on how your hands would feel if they were paws."

For several long moments, nothing happened. Then Zoe's hands twitched again, and a ripple of fur sprouted along the backs before disappearing.

"That's it, Zoe," Alexis said. "You're doing great. Don't worry and don't fight it. Just keep thinking about how your paws feel. That's it."

Rose tried not to gasp, or even move, so she wouldn't break her daughter's concentration, but watching parts of her body start to change was more than disturbing. Panic bubbled up and was forced down. Then, almost suddenly, Zoe's hands turned into paws. One instant they were child hands, the next cat paws with orange and white fur and extended claws.

Rose looked at the rest of Zoe. Her whole body was twitching now, fur rippling over her skin and not disappearing. She convulsed a few times, movements that made Rose reach for her. A look from Alexis made her stop halfway and sit back. But every maternal ounce of her wanted to take hold of her daughter to keep her safe from what was happening.

Zoe opened her mouth as she dropped onto all fours on the floor in front of Alexis. Rose expected a moan of pain or even a scream, but what came out was a sound her daughter had never made—a growling hiss. Just like a cat.

Rose forced herself to keep watching as her daughter's beautiful face changed and shifted to a tiger cub's face. Panic and fear rode her, until she had to sit on her hands to keep from interfering.

The minutes felt interminable. But everything seemed to finish in an instant. Though she'd watched the change, it felt like she'd blinked and a tiger cub stood in the middle of the living room.

An adorable cub, covered in the softest-looking fur Rose could imagine. "Can she understand me when she's like this?" Rose asked Alexis.

"Sure. She's still Zoe. She can think and understand just like she can in human form."

Zoe growled and then collapsed on the rug, rolling on her back, her little cat tongue lolling out, and a sound like a purr rumbled loudly from her.

"How do you feel, baby?" Rose asked her.

The cub that was Zoe bounced to her feet and charged Rose, bumping up hard against her legs and rubbing her head against her knee before bouncing away again and spinning in a circle, chasing her tail. Faster than she'd ever seen her daughter move, Zoe charged around the living room, running so quickly she was a blur.

This time, Rose couldn't hold back her gasp. "She moves so fast!"

Zoe paused to rub her face against Rose's leg again before making another rapid circuit of the room.

"Shifters do. At top speeds, you wouldn't even see us," Alexis commented.

"I've seen Vlad do that, but…" A new kind of fear and panic gripped Rose. "What happens if she runs away from me and gets into danger? I can't move fast enough to catch her. How can I protect her if she…I don't know, jumps into traffic or something? She's just a little girl. She doesn't understand a lot of dangers yet."

Alexis tilted her head to one side and frowned a little. "That is a bit tricky. Not something I've had experience with because I could always move as fast as my cubs. Vlad's going to have to help you."

"But we haven't even decided…" She trailed off. Zoe could still understand her, even if she wasn't paying a lot of attention. Rose didn't want her hearing things they hadn't actually explained to her yet.

Alexis moved to the couch, sitting next to Rose as they both watched Zoe getting used to her tiger shape. She stopped abruptly, too suddenly for her body, and ended up rolling head over tail into a wall.

Rose stood. "You okay, baby?"

Zoe popped to her feet, shook her entire body, then nodded and tore off toward the back of the house, skidding over the wooden floors. Rose started to follow, to keep an eye on her, but Zoe sped back into the living room before Rose even moved away from the couch.

When the cub plopped onto the rug in front of the fireplace and started licking her feet, Rose sat again.

"You'll work it out," Alexis said. "She's a good girl and you're a good mom. And you'll have support. I'll help where I can, if you want me to. Once she's introduced to our people, I'm sure you'll have a lot of volunteers stepping forward to help."

"Why?"

"She's a female tiger. All females are incredibly precious to our people." Alexis smiled. "Plus, she's absolutely adorable. She'll be capturing hearts all over the compound when she arrives."

Rose wasn't sure whether to be comforted or worried by Alexis' assurances. She didn't know how to feel about her daughter being thrown into this strange world, and she wasn't sure she *wanted* strangers fawning over her child just because she was female.

Alexis broke into her thoughts with a question. "Did Vlad mention that he can't sense Zoe?"

Rose blinked. "Yes. He said most tigers can sense each other, but Zoe is different. She can sense him, though."

"Really? Huh. Nila is the same. We thought it was just because she was human that we couldn't sense her. Zoe is most definitely a tiger shifter. The fact that we can't sense her either is…interesting."

"Vlad seemed to think so, too. Why?"

"It means there could be a lot more people like Zoe and Nila out there, and we wouldn't necessarily ever know." Alexis turned away from Zoe and very quietly said, "Our males don't bother using birth control with human women because we don't pick up the same diseases and we thought there was no possibility of a pregnancy. But now… Well, how many accidental pregnancies might have occurred from those couplings? How many children could have been born to shifter fathers without them even realizing?"

"Vlad thought I'd cheated on him when he found out I was pregnant," she murmured as quietly as she could, hoping Zoe was too distracted by her new shape to pay attention.

"That's probably not the first time that conversation has happened."

"So…there could be others like Zoe, in pain and not understanding why?"

Alexis sighed. "Hell. I hate that idea."

"Would some of them just…shift? Not fight it the way Zoe was?"

"Maybe. I don't know. This is all hypothetical. It's possible more humans than shifters have been born. Or it could still be Zoe and Nila are incredibly rare instances and there just aren't any others like them."

Rose watched her daughter roll around on the carpet, wiggling her back as if itching. "To be honest," she murmured, "I hope they are rare because I hate the thought of other children, children you'd never be able to identify, going through what Zoe has been through for the last year."

Alexis reached out and patted her hand where it rested on the couch. Both of them watched Zoe in silence after that. And Rose realized just how lucky they were Vlad had returned to them, even if his return heralded the start of a new and dangerous journey. The thought of how much worse things could have been for Zoe closed Rose's throat. She didn't want to even think about it. She might not completely trust Vlad, but she was extremely grateful he'd cared enough to come back.

# CHAPTER TEN

The process of Zoe returning to human form went smoothly, though once she was human again, she wanted to go instantly back to her tiger form and go outside to play.

Rose put a stop to that thinking immediately. "You are only allowed to turn tiger when I say so, never in front of someone you don't know, and never outside unless we're well away from other people. Do you understand? This is a secret and you have to be careful to keep it."

"But Vlad and Alexis know," she whined.

"Because they're tigers, too. They understand. Not everyone will. Okay? You have to mind Mommy in this."

"Fine. When I go outside and play tiger?"

"We'll find someplace, maybe go for a hike, and if I think it's safe, you can change. But," she said, interrupting Zoe's bounce of excitement with a raised finger, "you have to listen to all the rules and when I say you change back, you change back. No arguing. Do you understand?"

"Yes, Mommy," she said, trying to hide her pout behind a "good girl" expression.

Rose wasn't fooled for an instant.

Vlad returned just before lunch, his expression serious and contemplative.

"What's wrong?" Rose asked.

"My brothers have been…talking to other tigers, those sympathetic with my father's anti-hybrid stance."

"What does that mean to Zoe?"

"It means we'll have to be very careful with her, even at the elders' compound, even with the deal I'm working out with Elizaveta."

Alexis came out of the kitchen with Zoe trailing behind her carrying a plate with a peanut butter sandwich on it. "I'll talk to Victor," Alexis said. "I'm sure Elizaveta is already organizing things with him, but I'll make sure he sets stuff up even she doesn't know about." To Rose, she added, "My husband is in charge of the compound's security systems. He's a tech fanatic, so he's got bugs and cameras all over the place as it is. I'll make sure he's got Zoe under surveillance at all times so we make sure she's safe."

"I'm not leaving her side, so that won't be a problem."

The lunch dishes were barely cleaned up when Zoe started pestering them to let her go tiger again. After some discussion, they decided a hike in the woods, somewhere relatively private, would give Zoe a chance to test out her tiger form in the open.

Using Rose's SUV, they drove to a higher elevations, leaving the car parked in a small lot at the base of a hiking trail she and Zoe had walked before. Zoe stayed out in front of the adults as they walked the narrow path. The snow was only a few inches deep, so the hike was pleasant.

Vlad and Alexis both seemed distracted as they went deeper into the woods. When Rose frowned a question at Vlad, he said, "We're listening and scenting for other humans. Don't want to be interrupted."

True. She couldn't even imagine how they'd explain having a tiger cub out here. One more thing to worry about. How was she going to raise Zoe like this? She didn't want her discovered by human authorities who might try to experiment on her like she was some sort of alien. But she didn't trust the tiger shifters to keep her daughter safe either. A sense of isolation and the overwhelming task ahead of her tightened a band around her chest.

She startled when Vlad took her hand and squeezed, almost as if he sensed her distress. She forced a smile in thanks and was a little surprised when the tightness in her chest loosened. Glancing down at their linked hands, she realized she was starting to believe he'd stick around and support them, that she wasn't as alone in this new world as she'd felt.

That thought led down a confused path of mixed feelings. She didn't entirely trust him and yet part of her sort of did. But he'd kept information from her. Could she believe anything he said? Could she even trust her own instincts where Vlad was concerned? She still wanted him, yet without complete trust, did she dare give in to that want?

She couldn't explain exactly how she felt about him, even to herself, and she didn't have time to sort it all out right then, so she took his comfort and ignored everything else. Right now, her focus had to remain on Zoe.

They reached a place where the trail disappeared beneath the snow and there were no signs of human hikers going farther. They continued beyond that point, tramping through the soft whiteness until Alexis announced they were safe to practice shifting.

"Vlad, why don't you change and I'll stay in this form. That way we can handle anything."

Vlad brushed his fingers over Rose's cheek once before moving off into the trees both taking and giving privacy.

Rose watched him go, her stomach twisting with those unexamined emotions. When she looked back, Zoe was grinning at her. "What?"

"You *liiiikkke* him." She giggled into her hand, then threw herself against Rose's legs, wrapping her up in a hug.

Rose couldn't help but laugh. "We're here to play tigers not talk about who Mommy likes." She lifted one of her backpack's shoulder straps and said, "I brought plenty of spare clothes if you want to change while you're still dressed. It's pretty cold out here for getting naked."

"Naked! I not cold. I like naked."

Rose glanced at Alexis. "Is this safe? She won't freeze?"

"No. High metabolism. And a good fur coat once she changes."

"But can she change fast enough? She's only done it once so far."

"Trust me," Alexis said. "Okay, sweetie, time to go tiger. Remember, you are to listen to me and Mommy, and if we tell you to change back or to hide, you have to do as we say. Got it?"

"Yes."

"Vlad will stay with you, too, so you don't need to be afraid."

"Not afraid. I'm tiger!"

Rose pressed her lips together to keep from laughing again. She held Zoe's clothes as she wiggled out of them, taking off even her snow boots. Seeing her daughter standing naked in the snow was so contrary to her instincts to keep her warm, it was almost impossible not to wrap a coat around her again. But Zoe didn't seem to notice and she didn't shiver as she bounced on her toes.

"Can I change now?"

"You give it a try," Alexis said. "Remember, focus on how your tiger body feels, what it's like to have fur and paws…"

To Rose's surprise, the change happened very quickly this time. One minute, Zoe was a vulnerable little girl, and the next, she was a tiger cub, bouncing around in a snow bank as if she'd been doing this her whole life.

"How did she adapt so quickly?" Rose wondered aloud.

"This is natural to her. She just didn't know it. Now that she does, she won't ever have to go through those painful episodes again."

The reality of that almost brought Rose to her knees. Whatever else they had to worry about going forward, knowing she wouldn't have to watch her daughter writhing in pain was like a gift from God.

Vlad came out of the trees then, and Zoe launched herself at him, attacking with a little cub hiss and claws extended. Vlad jumped away, a move that sent Zoe tumbling through the snow. She stood up with her muzzle covered in white, sneezing to clear her nose, then she charged him again, bouncing around his feet and swatting at him to get him to jump away. He moved gently, letting the cub jump on his back and bite at him, taking the aggressive game easily.

"She doesn't normally play that rough," Rose said.

"Her tiger will. It's natural for our cubs to pretend to attack like that. It's how they learn to hunt—like a normal tiger."

"She'll want to hunt?"

"You squeamish about that?"

"No. I go hunting with my parents. We use bow and arrows or guns, though, not claws."

Alexis chuckled. "I find claws easier. But that's just me. Vlad can teach her what she needs to know. For now, this kind of game will get her skills up to where they should be."

They spent the rest of the afternoon moving deeper into the woods, Vlad leading Zoe as she explored. Rose had one brief heart-stopping moment of panic when Zoe took off so fast she blurred. Vlad gave chase, but they vanished into the woods, leaving only a faint trail of prints to follow.

"Damn it, I was afraid of this. Zoe Callaghan, you get

back here this instant," Rose shouted. She started after them, following the slight depressions in the snow.

She'd barely gone a few feet, when Vlad returned with Zoe dangling from his mouth by her scruff. She hung there without making a sound. When he gently set her down in front of Rose, Rose glared at her daughter. "What did I tell you about running away?"

Zoe dipped her little cat head and butted against Rose's calf.

"You're forgiven. Don't do it again."

Zoe bounced up and pranced into another mound of snow, flopping around and covering her thick fur in white.

"You handled that very well," Alexis said, settling a comforting hand on her shoulder.

"Inside I'm a mess," Rose assured her. "If we're alone and she does that, I can't catch up."

"She'll learn not to run away, and until she does, Vlad can catch her."

Rose wasn't sure what to say to Alexis' assumption that Vlad would always be around when Rose or Zoe needed him.

She watched the huge male tiger pretend to fall over when the much smaller cub swatted him across the nose. Zoe danced and hissed and growled as if she'd just brought down an elephant. But when she pranced too close to Vlad, he swiped out and gently pushed her over. Zoe leapt back to her feet and jumped on his side. Alexis laughed.

"He's good with her," she murmured.

Yes, Rose thought, he was. She wasn't even a little

surprised that Vlad made a wonderful father. She'd known he'd be from early in their relationship.

But would he continue to accept the job?

* * *

Not long after they put Zoe to bed that night, Alexis excused herself, saying she needed to start making her own calls to ensure their trip to meet with the elders went smoothly. She left the cabin with a little wave, leaving Rose and Vlad alone in front of the fire.

"It was a good day," Vlad said into the silence.

"Much better than I expected." Rose turned on the couch to face him. "You're very good with Zoe. Thank you. She really had fun 'playing tiger.'"

He smiled and Rose's stomach tumbled around in a crazy dance. In the quiet darkness, with her daughter safely asleep and Alexis gone, Rose could finally think about something other than fear and worry. Her heartbeat sped as Vlad's always-yummy scent drifted around her, and the heat of his body, close to hers on the couch, warmed her.

His expression turned serious, matching her mood, and he reached up to cup her cheek in one warm palm. "I know there's still a lot…unsettled between us," he said, his voice deep and quiet. "But I want you to know, I'm not going anywhere. I'm in your life to stay now." He rubbed his thumb gently along her cheekbone. "How much or how little you want me around is up to you."

"I'm not really sure what I want now," she admitted. "I've spent more years hating you than loving you."

"If I could change things, I would, Rose. You know that, right?"

"I think I do. I want to believe that. And so you know, I don't hate you anymore."

His lips lifted in a sexy half smile. "Glad to hear it."

"But I still can't trust you entirely. You hurt me bad when you left, and that ache is still there."

"It hurt me to leave," he said. "I haven't been the same without you. In fact, even before finding out it was possible for us to have a baby together, there were a few times I thought of coming back, because being without you made life feel…wrong."

"Vlad." Staring at him in the low lighting, it was like no time had passed, like they were back in the heyday of their affair, in love and talking about marriage. Before she knew tiger shifters existed. Before she'd gotten pregnant.

In fact, they'd spent many nights in settings just like this, a cabin in the mountains, snuggling in front of a fire after a day of hiking snowy cliffs.

He'd never made her feel odd for her thrill-seeking nature. He'd gone with her into the adrenaline jolt of adventure. And at night, when they came together, it was another kind of rush, the ultimate thrill.

Could they ever have that again? Did she want that again?

She'd changed in the last four years. Being a single parent to a child with medical problems hadn't destroyed her love of thrill and adventure, but it had certainly made her more cautious and realistic. She didn't have time for many of the distractions of youth anymore. And she didn't dare to do something that could get her killed because she had a child to take care of now.

Her life wasn't simply her own anymore. In many ways, she belonged to Zoe as much as Zoe belonged to her, and she lived to ensure her daughter was safe and loved.

He didn't know her this way. Would he even like this more staid version of herself? She was happy with the woman she'd grown into, and proud of the way she'd handled being a single mom, but that didn't mean he'd love the person she'd become.

She realized if he couldn't, if they didn't fit now, they might have been doomed from the beginning. She would have always grown into this person, she was certain of that. Even having a husband wouldn't have changed her approach to parenting or the changes she was willing to make to be a mom.

"We don't really know each other anymore," she murmured. "I want you to have a relationship with Zoe. I think it's important—beyond the whole shifter thing. But you and I? There might just be too much history between us."

"You're right in that I don't know you as well as I'd like. But I can see the kind of mother you are, and the woman you've become. The strength you always had has deepened and matured. And I like it."

He raised a hand and cupped her cheek, stopping her when she opened her mouth to respond. "I want to give us a chance, Rose. I don't have the words, I don't know the right things to say. I don't know how to earn back your trust. I just know I want you still, always, and I'm prepared to do whatever it takes to win you back."

Her chest tightened with all the emotions welling up. When he leaned close, she didn't pull away. And when his lips pressed against hers, all the old feelings and need came roaring back with the same power that had always been there—was still there. She fell into him, tunneling her fingers through his hair and holding him close.

He tasted so good, so right. His arms came around her, pulling her close. Memories of times past, of the nights they'd spent in each other's arms, gave power to the moment. When she was sure he wouldn't pull away, she released her hold on his head and ran her hands along his shoulders, down his back, remembering and savoring his hard, muscled body. His shoulders drove her crazy. She couldn't get enough of them.

But she wanted less clothing in the way. She'd seen him naked several times recently and those images joined with her memories, sending waves of desire right to her core. Last night, just touching his bare skin under his shirt had scorched her. The thought of stripping him and exploring his beautiful body again robbed her of all sense. In that moment, she didn't want to think and she certainly didn't want to worry. She wanted to throw caution to the wind and take what she'd missed so much these last few years.

It had been a long time since she'd felt like a sexy, vibrant woman. She'd spent a lot of time being Mommy and trying to forget her heartbreak. In those years, she'd pushed her desires and needs as a woman to the back of her mind—something she'd worry about in some distant future when she had time.

Since Vlad had returned, all those suppressed needs had roared back to life. She'd resisted the lure of them last night because there was still so much unsettled between them. Tonight, she was losing the fight. Wetness seeped between her legs, her breasts felt swollen and ripe, her body tingled and sparked.

And it felt so good.

Only Vlad could do this to her. Only Vlad had ever let her be herself, completely and totally, giving her a freedom no one else ever had.

She wrapped herself closer, practically crawling onto his lap. Her responsible mommy brain paused a moment to listen for any tell-tale sounds of Zoe waking up, and when she heard nothing, she dove back into the lust and need, the feel and taste of a man she'd loved and wanted even when she'd hated him.

The feel of his hands caressing down her back, across her hips, down her thigh, made her wiggle against him, trying for a closeness she'd only get if they were naked.

That sounded so good. A naked Vlad, in her bed, his hot hard body at her command.

A bed. They needed a bed. Alexis was supposed to be sleeping in her bed. But *he* had a bed. Yes, a bed was just what they needed.

Some part of her thought maybe she should stop. They still needed time. Nothing had really changed from last night to tonight. In fact, learning he'd held some information back had shaken whatever trust in him she was starting to feel. They had to get to know each other again. They had to find a new balance, start a whole new relationship. They were parents. They *couldn't* just give in to their lust without consequence.

Another part of her thought, *This is Vlad, the father of your child. The man you always thought you'd marry. The one man you loved so much, you haven't been able to even consider another man since meeting him. He's yours.*

She liked the way that voice thought. She decided to listen to that one. Just this once. Because she needed this, needed him, more than she needed her next meal. And she was a woman who loved her food.

# CHAPTER ELEVEN

"Would it be rushing you to say let's go back to your bedroom?" Rose asked between kisses.

He groaned, his big body trembling. In the next instant, he stood with her in his arms, the move so fast she gasped.

Capturing her mouth again, he carried her to his bedroom, bumping open the door, then reaching down to shut it silently. The fact that even now he was concerned and aware enough not to wake Zoe left her giddy, and the love she'd worked to forget overwhelmed her. They may have to start over and get to know one another again, she may still have to figure out how to trust him again, but falling in love with him wouldn't be a problem. She was already there.

He settled her onto the bed, then straightened to strip off his shirt. She reached for him the instant he stretched out next to her, her hands roaming over the planes of hard muscles she remembered so well. And yet he was brand new to her. She set about relearning all the dips and rises, the lovely ridges of his abs, the way he sucked in a breath when her fingers brushed against his ribs. When simply touching him wasn't quite enough, she slid down to run her lips across his chest, down the center of his stomach, flicking her tongue against the skin just above his jeans.

Oh, the sounds he made, those deep groans, growls, and hisses. She'd always loved listening to him, thrilling in his pleasure. She rubbed her hand over the hard ridge of his cock, through his jeans, and when his hips bucked, she grinned.

He rewarded her efforts by flipping her onto her back and indulging in his own exploration. He removed her t-shirt and bra, then dipped his head and took her nipple into the heat of his mouth. The feel of him sent a sharp shock of lust straight to her core. She squeezed her thighs together to contain the pressure building too fast.

"I've missed you so much," he murmured as he kissed from her breast down the center of her stomach.

Everything in her clenched and tightened, straining and coiling, the tingles of sensation almost painful. "I've missed you, too," she panted. Then groaned as he slipped a hand under the waistband of her jeans, not far, just enough to tease and torment.

He brushed his fingers gently just above the line of her underwear. She gasped and her hips bucked. For long moments, he did nothing more than drop light, wet kisses over her stomach and brush the skin along her lower abdomen, teasing at the elastic of her panties but never quite dipping beneath.

The teasing drove her to the very edge of screaming. Her every nerve jumped and fired. Her body clenched tight, straining toward more.

"Vlad." His name came out low and husky between her clenched teeth, both a plea and a demand. If he didn't remove her jeans soon, she was going to do it herself.

His chuckle tickled her stomach, sending another wave of tingles through her. Her nipples were peaked and so sensitive even the gentle brush of air in the room felt like a delicious torment.

"You always were in a hurry to get naked," he said as he finally, finally unbuttoned her jeans.

"All the good stuff happens when we're naked," she said, wiggling to help him get her jeans and underwear off. "Speaking of which, lose the rest of your clothes. Now."

His laugh was dark and husky, a seduction all its own. He stood long enough to shuck off the rest of his clothing, but he stared at her the entire time. Now naked, she arched and stretched under his gaze, feeling like the sexiest woman on Earth. The way his dark eyes narrowed and his breathing sped as he stared only made her hotter.

"You got a new tattoo," he commented, his tone almost an octave deeper now.

She'd wondered if he'd notice. To her extreme pleasure, he knelt on the bed and brought his face close to the little red heart she had on her inner right thigh. He traced it with one finger. It was a simple enough design, but he studied it like it held some secret.

"It's beautiful," he said, before kissing her right on the tattoo.

She shivered and her muscles clenched.

"Why this, and why here?"

"Because of Zoe. I got it right after I found out I was pregnant, before I even told you. It was going to be my second surprise."

He looked up at her as he stroked his thumb back and forth over the heart. "It's perfect. I'm very sorry it's taken me four years to see it."

"I can think of a few things you might consider doing while you're down there that could make up for that."

He grinned, a deliciously wicked expression that set her pulse pounding. Then he turned his full attention back to the little tattoo. "You still have the other two? I've been wondering all week."

"You'll have to see for yourself."

"Can't wait." He flicked out his tongue, a quick lick along her inner thigh, then pushed her legs farther apart and settled between them.

She had to bite her hand to keep from screaming when he settled his mouth over her heat and licked into her. Her clit was so sensitive, so ready for his tongue, she was trembling and close to orgasm within moments. She panted and groaned and tried desperately to hold back so she could enjoy the feel of his mouth on her for just a little longer, but her body worked against her. She tightened and tightened and then broke apart with a rush of pleasure.

He continued to lick her gently, but she was so sensitive after the orgasm, her body jerked and twitched with sensations that were a little too close to pain.

She gripped his hair and sat up, forcing his mouth away

from her. "Too much," she said. "Need just a little time to recover."

He kissed the inside of her knee and said, "Fair enough. I have a lot of other places I want to explore." He brushed his hand over her curls. "I'll just make my way back here."

She couldn't bring herself to argue.

"Now, let's see about those other tattoos."

He flipped her onto her stomach so fast she gasped, then giggled. She closed her eyes to savor the feel of his big hands stroking down her back to her bottom. He traced a finger over the sugar skull she had on her left ass cheek and hip, and she trembled in response. God, everything he did sent her close to the edge. He kissed the intricate artwork, then nibbled his way up, pausing at her lower back to lick the little dimple she had above her bottom, before dragging his lips along her spine. She arched, her hips lifting of their own accord.

With one hand still on her ass, he nuzzled her second tattoo on the back of her shoulder. This one was a small, single-color Celtic cross.

"I remember the first time I saw this one," he murmured against her shoulder. "On the ground watching you start your climb. I kept getting distracted from my gear checks, trying to catch sight of this whenever your tank top moved enough to show it. My belayer actually had to punch me in the arm to get my attention. I was so distracted by you, I thought for sure I'd miss a hand or toe hold and drop." He licked her shoulder blade. "The fall would have been worth it."

"You could have just asked for a better view," she said,

lifting up to look at him over her shoulder. "I was hoping to give you a closer look at both my tattoos."

"Then I really would have fallen to my death."

"I would have waited until we finished the climb."

"Yeah, but if you'd offered before we started, I wouldn't have."

She laughed quietly, then sighed and moved her head to one side as he nibbled the skin between her shoulder and neck. He made her feel so desirable, so feminine. How had she managed without this for four years?

He kissed his way to the other side of her neck, pausing at her nape to nuzzle a spot that was particularly sensitive. She shivered. When he started kissing down her spine again, she had to bury her face in the pillow to keep from groaning too loudly, and when his lips moved across her butt, she bit the pillow, hard.

"I love how sensitive you are," he murmured.

His breath was hot against her skin.

He traced the elaborate, multi-colored design on her butt again, his fingers running over the flower vines that twined round the skull and across her hip. "How'd you manage to get this without having an orgasm in the tattoo parlor?"

Her laugh turned into a muffled gasp. "The pain offset the pleasure," she said when she could manage to speak. "A lot."

"Probably for the best. I'd hate to be jealous of a random, anonymous tattoo artist."

"Not anonymous."

"Oh?"

The growl in his voice made her grin as she looked over her shoulder at him again, her hair dropping across one eye. "She's the only one I ever use. Very skilled." She pushed the mass of her hair out of the way so she could see his expression better.

He paused. "I'm not sure whether to be jealous or turned on now. I'm leaning toward turned on."

"Since we're naked and in bed together, I should hope you're turned on," she said dryly.

He grinned, that wicked smile she loved so much. "More turned on."

"Would you really share me with a woman?"

"No. But I like the fantasy."

She tossed a pillow at his head. He retaliated by biting her ass, none-too-gently. The sensation went right to her core and her body clenched in reaction, winding tighter and closer to another orgasm, just from having his mouth on her.

"You keep this up, I'm going to be too worn out for the actual intercourse part of the night," she said.

"I doubt that. I remember you having a great deal of stamina."

"I'm out of practice." More quietly, she said, "It's been a while for me."

He stopped kissing her, though his hand continued to caress her butt. "How long?"

She kept her head down, shy to admit this truth because it revealed so much. "Since you. I haven't been with anyone since you."

He remained so quiet, she forced herself to look at him.

Something she couldn't read moved through his expression. In a blink, he moved up the bed, rolled her onto her back, and kissed her, deeply and with so much passion she was overwhelmed. She wrapped her arms around him, trying to tell him with her kiss how much she'd missed him, in ways words just couldn't express.

He settled between her legs, his cock nudging against her entrance, but for a long moment, they just held that position, caressing and kissing as if they had all the time in the world. When he pushed a little farther, almost entering her, a strange but important thought invaded her passion addled brain.

She pulled his head up so she could look him in the eyes. "I'm not on birth control. And I don't have any condoms. We never worried about them because we thought we couldn't get pregnant, but we did. Which means we can again. I know we were together for two years before it happened last time, so it's not likely to happen tonight, but…"

She swallowed. She couldn't even consider pregnancy at the moment, not with everything going on with Zoe, not with the way her world had been upended, and certainly not with a man she was still learning to trust again.

He grimaced and in the dim light she could swear she saw color climb into his cheeks. She had to be imagining that. His skin tone was too dark and the room was shadowed, the lights out.

He said, "I have condoms in my bag."

"What?"

He rolled his eyes and looked away.

She took his face in her hands and forced him around to meet her gaze. "Are you telling me you planned this? You intended for us to end up in bed together again?"

"It wasn't exactly a plan. Wishful thinking maybe, but I didn't intend to rush you into anything."

"And you thought of birth control, even though we never bothered with it before?"

"Like you said, we can get pregnant. I didn't think you'd want to take that chance yet. Maybe after you forgive me and marry me, we can talk about it, but—"

"Wait." She put a finger over his mouth. "Did you just say marry you?"

"Of course. What did you think I wanted?"

"Well how the hell should I know? We have been… estranged for four years. You just came back into my life. And there's all this other stuff with Zoe."

"I know. Which is why I haven't brought it up. But I meant it when I said I would be here for you, Rose. Any way you want me. If I get my way, eventually you'll marry me. I won't rush you or pressure you, but it is what I want."

"And in the meantime, you brought condoms."

He grimaced.

"That was very presumptuous of you." She stopped him when he opened his mouth. "And very thoughtful."

In fact, his actions did more to prove his honorable intentions toward her then he could have guessed. Because if he was here to coerce her into marrying him, the best way to do that would be to get her pregnant again. The fact that he wasn't actively working to manipulate her that way made her heart swell. She pulled him close and kissed him.

When he raised his head again, she was panting and no longer thinking clearly.

"Does this mean I should go get one of the condoms?" he asked, sounding breathless too.

"One. Or two. Depending on *your* stamina."

He kissed her hard once and leapt away so fast the move made her bounce and the bounce made her giggle. He was back as quickly, with two condoms. He set one aside, slipped one on, and returned to kissing her before she had time to feel the chill in the room.

This time, when he nudged between her legs, she angled her hips and opened to him, eager to finally have him inside. For just an instant, the feel of him stretched her so fully she wasn't actually sure she was ready. She was more than eager and wet, but she was also very tight after four years of celibacy—despite having a child in that period of time.

Then he settled in fully, her body adjusted, and all she felt was the zing of satisfaction, a wholeness she'd almost forgotten. She gripped his shoulders and rocked against him, and the power of her need took over.

"You feel so perfect," he said against her neck. "I've missed the feel of you so much."

"You, too," she said, "Me, too."

They rocked together, petting and kissing, the sound of skin slapping against skin filling the room, and the scents of sweat and sex swirling around them. She let herself go, wallowing in the freedom to just be and feel, take and taste. And love. Her orgasm built until she couldn't hold back, but with Vlad she didn't need to. She charged into the abyss and kept him close as he followed.

They lay in each other's arms, hugging, silent for long moments after. She came down slowly and made no move to break the moment. She wanted to stay just this way for the rest of the night.

Vlad was the first to raise his head. He held her gaze and that emotion she couldn't quite decipher moved through the depths of his dark eyes. Finally, he kissed her lightly and rolled off. "I'll be right back. Just want to clean up."

To her pleasure, he took the time to tuck her under the blanket first, then he paused at the bedroom door.

"What are you waiting for?" she asked.

"Just listening. Making sure Zoe doesn't get up and catch me walking around like this." He flashed her a grin and left for the bathroom.

She rolled to stare at the door, a little awed and more than a little scared to face the fact that she was madly in love with Vlad. Again. Still.

Forever.


Vlad finished in the bathroom then walked out to the living room. Alexis had returned not long ago, his sense of her being in the house the only thing that had disrupted his focus on Rose. He was still a little overwhelmed, his body humming from having her in his arms again. And he was looking forward to going back and proving his stamina by making use of that second condom.

But first, he wanted to know what Alexis had put into place for the trip to the elders.

He thought he'd been protective of Rose and Zoe before this. Now, his protective instincts were pushing him to run away with them, keep them safe and well away from any other tigers. He couldn't, but everything in him wanted to.

Alexis sat on the couch, reading something on her phone.

"Victor has put his security team to work setting up safe rooms in the compound for all of you," she said without preamble, still looking at her cell.

"Good." That would augment the things Elizaveta was supposed to be doing.

He'd had to go through her assistant to start the arrangements because it was almost impossible to talk to an elder directly over the phone. Most of them just didn't do it. But going through an intermediary worried him. Most elders trusted their assistants with every aspect of their affairs. But all his life Vlad had seen the way money could swing loyalty. He'd used that fact frequently himself. When it came to Rose and Zoe, his trust in other people's moral fortitude was very limited.

"Any other news?" he asked.

"Victor says Elizaveta is thrilled." Alexis glanced at him and rolled her eyes.

"Should I be pleased or afraid?"

"Terrified." She set her phone aside. "Elizaveta will ensure you have official safe passage, and Victor will make sure you have official security. I'm going to go in with you, just to add a little muscle." She grinned. "I've asked a couple of Trackers I trust to meet me there so we can provide you with the physical security you'll need."

"I can handle that part."

"I'm sure you can. But we want to make a show of it. We need everyone aware that Zoe isn't vulnerable or without support within the community. Nila didn't have this going in, and it left her open to attacks. We don't want anyone thinking that's an option with Zoe. Outside of those like your brothers, you still have the elders to worry about and… Do you know about the split among the Trackers?"

He nodded.

Just like the rest of the community, the Trackers were divided over the issue of human-tiger mixes. Some of them sided with Elizaveta, some were on the fence, and some were with the elders who didn't want hybrids in their midst. His father had used the Trackers who agreed with his stance when he went hunting for Nila. They hadn't directly helped him go after her, but they'd actively thrown the other Trackers off his trail, giving him time to try to kill her. Since the Trackers were essentially the police force of the tiger shifter world, having some of them help a wanted criminal had damaged the organization's reputation.

Many of those who'd aided his father hadn't been identified by the elders yet, either. Vlad was still working on uncovering them all himself. He had to work carefully to avoid making his brothers question why he was looking for them.

"Then you know," Alexis continued, "that even within the compound, even with all the resources we've set up, there are some we can't trust, and we don't know who they are."

"I don't trust anyone right now." When she raised her brows, he said, "No offense. I suppose I'm trusting you to a certain extent. But you'll understand if I stay on guard around all tigers."

She snorted. "Yeah, I can't blame you. If she was my baby, I'd be viciously protective, too."

"I've heard you already are."

She grinned at that. "Guess it comes with being a parent. And speaking of which, how do you like the job so far?"

He thought of that beautiful little girl, sound asleep in the other room, the way she'd taken to her tiger nature as if she'd always expected it to be part of her life, the way she ordered him around when she was in human form, and the way she'd play-attacked him in tiger form. He smiled softly. "Love it."

"Good. I assume you and Rose are…reconciling?"

"Working on it."

"Then I assume you intend to stick by her and Zoe in the years ahead."

"I do. Why do you care?"

"They're going to need you." She glanced back at the hallway leading to the rooms. "There's been a change… A few of the females in the generation just before my daughters, they're coming into their first estrous early. We've been keeping it pretty quiet."

"Who's we?"

"Elizaveta and me, the girls, and a handful of scientists Elizaveta trusts."

"How do you know?"

"I work with most of the female tigers in the US."

He raised his brows. "Work?"

"Self-defense training. Remember Su-jin Lee-Bennett?"

Vlad sucked in a breath. Everyone remember Sujin's murder. It had rocked the community because her murderer was human.

"Well, after, it was decided the females needed to learn how to defend themselves properly. Instinct is all well and good, but training goes a lot further."

The conversation suddenly made him very grateful Rose was a highly trained martial artist. They'd have to be sure Zoe got training, too. Thinking about Su-jin's death, especially now that he had a daughter of his own to worry about, was too uncomfortable, so he went back to the original topic. "How early is the early estrous?"

"Two started at twenty."

"That early?" Most tiger females didn't come into their first estrous until around twenty-five.

"One girl had her first estrous at nineteen. We're not making this common knowledge. They're all too young to go into the Mate Run."

"Theories about why it's happening?"

"The extinction threat. We're still right on the edge. The few scientists Elizaveta trusted with this have theorized the earlier estrous is a way for females to start breeding earlier so they have a longer reproductive life."

"Why now? Why not a century ago? Why not two centuries ago when the problem first became serious?"

She shrugged. "Got me. But it's the only logical explanation we have at the moment. The thing is, this probably means my daughter's generation will have more females coming into estrous early. The secret won't remain a secret much longer. The males will get wind and will expect these girls to start running."

"Why are you telling me all this?"

"You have a daughter. A tiger daughter. Mixed or not, she's a shifter, and she will be pressured to run. I know it's years down the road, but you should know you might reach that point a lot sooner than you expect. It's hard to tell with a hybrid. We have no way of knowing what road her biology will follow. But she's going to need a strong advocate on her side. The best person to do that is her father."

The urge to run away and keep Zoe and Rose hidden from his people got even stronger. "I'll be with her," he said. "I'll keep her safe."

"Good. Now, I'm going for a run. I'll be back in a few hours." She winked and ambled toward the front door, pulling her shirt off as she went.

Giving him and Rose some privacy from shifter hearing.

Privacy he intended to take advantage of. He paused in the hall outside Zoe's door, assuring himself she slept soundly, surprised at how much he needed to check on her and how often. He found himself listening for her breathing almost automatically.

So this was what it was like to be a father.

Had his own father ever done this? Was there a time, ever, when his father had felt this protective instinct for him? He shook off the thought. He didn't intend to be a father like his. He would be his own man, as he'd always been, and a better parent to Zoe.

As he made his way to his room, and Rose waiting in his bed, he hoped she'd give him the chance to experience what it was like to be a husband, too. Things between them were good at the moment, but she still didn't trust him. And he wasn't confident she'd even want him in her life after she faced the rest of his people.

He just had to prove to her he could keep her and Zoe protected and safe.

"What kept you?" Rose asked when Vlad came back, closing the door quietly behind him.

"I wanted to talk with Alexis, see what she'd set up for our trip, and what she'd found out about the reception we can expect."

Rose narrowed her eyes and glanced over his body. "You're still naked."

He glanced down, as if he'd forgotten. "Yes. Zoe's still asleep so there wasn't a chance she'd catch me."

"I wasn't thinking about Zoe catching you. You sat out there talking with Alexis while you were naked."

He chuckled. "I told you, we tigers don't really pay much attention to nudity. I actually didn't think about it."

"Did Alexis?"

"Alexis is happily married and old enough to be my mother."

Rose gaped. "She is? She looks maybe right on the edge of turning forty."

"She's almost fifty-two." He paused. "Yeah, I guess she's not quite old enough to be my mother. Close, though."

"She couldn't have had you at twenty-two?" To Rose, who'd gotten pregnant just before she turned twenty-four, Alexis sounded more than old enough to have a thirty year old son.

He crawled up beside her on the bed and pulled her into his arms. "Female tigers don't go into estrous until around twenty-five." His brows furrowed as he said it, as if he was leaving something out.

"What? What are you not telling me?"

He sighed and rubbed her arms. "It's not a big deal, yet. But a few of our females have started coming into estrous…early. Really early for tigers."

"What age?"

"Twenty. One even at nineteen. It'd be like nine and ten year old human girls getting their periods."

"That does happen sometimes."

"True, but it doesn't happen in tigers. Females might come into estrous as early as twenty-four. But nineteen and twenty is really, really young."

"Ah. The extinction thing?" She snuggled closer, savoring the warmth of his skin against hers.

"Likely. It's being looked into." He shook his head and

kissed her. "Anyway, that's not something we need to worry about."

"For now. But Zoe will come to maturity someday."

"I don't even want to think about it."

She chuckled. "You sound like a father."

His expression softened and when he kissed her this time, it was a deep, deliciously heated kiss.

"Where's Alexis now?" she asked when she came up for air. The idea that Alexis would hear them easily was a little embarrassing. Rose wasn't quite *that* adventurous.

"She went for a run. A tiger run. For a few hours." He nibbled the skin along her throat. "So we have some privacy. I checked, Zoe's still asleep. It's just the two of us."

"Really?" She traced her fingers along his arm, angling her head so he could kiss his way along the other side of her neck. She shivered as the heat and need built again. "And what should we do with that privacy?"

"I think we should use that second condom."

"You…up for that already?"

He took her hand and pressed her palm to his erection. "What do you think?"

She wrapped her fingers around his cock and stroked him. "I think you've got a lot of stamina."

He spent the next two hours proving it.

# CHAPTER TWELVE

They spent the next three days teaching Zoe how to be a tiger and lining up their plans for the trip to West Virginia. Rose's parents weren't happy about the side trip, because she wouldn't let them go with her. Since one of Vlad's brothers had been to see them again, they were as worried as Rose. But a two-hour conversation on Vlad's secure cellphone convinced them to remain behind.

Her dad did tell her who she could go to in West Virginia to borrow a gun or three, though.

"As many as you need," he'd said.

When she'd told Vlad she intended to pick up a few guns before going to the elders' compound, she'd fully expected a fight. After all, this was the US seat of his people's governing body. Strangers bringing weapons into the center of power for a government was typically frowned upon.

He surprised her by encouraging the idea, even offering his own contacts for weapons and ammunition.

"We'll make sure to pick up any gear we might possibly need," he said. "I want us ready for any contingency. You armed with more than your various black belts will be good."

"You should have an escape plan in place, too," Alexis added. "In case everything goes wrong. Victor, myself, and the few people we're trusting with your safety will be able to help and cover your backs, but if things get out of hand, leave the compound and go into hiding until we can work out a better plan."

"Jesus, why are we doing this?" Rose asked, not for the first time.

They were sitting in front of the fire, Zoe napping on the rug. All the tiger play wiped her out and ensured she slept well at night as well as took a nap during the day. Rose smiled at her. Zoe hadn't taken regular naps since she was two—except after episodes. Seeing her sleep because of simple exhaustion from playing made Rose's heart happy.

There hadn't been even a hint of an episode since Zoe had learned how to let her tiger out. Vlad was even teaching her the "play" hunting, which tiger cubs all apparently learned, because she'd taken to being a tiger so well.

If it weren't for the threat and complication of introducing her to a greater tiger shifter world—a place where she'd be revered, valued, seen as a commodity, and reviled as an abomination all at once—Rose would be completely content with the way things had gone.

She glanced at Vlad. "We can't just run away and hide, huh?"

He smiled faintly and shook his head. "Though, I have considered it. More than once." He shrugged. "A lot actually."

The fact that he was thinking the same things she was made her feel better. The last three days had been so wonderful, almost dream-like. This was what she'd imagined her life would be like with him. Well, without the tiger part of course. Her days with Zoe and Vlad as a close family; her nights in bed with the man she loved, finding new ways to excite and please each other.

The contentment of the last few days made her feelings for the tigers complicated. If not for the threat Vlad's brothers posed, would he have returned to them? Would they all be here together?

A part of her still wondered if he'd stay. When all was said and done, when the thrill of the danger wore off, when the reality of parenting sank in, would he still want this life? Vlad was as much of an adrenaline junkie as she was.

And he'd left before.

She shoved down that mean little voice. He'd left because he'd believed she'd cheated on him, and while he should have known better, at the time he couldn't have realized Zoe was possible. Rose had to let go of her resentment for his distrust if they were to have a future together. But the pain of his abandonment still lingered and made trusting him so difficult.

Going into the elders' compound meant she was putting her life and the life of her daughter in his hands. She knew he'd guard their backs, and that was at least something, a level of trust that was a good start. She just had to find a way to give in to it and stop doubting that the contentment of the last few days could be their future.

"You all packed?" Alexis asked, breaking into her thoughts.

"We're ready. I think Zoe would like to stay here and keep running around in the snow, but she's pretty excited about being on an airplane, too."

They were all leaving early the next morning, driving directly to Sky Harbor airport. Vlad's brothers had left the area the day before. One had gone to Alaska of all places. The other two were back on the east coast. So going into Phoenix was safe for the moment.

Rose was more nervous than she'd ever been about any trip she'd ever taken. Zoe just saw the adventure.

She was definitely her mother's daughter.

Alexis stretched her arms over her head and sighed. "I need to go for a run if we're going to be on the road all day tomorrow. I'll be back in a few hours." Before standing, she patted Rose's knee. "Don't worry." She left the cabin wearing only a long-sleeved shirt, jeans, and boots.

"She's going running like that?" Rose asked.

"She'll hike to a place with privacy and turn tiger."

"How long can you go without letting your tigers out?"

He shrugged and scooted closer to her, his arm around her shoulders. "Depends on the individual. I can go for weeks if necessary. It gets easier as we get older. But we get restless and a little achy if we go for too long. Like when you spend too much time sitting and your body starts to get edgy for some exercise? It's like that."

"No pain?"

"No pain. You're still worried about Zoe?"

"It's hard to believe after more than a year of her episodes, we won't have to go through that ever again. I'm so relieved and yet I still feel like I'm waiting for the other shoe to drop."

"She won't have the pain again. But I'm afraid we do have another shoe waiting."

"The other tigers." She didn't have to ask. They'd gone round and round this same conversation for days.

He nuzzled her neck. "You know, we have to leave so early and we probably won't have much privacy for the next week." He bit her ear, tugging gently at the lobe. "Zoe'll probably sleep another half hour or so."

She smiled as he kissed his way down her throat.

"Want to sneak into the back?"

"Have to be quick," she warned.

He picked her up and before she could gasp, he was closing the door to his bedroom.

"*Dios*, that was fast," she breathed, her heart thumping with so much excitement that she might have been embarrassed with anyone but Vlad.

He chuckled and pressed her against the wall, her legs wrapped around his waist. "So we have more time for this part."

He kissed her, and the taste of him swept her up, tumbling her into that wonderfully erotic place only he could take her.

Her hands moved over his shoulders, gripping hard as she ground herself against his erection. "Better get our clothes off," she muttered before kissing him again.

He set her on her feet, stripped, slipped on a condom and pulled her back into his arms before she could do more than push her jeans and underwear off. She chuckled. "You're taking the 'quick' thing seriously."

"Don't want to take time away from the fun part." He cupped her heat, rubbing a finger along her entrance, dipping into her once before moving his finger to her clit.

She dropped her head back against the wall, biting back a groan.

"I love the way you look when I have my hands on you," he said, circling her clit in just the right way to make her moan.

She bucked against his hands as her orgasm approached fast enough to surprise her. "I love having your hands on me." She gasped and gripped his shoulders tighter, coming up on her toes when everything in her tightened.

He nuzzled her neck, pushed the collar of her shirt aside with his mouth, and bit down on the sensitive skin between her neck and shoulder. The sensation sent her careening into her orgasm, everything in her bursting apart in a breathless moment.

She would have slipped to the floor in a boneless heap but for his strong arms. He lifted her, wrapping her legs around his waist again, and slid into her. And, just like that, her body lit up again. The friction of his cock stretching her set her nerves jumping with sensation. With each thrust, she tightened and squeezed him, wanting every part of him. He was hers, for this time, in this moment, he was all hers and she took every hard pounding thrust with possessive demand.

When he came, she watched his release, the way his muscles tightened, his jaw rock hard, his eyes closed, and she triumphed in knowing she'd done that to him.

He hugged her close as they both settled slowly, then he pulled back and kissed her. After a quiet moment when she could tell he was listening for Zoe, he patted her ass, right on her tattoo. "We'd better get dressed in case she wakes up."

Rose grinned as he set her on the floor and kissed him one last time before she let him go clean up.

Slipping into her jeans, she once again had that content, nostalgic sense that this could be their future. Sneaking off for a quickie during naptime. Dressing fast afterward, so they didn't get caught. Almost like a normal family life…

Except their lives were never going to be "normal."

She sighed as the worries descended again, dampening some of her afterglow and contentment.

She was back on the couch watching Zoe sleep when Vlad joined her.

"What happens if your brothers show up at the compound while we're there?" she asked.

He pulled her into his arms. "Back to worrying?"

She chuckled, but without much humor.

"They can't do anything to you at the compound," he said. "You'll be surrounded by bodyguards."

"But Alexis thinks we need an escape strategy. That's a very ominous suggestion."

"She's a retired Tracker. She's both paranoid and cautious."

"You're letting me bring guns into the compound. She's not the only one paranoid and cautious."

He shrugged. "Despite my increased efforts the last few days, I still can't figure out which specific elder was helping my father go after Nila. I'm not entirely sure my father even knew, except that he had support through intermediaries. Then there're the unknown anti-hybrid Trackers out there somewhere. We're walking into a very volatile situation without all the information. That calls for a little paranoia."

He cupped her cheek in one hand and kissed her gently. She wanted to fall into that kiss all over again and forget the worries plaguing her, but Vlad pulled back to continue.

"I *know* this trip is the only way to ensure you'll be safe," he said. "Without the backing of the elders, without formal recognition under our laws, you and Zoe are vulnerable. But until the elders give you their official support, we have to stay on guard."

"If one of the elders doesn't like…people like Zoe and Nila, if there are tigers like your brothers we can't trust, how can official recognition help us? Won't the fanatic bigots still come after Zoe?"

"It's a perception thing. Once the elders, as a group and ruling body, grant their protection, it would make them look weak and useless if something then happened to those they're protecting. Which means they take those oaths very seriously. Otherwise, they risk being overthrown."

"What's the hitch?" She could hear it in his voice, something he was hesitant to admit.

He sighed. "The hitch is *getting* them to give Zoe their protection. The debate with Nila was extensive, but at the time, she was the only one and they needed her to help them study how those like her could even exist."

"Why haven't they asked you to help with that research? You're the child of a woman who could have children with humans."

"They assumed I wouldn't cooperate. I haven't come out as believing anything different than my father and brothers yet."

"Because of Zoe?"

"And you. Any hint would have endangered you both. I was playing a game. Which I lost, or we wouldn't be in this position."

She dropped a kiss on his lips. "We would have always been in this position. It was just a matter of time." She frowned a little. "The elders wouldn't just…coerce you into helping?" She didn't trust them not to try throwing Zoe into some medical lab to poke at her like an experiment. She was absolutely not going to allow that, but the fact that they might try was an ever-present worry.

"We're free agents," he said. "The elders make laws and rule us, but they can't order us to participate in medical tests without our permission. That kind of abuse of power would definitely lead to a bloody uprising, and we can't afford that. We're too close to extinction as it is."

"Sounds like a very delicate balancing act."

"It is. Makes me glad I'm not an elder."

"Is it possible one day? I mean, how does one get to be an elder? Besides living a long time."

He chuckled. "Though most of them are very old, the title elder isn't simply an indication of age. They don't get to be in that position just by outliving their contemporaries. They have to be extremely powerful and very rich in their own right. Then there are debates and arguments and votes to approve a new one."

"The rest of the community or just the other elders?"

"Both groups have to approve. Takes a lot of machination to make it onto the council. Means every one of them is smart, powerful, manipulative, and cunning. Not people to take lightly."

"Why are we going again?" She raised a hand when he started to answer. "I know, I know. I do understand. I was just whining. But I have to admit, I'd rather take Zoe into hiding."

"Me, too."

She tilted her head to look at him. "If we did go into hiding, where would you want to go?"

"Alaska."

"Where your brother just went? Really?" She loved Alaska. She and Vlad had even taken a trip there, kayaking in the sea surrounded by ice floes. It had been a spectacular adventure.

He stared at the cold fireplace as he said, "I have a house there. I bought it…a month before we broke up." He faced her. "For you. It was going to be an engagement present if I could get you to say yes."

"You were going to propose?"

He brushed a finger over her inner thigh, indicating the heart through her jeans. "'Bout the same time you were getting this tattoo, I was trying to find the right ring."

Her heart did a little dance at his admission. God, all the time they'd wasted. She leaned close and kissed him again, not even sure how to express all the feelings welling up in her. Before the kiss got too serious, Zoe stirred, flopping into a new position on the rug—a sure sign the nap was coming to an end.

Rose sighed and rested her forehead against his for a moment before pushing back. "I'd better get dinner started."

She was pulling vegetables out of the refrigerator when Vlad joined her, leaning against the counter, frowning slightly.

"What's wrong?" she asked as she started washing lettuce. That look didn't bode well, and was a real mood shift from just a few moments ago.

"I need to tell you something, and I've been hesitating."

"Oh no." She paused to stare at him. "Now what haven't you told me?"

He winced a little. "This is… Other tigers are likely to bring this up while we're at the compound. I want you to hear the story from me."

"What are you talking about?"

"I told you my father killed my mother."

She nodded but didn't say anything. He looked too pensive and she didn't want to interrupt what he had to say.

"My brothers believe it was a suicide because that's what my father told all of us. He claimed when he found out she'd had a baby with a human, she'd been so ashamed she killed herself. My brothers bought that story because they share my father's prejudices."

"You don't believe it, though?"

"He admitted to Nila he'd killed my mother. It's common knowledge in the community now." He swallowed visibly and looked down at the floor. "But even before that, I knew he'd murdered her. It's my fault he found out about Nila in the first place."

She wasn't sure how to react. A part of her wanted to comfort him and ease the guilt she saw plainly in his body language. Another part wanted to throw questions at him. Instead, she kept working on dinner, giving him room to tell his story in his own time.

"I was visiting my parents in their home in Russia," he said. "I was…out of sorts. My mother and I were always very close. I look a lot like her, which is unusual for tigers. Most of the time, sons resemble their fathers, daughters their mothers. There's a little mixing but for the most part, tigers bear the strongest resemblance to the parent of the same sex. My father was very Russian looking, with blond hair and blue eyes." He gestured at his face. "There's very little of him in me."

She couldn't help but say, "I'm glad to hear it since he murdered your mother and tried to murder your sister."

He tilted his head in acknowledgement of the point. "At any rate, the fact that his oldest son didn't really look like him was always an issue between us. It tainted our relation-ship. He…didn't like me as much as my brothers—all of whom look more like him than I do. Anyway, because my father and I had a cold and distant relationship, my mother tried to make up for it by loving me more. We were very close."

"Oh, Vlad. Her murder must have really torn you up." Rose couldn't imagine losing her own beloved parents yet. She dreaded the day and was kind of hoping they'd live into their hundreds so she wouldn't have to deal with it for a long time.

"Worse because it was my fault."

"How?"

"On that particular trip to Russia, my mother pestered me until I admitted what was bothering me—that after four years, I still couldn't get over you. I'd tried. I'd even done a few Mate Runs right after, thinking if I got a tiger shifter mate I'd be able to stop loving you."

She kept her gaze on the vegetables she was chopping, trying not to feel hurt at that admission, but it still hit her in the chest like a punch. He'd left her and then gone looking for another woman, someone he could have children with. The thought actually brought tears to her eyes. She blinked them away so he wouldn't see.

"I didn't put much effort into the Runs. I never caught a female and really didn't try. After a year of pretending, I stopped running. That pissed my father off. I'm his oldest and he expected me to get a mate and have children. He actually thought all his sons would get mates, which is ridiculous. That never happens. There just aren't enough tigresses."

He waved off the slight change in direction and went back to the topic. "When I told my mother I was still hung up on you, even though you'd cheated on me, and I was considering trying to get back together with you, she encouraged me. She said I should trust my instincts, and then she admitted that maybe it was possible for your baby to be mine."

"She told you?"

"We both thought my father was out of the house and that we had complete privacy. We would have been able to feel him if he was in the house, or any other tiger for that matter, so she felt safe. Up until this point, the only tiger who knew about Nila was Elizaveta. My mom went to her when she found out she was pregnant, and Elizaveta helped her keep the secret."

"Why did it have to be a secret?"

"Because of tigers like my father, my mother was terrified her child would be killed, terrified Nila's father, Leo, would be killed, and Elizaveta wasn't ready to make knowledge of hybrids public yet. She was still researching and didn't want to get my people's hopes up or start a war against hybrids. Especially if Nila's conception turned out to be a fluke and not something we could duplicate. Elizaveta wanted time. My mother wanted Nila safe. So they kept the pregnancy a secret and when Nila was born, they left her with her father. My mother went back to the Mate Run to get a tiger mate."

"Why on earth did she marry your father? Given the way he felt about hybrids."

"She didn't know about his extreme beliefs until well after their wedding. I asked the same question when she told me about Nila. She was pregnant with their second child—the twins as it turned out—before he showed her any hint of his beliefs. At that stage, she'd fallen in love with him and was happy with their pairing. She thought his ideas were just vague feelings, nothing too extreme, so she stayed with him."

"When did she learn how…deeply he held the belief that hybrids were a bad thing?"

"I was about fourteen and my father announced to a group of powerful tigers that he'd kill any hybrids he found. That's when the true depths of his fanaticism started to show. She stayed with him at that point to protect Nila. She didn't want him getting even a hint that she disagreed, because she was afraid he'd try to find out why. My father is…was very smart and cunning. I'm still surprised she kept her secret as long as she did. Just goes to show how smart she was."

He paused and Rose watched a range of emotions move through his expression, most of which were difficult for her to see—a lot of pain and bleakness.

He sucked in a breath and continued. "Anyway, we had this long talk where she admitted all this history to me, swore me to secrecy, but said I should consider going to you and trying to reconcile because it was entirely possible your baby was my child. I was both thrilled and devastated. I went for a run to consider it all."

He gripped the counter, and Rose saw his knuckles go white. She heard the granite crunch and gasped. "Vlad?"

He released his hold and flexed his fingers. "Sorry. This…" He shook his head and crossed his arms over his chest. "When I got back, I could tell my father was home, but I couldn't feel my mother anymore. I didn't think that was a big deal until I came into the living room and saw my father standing over my mother with blood on his hands, glaring down at her dead body."

"*Madre de Dios*."

"He'd ripped her throat out. Her head was barely still…" He swallowed hard. "And when he saw me, he didn't show any signs of guilt. He didn't even hesitate when he said she'd killed herself."

"How the hell would she have ripped out her own throat?"

"He said she'd slit her throat with a knife—even though there wasn't one around. He explained the blood on his hands by claiming he'd tried to put pressure on the wound and keep her from bleeding out before her body could heal. But the wound was clearly not from a knife slice, and the blood on his hands was *not* from trying to save her life."

"What did you do? What did he do?"

"He said we had a problem to solve. My mother had committed a crime—which was why she'd killed herself, out of shame—and it was up to me and my brothers to fix her mistake. When I asked what crime, he said she'd given birth to a half-breed abomination and that disgusting offspring had to die."

"Oh, my God. Vlad, what did you say? How did he know?"

"Later, after he'd rallied my brothers to his cause, I went through the house, trying to find out how he'd heard us. He was definitely *not* there when we were talking. He had the fucking place bugged. I don't know why. Paranoid.

Or maybe he already suspected my mother of something. Can't ask him now. Didn't dare ask him then."

She flinched a little at his curse and glanced toward the living room. To her relief, Zoe was still asleep. She looked back at him. "Did you go to your authorities?"

"I pretended to be on his side."

"How could you do that when you knew the truth?"

"He asked me about you, Rose. With my mother's blood still on his hands, he asked me if your baby could possibly be mine."

The knife she held clattered onto the granite countertop. She snatched it up and stared at him. "You lied to him to protect us?"

"Of course. Even if Zoe wasn't mine, I couldn't risk him thinking she might be."

"What did you tell him?"

"That I knew for a fact you'd had an affair because I'd tracked down the man in one of my 'grief stricken' periods. I even told my father I came close to killing the man. Poured enough real emotion into my lie that he believed me."

"You're sure?"

"If he hadn't, he would have sent someone after you and Zoe while he was hunting Nila. Tigers can…sniff out lies. Scent gives away a lot of emotion. But I've spent my entire life learning how to hide who I am and what I really feel from my father. I am very good at deception now."

That comment made her more than a little nervous, but she pushed the worry aside for later. "If he believed you, how did your brothers get suspicious?"

"They found out I was planning a trip to see you and with that trip coming only five months after we discovered Nila… It's not hard to see why they might have gotten suspicious. I tried to keep my plans to myself, but obviously, I'm not the only one spying on my siblings."

"You have a very dysfunctional family, Vlad."

He snorted.

She started to say more, but noise from the living room stopped her.

"Mommy?"

"In the kitchen, baby." To Vlad, she said, "We'll have to finish this later."

"Not much more to tell, just thought you should know before our trip."

Zoe wandered into the room then and they switched subjects, but the conversation had left Rose with many more questions. Not the least of which was…if Vlad could lie so well he could fool his own father, would she ever know if he was lying to her? Her trust was already tentative and shaky at best. How could she trust him if she couldn't believe anything he told her? All that talk of a house in Alaska, a ring hunt, his intentions to propose, had any of that been true or just a lie to make her feel better about their relationship?

And would she ever know the truth?

# CHAPTER THIRTEEN

Rose was putting dinner on the table when Alexis slammed into the cabin. She looked flushed and anxious.

"Vlad, your brothers found out about this place. They never left Arizona, and they're on their way here right now. We need to leave tonight."

Vlad held up his phone. "Just got the word."

"What? How?" Rose asked. "It's impossible. This cabin isn't linked to my family at all except through a friend."

"Fuck," Vlad muttered.

"No cursing," Zoe corrected him.

He gave her a little smile. "Sorry." To Rose, he said, "They've been searching. They must have come across the link and are heading here to check it out. Thought they were checking *my* homes first after Yuri booked the flight to Alaska."

Unfortunately, it looked like the flight was a diversion. "What now?" Rose asked.

"If they found this cabin, they know more than I thought they could so soon. They likely know about our flights tomorrow," Vlad said.

"Does that mean it's not safe to go anymore? Not that it was safe anyway."

"Still the best way to protect you and Zoe is to get you in front of the elders," Alexis said. "But we're going to have to get there by a different route. Can't afford to follow a plan the Dubrovskys might know about."

"Mommy, what wrong? Thought we were still on vacation?"

"We are, baby, but we have to change our plans a bit. You sit down and eat. I'll go get our bags."

Alexis sat with Zoe and helped her put together a plate, while Rose hurried to the bedroom. Vlad followed.

"What are we going to do now?" she asked as she pushed the rest of her and Zoe's gear into their mostly packed bags.

"Drive to Colorado and take a flight from there."

"Why Colorado?"

"Not tiger territory. There's only one tiger in the entire state and he's a Chernikov." He frowned. "Actually make that two tigers, now that he's got a mate."

"Chernikov? Related to Elizaveta?"

"Her grandson. He's one of the men Alexis considers a brother. It's his youngest brother who's engaged to Nila."

"Ah, so he's not a threat. Why no other tigers there?"

"The state's traditionally werewolf territory."

"Werewolves? Are we going to run into werewolves?"

"No, no. It just means we won't accidentally run into any tigers, and my brothers won't have extensive resources there—no reason to."

"How about your resources there?" She went to the gun cabinet to get her father's rifle. She held it a moment, considering. She couldn't take it on the flight and she didn't want to abandon it. She should leave it here so her father could collect it.

"Skimpy, too," Vlad answered her question.

"Can we get a last minute flight? That's gonna cost a fortune." She locked the gun back in the cabinet. She was going to feel a little naked driving all the way to Colorado without it. After seeing how fast Zoe and Vlad could move, she wanted more than her own fighting skills if they had to face any other shifters along the way.

"Money isn't the problem," Vlad said. "Space on a flight might be. And my brothers waiting at Yeager is a definite problem."

"They're coming here. They can't be in two places at once."

"There are three of them. They split up before, they'll do that again. And if they think Zoe is a hybrid, they won't be working alone to get to us before we reach the compound."

"So we fly in somewhere else and drive a little farther than planned."

He smiled. "My thoughts exactly. We'll take whatever we can get that's close but not directly there."

"We still have time to pick up the guns from my father's friend?"

"We'll make time."

She nodded, but a slight tremor shook her shoulders. "That cabin in Alaska sounds good about now."

"Except my brothers know about it." He pulled her into his arms. "We'll take care of this. Zoe will be okay. I promise."

She kissed him, quick and hard, then finished getting her bags together. By the time they were done, Zoe was halfway through her dinner. Rose was too worried to eat, but she forced down a little to keep up her energy and cleaned up as Alexis and Vlad loaded their gear into the cars.

They decided to leave her SUV there as a diversion. Vlad would take her and Zoe in his rental to Colorado. Alexis would cross into New Mexico and fly out from Albuquerque—another diversion.

"Good thing you had a nap," Rose said to Zoe as they finished putting the house in order. She didn't want to leave it a mess. "We've got a long drive ahead of us."

"Like driving."

She could tell from Zoe's expression she was more worried than happy about this change of plans, though. "It'll be okay, baby. I promise. We've just got a lot of driving and flying ahead of us."

"Okay, Mommy."

Rose's heart squeezed at the little hitch in her daughter's voice, and a deep seed of anger took root. Damn this stupid shifter business. Zoe had been through enough in her short life. As they headed out into the dark night, she swore by all that was holy, she'd make sure Zoe didn't have to worry about running away like this again. Whatever it took.

*  *  *

With all the fear and anxiety riding Vlad throughout the journey, all the worry about his brothers somehow catching up to them, he was a little surprised when they reached the elders' compound forty hours later without any trouble.

"Was that too easy?" Rose asked as they drove through a huge security gate. "Or did we just outsmart your brothers?"

"Good question." He wasn't entirely sure. "Just stay alert. We won't be able to relax until the elders give Zoe their backing, and the way the bastards talk, that could take days."

"Days? Ah, hell."

"You guys cursing," Zoe scolded. "Ah ah ah."

Rose shook her head and grinned. To Vlad, she said, "This is what I get for imposing a no-cursing rule in my home. My daughter throws it back in my face. I blame my mother. I get the prohibition on 'bad words' from her. My dad can cuss up a storm when he wants—especially when Irish rugby is on."

"Grandpa gets in trouble when he says fuck."

Vlad choked back a laugh.

Rose rolled her eyes and tried not to laugh, too. There *was* something very funny about a three year old saying "fuck" even though it was completely inappropriate. But her mother would kill her if she heard it. "Exactly right, baby. You shouldn't say that word either."

"'Kay, Mommy."

The drive from the gate up the long, forest-lined road to the interior of the compound took enough time that Zoe started asking for a potty stop.

"Almost there, sweetie. Can you wait a few more minutes?" Vlad pulled into the parking lot, looking around, anticipating ambush. What he saw surprised him.

Alexis, backed by a dozen other tigers, was already waiting to greet them. She broke from the group as he climbed out of the rental car.

"Thought you might feel safer with an escort," she said quietly. "Did you have a fun trip, Zoe?"

"Yay! We drove lots. Need a potty."

Alexis chuckled. "Well, we'd better get you to one quick." To Vlad and Rose, she said, "These are Trackers I trust. They'll guard our backs. You're safe now."

Rose released a breath and her shoulders sagged for just a moment before she straightened again. Vlad couldn't quite believe what he was seeing. He was the son of a known murderer, under suspicion himself for playing a part in Nila's kidnapping. Yet Alexis had rallied support to keep his daughter safe.

"Thank you," he said to her as he pulled their luggage out of the rental.

She waved it off.

Inside, the huge entry was brightly lit and outwardly welcoming. All the corridors in this part of the compound were lined with pale marble floors and white walls, the walls holding paintings and sculptures of nature scenes and tigers. The high ceilings gave the building an open, airy feeling that kept the average tiger shifter from feeling confined and squeezed. The designers of the building had intended for it to be imposing too, and from the awed look on Rose's face, they'd succeeded.

Their group had barely cleared the main door when Alexis' husband, Victor, joined them.

Alexis and Victor signed to each other for several moments, then Alexis said aloud, "Everything is in place. We'll get you all to your rooms in the guest wing. After you've rested some, the elders have arranged a meeting. Zoe will have to attend that." After a bit more signing with her husband, she said, "They've agreed to an open meeting so any tiger in the compound can attend."

"Is that good or bad for us?" Rose asked.

"Good," Vlad said, both surprised and relieved by the news. "With the entire community watching, they have to keep things...on the up and up."

"Safer for Zoe?"

"Yes."

Nila had had a closed meeting with them when she'd finally been brought to the compound. According to gossip, she'd handled herself well, and the elders had behaved, if not well, then at least typically for them. Still, Vlad hadn't been looking forward to having his daughter alone in a room with them—especially knowing one had been helping his father.

Rose stayed close to his side, holding Zoe's hand

tightly, as they were escorted through the massive corridors toward the wing of the compound reserved for guests.

"Is he deaf?" she murmured to Vlad, nodding toward Victor. "Not sure why, but that surprises me."

Victor glanced over his shoulder and shook his head, grinning.

"He hears just fine," Vlad told her. "He's mute. That's the reason for the sign language."

"I'm still surprised."

"Long story. Childhood injury. A lot of tigers consider him defective."

Alexis glanced back this time, her eyes narrowed.

"I'm not one of them," he said, raising his hands, palms out to appease her.

She nodded and looked ahead.

"You probably shouldn't aggravate our security detail," Rose murmured.

They'd just arrived at their rooms when one of the elders' assistants stopped them. He stood with his spine stiff, regarding them with a neutral expression. Vlad breathed in the man's scent, trying to pinpoint his identity. He was…Luke Chang, assistant to Wu Qiang, one of the "wait and see how the hybrid thing progresses" elders. Vlad was more than a little surprised to see one of Qiang's people before any of Elizaveta's.

"Welcome," Luke said to Rose directly, ignoring Vlad. "I hope you'll find our hospitality suitable. When you are comfortable and settled, Elder Wu Qiang would like very much to meet your beautiful daughter."

Rose narrowed her eyes and glanced at Vlad. "I under-stood we'd be meeting all the elders later today."

"Of course. He simply wished a quieter introduction in a setting that won't intimidate the child. The meeting promises to be…something of an event. As you no doubt realize, your daughter is very important to our people. Qiang would like the opportunity to make her acquaintance prior to all the chaos."

Rose glanced at Vlad again. Vlad stared at the assistant as he took in his scent. Nothing. He got nothing from him. Damned man worked for an elder. Of course he'd be able to keep his intentions and feelings out of his scent.

"I'm not sure we'll have time," Rose hedged. "We've had a long journey and Zoe needs to sleep before the…chaos."

Zoe scooted closer to Rose, half hiding behind her. Luke's eyes narrowed almost imperceptibly at the move. Vlad noted it too and wondered if Zoe was just shy around all these strangers or if she'd managed to pick up some-thing from Luke that Vlad couldn't.

Their people lived on instincts they couldn't always properly explain. Vlad was inclined to trust Zoe's.

"There will be time after the official meeting for quieter introductions," Vlad said, forcing Luke to acknowledge him.

"Of course. It was a hopeful request." He tipped his head a little as he considered Vlad. "But we must always bow to the wisdom of a parent."

Vlad wasn't sure what to make of that comment—was it a reference to his own father or to Vlad's parental relationship to Zoe? If the former, did that mean Qiang was less neutral on the subject of hybrids than they'd all assumed? He wasn't one of the elders Vlad had suspected of working with his father, but that didn't mean he *wasn't* the one. If the reference was to Vlad being Zoe's father, the assistant had come damned close to spilling the beans and telling Zoe something they hadn't told her yet.

He glanced at his daughter. She was watching Luke with a wary, narrowed gaze.

He was pretty sure she was too young to understand the undercurrents of this conversation, but it was hard to say with kids her age. He and Rose needed to talk about how to tell Zoe the truth. But that would have to wait for a better time.

Vlad said, "Tell Qiang we're honored by his request, and Rose and I will discuss the possibility of a more private conversation with all the elders after the formal introductions."

Luke bowed his head in a perfectly polite and neutral acknowledgement, then left.

"Was that…unexpected? Odd?" Rose murmured as they went into the room she and Zoe would share.

"Odd," Vlad confirmed. "But I should have expected it as soon as we found out the meeting would be public."

"The elders don't hold public meetings like this often," Alexis said from the doorway. "I imagine most of them are looking for ways to do things privately. They like to keep their machinations secretive and are more inclined toward closed door proceedings until decisions have been made."

"Why aren't they doing that now, then?" Rose asked.

"Elizaveta insisted on taking things public," Alexis said. She glanced after Zoe, who'd disappeared into the attached bathroom. "Given the circumstances. She used Zoe's age as the justification."

Vlad took Rose's hand and squeezed it to forestall any more questions as Zoe came out of the bathroom. He was sure his daughter could tell things were tense and this was a scary situation. She might be young, but Vlad didn't want to make matters worse by saying more out loud while she was listening. Rose seemed to feel the same way because she dropped the topic.

Without a word, Zoe crawled onto one of the two huge beds in the large and luxurious room. Rose tucked her in while Vlad checked the locks on the various windows. They were three stories up, but that was nothing to a tiger. Alexis silently pointed out the cameras trained on the windows and main door, positioned so Rose and Zoe would be able to use the bathroom and sleep in complete privacy, but Victor's security team could keep all possible entrances into the room under close watch.

Alexis left them with three of the Trackers to guard their doors and assurances that they'd be safe enough to sleep. Vlad waited until Rose and Zoe were settled before going across the hall to his own room. He didn't like staying separate from them, but Rose had been hesitant to have him in the same room with them when Zoe didn't know he was her father yet. Since the entire situation was already uncomfortable, he didn't want to make things worse.

"If you need me," he told her before he left, "just call. I'll hear you and be here immediately."

She cupped his cheek and gave him a quick kiss. "Thank you. I hope I'll be able to sleep." She glanced back at Zoe who was already snoring softly. "At least she's too tired to stay awake fretting."

"You'll be okay," Vlad assured, then kissed her, a lingering kiss this time, before leaving so she could rest.

They had a serious ordeal ahead of them. They needed all the rest they could get.

CHAPTER FOURTEEN

Rose sat staring at the *still* talking panel of elders while she cuddled Zoe. Her daughter had crawled onto her lap the minute they sat down and refused to be moved, which suited Rose just fine. She didn't trust these people, and she sure as hell wasn't going to allow them access to her child without her say-so. Vlad stood as a reassuring presence just at her left shoulder. He refused to sit, an action that only confirmed the danger for Rose.

The huge meeting room was as impressive as she'd expected for a seat of power—bright white walls, a long wooden table on a dais where the elders sat, the shiny dark marble floor covered with a soft red rug, and gold-leaf details adding an air of wealth. The lighting was mellow but bright, almost like sunshine, and sound carried easily around the room without echoing, which surprised her given the size of the place. The ceilings were arched overhead and painted with a beautiful mural of a nature scene filled with tigers.

The rows of seating lining the two shorter walls of the long rectangular room were filled to bursting with people, all but two of them men. And one of the women was Alexis. Rose could only assume they were all tiger shifters. Since arriving, she hadn't actually encountered a tiger walking through the huge corridors, though. She wasn't sure why, but she'd imagined the place full of free-roaming big cats.

Zoe focused exclusively on the ceiling mural while the elders debated her future. Rose couldn't blame her. Most of the surrounding crowd was staring at Zoe with an unnerving intensity. Rose couldn't be sure what any of them were thinking, but the atmosphere of the room was charged.

Rather than glare off all the staring strangers, which Vlad was doing for her anyway, Rose kept her attention on the group of officious elders talking over each other in a cacophony of noise. She'd made a few attempts to speak, but there was no hope of getting a word in while they all tried to out-argue each other, so she gave up and instead studied them.

She refused to let them take over her daughter's life, but they would have to be a part of it—if Vlad was right— so Rose wanted to know what kind of people she was dealing with.

Elizaveta Chernikova was hard to miss, being the only female elder, but Rose suspected she'd be hard to overlook anyway. She was a tall, slim woman with sharp, angular features and beautiful white-silver hair. Her blue eyes were narrowed at the moment, and she was the only one not speaking. She wore a beautifully tailored white pants suit and a black silk blouse, an outfit that spoke of power and wealth.

Despite knowing she was an "elder," Rose found it impossible to tell how old she was. The silver hair, pulled back into a severe bun, was the only sign of advanced age. Her pale features were mostly smooth, with only a few lines around her eyes and mouth, a mouth that was set in a firm line that gave away nothing of what she was thinking. In fact, beyond the slight narrowing of her eyes, she showed no sign of emotion at all.

Rose had to force herself to look at the others. Elizaveta was a powerful presence and Rose kept finding herself watching the older woman for signs indicating her thoughts.

There were eight others at the table—a full house, according to Vlad. Despite the formal introductions, though, she'd completely lost track of most of their names. She'd made a point of remembering who Qiang was since he'd requested a private meeting with Zoe. And she'd managed to retain the name of the last elder introduced— Pavel something-or-other—who spent most of his time glaring at Elizaveta. But the rest, she just couldn't keep track of, so she'd assigned them numbers based on where they sat along the dais, with Elizaveta being One and Pavel Nine.

Of those unnamed elders, one stood out for being outspokenly pro-hybrid—that was Elder Three. He kept staring at Zoe with a sort of awe and admiration that made Rose very nervous. Elder Six was blatantly anti-hybrid and made no effort to disguise his feelings. The rest were much more difficult to judge. Each one argued multiple sides of the debate and often contradicted themselves—she suspected sometimes just to be contrary.

She was almost grateful for Six's obvious disdain. At least she knew where he stood.

Seven's arguments were quieter than Six's, but no less violent in intensity. Rose didn't know how he felt about hybrids in general, but he definitely didn't think their presence was the answer to the biological problems faced by the tigers. He waffled a little when it was pointed out that Zoe could shift, and it was this point that finally brought the attention of all nine elders squarely to Rose and her daughter.

"Show us," Seven demanded. "Shift."

"No," Rose answered. "She's not a trick pony here to amuse you."

Vlad settled a hand on Rose's shoulder but didn't otherwise comment. Seven lifted his gaze to Vlad.

"Your father would be disgusted by this…child. How does that make you feel?"

They were all being very careful not to call Vlad Zoe's father out loud—at Rose's insistence—but they kept dancing very close to the line, and every time it made Rose cringe.

"My father's feelings have very little to do with this, as he's dead." Vlad's voice was even and steady, no hint of insult or worry.

That sound did more to calm Rose's anxiety than anything else. She squeezed Zoe in a firm hug and met the elders' stares with as neutral an expression as she could muster. She was raging inside, and she was sure they smelled it, but that didn't mean she had to put on a show for them—any more than her daughter did.

Elizaveta finally spoke up. "It would be helpful to be certain she can shift."

"She can. I wouldn't be here otherwise," Rose said.

"I can vouch for her ability," Alexis spoke up from the crowd just as Seven opened his mouth. "I helped teach her to control it."

Seven settled a little, folding his hands on the table, and considered Zoe.

Zoe turned her head into Rose's neck and murmured, "Are they done yet? They very loud."

Rose smiled. "Yes, they are loud. But I don't think they're done just yet, baby. You doing okay? You hungry or thirsty? You need to use the bathroom?"

"I good. I can go tiger if you want, Mommy."

"That's okay, baby. You don't need to now."

"Alexis' word is unquestionable," Seven admitted grudgingly. "Do you realize what this means for you, Ms. Callaghan?"

"Me? We're talking about my daughter."

"Yes, but you are a human woman who can conceive with a tiger male. And you produced a tiger child. *A daughter.*"

"What are you getting at?" A niggling of worry started

to creep in through Rose's primary concern for Zoe. Vlad's hand tightened and he stepped closer.

"Your genes must be compatible with tiger genes for this to have happened. And you produced a daughter."

"You keep saying that. I know I have a daughter."

"Daughters, and females who can produce them," Qiang spoke up, "are extremely important to a population in which female births are rare."

"This means not only is Zoe a blessing," Three said, which earned some grumbles and glares, "but so are you."

"Me?"

"What they are trying to say," Elizaveta said, "is that your status is as much at debate here as Zoe's."

Vlad moved from standing just behind her to just in front of her. "She's my mate. That's her status."

Elizaveta raised her brows but otherwise didn't comment. The rest of the table, on the other hand, erupted into conversation. So many voices at once, Rose lost track of who spoke.

"You left her many years ago. She is eligible for new mate selection."

"She can't run. She's human."

"He must get her pregnant to claim mate status."

"She should be given a choice like the other one."

"The other one *is* a hybrid. This one merely gave birth to a hybrid."

"But she *gave birth* to one. She can procreate with our males."

"She's human, the rules are different."

"Mated males don't have to get their females pregnant again to keep them."

"They do if they give up mated status by leaving."

In the midst of all the mayhem, Rose's head spun. She'd spent this entire time worrying about Zoe and what Zoe's life would be like among the shifters. It never even crossed her mind they might try to control her own life. She was about to stand up and put that idea right out of their heads when Vlad's deep voice boomed out through the cacophony.

"Mikhail Chernikov doesn't have to get my sister pregnant to keep her," Vlad said.

Silence descended for several long moments as everyone stared at him. Looks were exchanged. Everyone but Elizaveta frowned.

"We don't even know if Nila can have children with a tiger," Seven commented.

"All the tests say she can," Elizaveta said.

"We don't know if they'll be tiger, though," Five said.

"Nila and Vlad are of the same family. They have the same odds of tiger or human children," Elizaveta said.

Rose winced. Again. This conversation was too close to telling Zoe who her father was. They needed to tell her the truth soon before some stranger slipped up.

"But Ms. Callaghan has proven she can have a tiger child, so her status must be different," Two said.

Rose hugged Zoe closer, trying to sort out the arguments. Then Vlad spoke again, commanding the elders' full attention.

"A precedent has been set," he said. "The hybrids are

treated differently. They must be because not all of them will be able to shift like Zoe."

"Ms. Callaghan is not a hybrid," Qiang pointed out the obvious.

"Exactly. She has no relationship to our people, beyond her daughter. You didn't ask Nila's father, Leo, to consider taking a tiger mate."

"Don't be ridiculous," Pavel snorted. "*He's* unnecessary to us. Zoe's mother, on the other hand, can help us."

Rose narrowed her eyes at being referred to as "Zoe's mother" and not by her own name. At least the other elders had the decency to refer to her by name.

"If she chooses to help us," Vlad said. "But you have no jurisdiction over her or who she mates with. She holds no blood relationship to the tigers beyond her daughter."

There was another pointed silence and then another round of debate.

"He's right. She's neither tiger, nor hybrid. She's human, not a part of this community."

"A valid point. We didn't expect Nila's father to try producing more hybrids."

"Because we are not trying to produce a race of hybrids. Using them to stave off extinction is one thing. Allowing them to overtake full blooded tigers is abhorrent."

"Even so, every female who can produce females capable of mating with tigers is significant and important to our hopes of survival."

"Again, she is human. She's not one of us—even partly one of the community, as she would be if she were hybrid."

"Her daughter will be part of our community because she's a shifter, hybrid or not. We must allow for her mother."

"Not if we adopt her daughter." This last came with a slight sneer from Pavel.

Rose stood then, cradling Zoe, her eyes narrowed. "No way under heaven or hell are you even contemplating taking my daughter," she said. "I will kill anyone who tries."

The entire room fell silent, except for a quiet shuffling of feet. The already electric atmosphere seemed to crackle with tension now. Rose didn't back down. She glared at each and every elder, making sure they saw—and smelled—that she was deadly serious.

She would run away with Zoe before allowing these… people to consider trying to cut her out of her daughter's life. They had no right. No legal ability to take Zoe. Which didn't mean they wouldn't try. So she wanted them to know what they'd face if they did.

A very vengeful momma.

As she glared them down, Vlad stood at her side. She could practically feel his tension. When she allowed a single glance at him, he was glaring at the elders, too, poised and ready to fight. She faced the bastards again with a snarling smirk.

Elder Two spoke into the silence. "Child, like it or not, there is very little you *could* do against us, if the vote turns against you. You might consider diplomacy."

"This isn't a diplomatic situation," she said. "And if you think I couldn't do anything to hurt you, try me."

"You're human," Pavel said. "You aren't strong enough, or fast enough, or…anything enough."

She met his gaze without flinching. "A bullet to the brain will kill you. I'm a hunter. Don't push me."

"I could disarm you before you could shoot."

"You threaten my daughter, you will see how fast I can shoot."

"Enough," Elizaveta said into the argument. "We are not going to take this woman's child from her, you idiots." She shook her head.

The "idiots" outburst was the most emotion Elizaveta had shown up to that point in the debates.

"Would you think to threaten the child of a tiger mother? No. You would not because she would kill you. Ms. Callaghan might be human, but she is defending her daughter. You would be fools indeed to underestimate that. Stop talking such nonsense, or you will send her and her precious daughter into hiding. And I would not blame her. In fact, I would help her. And you know well I can hide much from you. If I hear any more talk about taking this child from her mother, *I* will get violent. Are we clear on this point?"

There were a few grunts and one or two nods. The tension went out of the room with Elizaveta's speech. The elders relaxed back into their seats and the surrounding audience settled again.

"Good," Elizaveta said. "Now, my dear, please be seated. You are not under threat here." She said this last with raised brows as she looked down the length of the table at the other elders. None of them made eye contact.

Rose hugged Zoe a little closer but didn't take her seat.

For the first time since entering the room, Zoe looked at the elders. She stared with her huge dark eyes then said with that oh-so-familiar stubborn jut of her chin, "Staying with Mommy."

Rose grinned and kissed her cheek. Elizaveta's lips compressed as if she were holding back a smile. Three smiled, his head tilted as he considered Zoe. The other elders exchanged looks and raised brows.

Vlad rubbed a hand along Zoe's back. "She's definitely a tiger," he said.

"Yes, am tiger," Zoe confirmed.

This time Elizaveta did smile and chuckles sounded from the crowd.

"Well." Elizaveta stood and addressed the room at large. "After that, I think we should allow our guests a break. We will reconvene in two hours."

With that, the room emptied. The elders filed out one of the two side doors, while the rest of the crowd exited through the main door in a quiet hum of conversation.

"Threatening to kill the elders," Vlad said as they waited for the room to empty. "Ballsy."

"Serious."

"They are faster and stronger than you."

"I don't give a fuck."

"Cursing, Mommy."

"Sorry, baby." She kissed Zoe's cheek.

"I know you're well trained," Vlad said, "but you haven't even seen our top speeds yet. It's not something most humans have time to react to..." He trailed off and his gaze turned inward, frowning slightly at some inner thought.

She bumped his arm, and when he focused on her again, she looked him right in the eye. "I don't care how fast tigers are. If they threaten my daughter, I will do whatever it takes to protect her."

He cupped her cheek. "I'm trying to tell you, you wouldn't be alone. It won't matter that they're fast because so am I. I'll be with you to keep her safe."

She rubbed her cheek against his hand. "Thank you."

"I there too, Mommy. I tiger!"

She hugged Zoe tight. "Thank you, too, baby. You're a great tiger."


They returned to their rooms for the break so Zoe could rest. She insisted she didn't need another nap, but she fell asleep two minutes after being forced to lie down.

"She's been through a lot in the last few days," Rose commented, watching her daughter sleep. "I'm surprised we haven't had more tantrums and fussing."

Vlad hugged Rose from behind, holding her close and breathing in her lavender and cardamom scent. The meeting had gone…as well as he could have expected, he supposed. He'd been afraid they'd try to twist Rose up into their machinations, so he hadn't been entirely surprised when they suggested she follow tiger law to select a mate. What he hadn't expected was for the elders to threaten to take Zoe away from her.

They had no legal right to do such a thing—under human or tiger law. And because he was the father, his position on the matter covered the tiger side of things anyway.

But just because they didn't have a legal right didn't mean they wouldn't try it. Especially since Rose had insisted they not refer to Vlad as the father out loud yet. She'd done it to protect Zoe until they could tell her the truth themselves. He understood that. But to the community, it could look as if Rose was refusing to claim him as mate and father to her child, and that caused complications.

His instincts screamed at him to get Rose and Zoe out of there and hide them away somewhere no tigers could find them.

His practical side knew he couldn't do that. This had to be settled, here and now, with the entire community watching. The way the elders dealt with Rose and Zoe would set precedents going forward, even more so than the rules already established for Nila, which was why the process was so damned convoluted and drawn out. But once settled, the two people he loved most in the world would be safe. That hope was worth staying and fighting for.

He watched Zoe as he cradled Rose in his arms, overwhelmed with how easy it was to love his daughter, how easy it was to love Rose again. His soul belonged to them completely now. What would he do if anything happened to them?

Against Rose's ear, he said, "Should we leave so we don't disturb her? I'd like to talk a little before we have to go back, but I don't want to wake her."

Rose hesitated and he couldn't blame her. He didn't want to leave Zoe alone either. But they needed to talk.

"I'll hear if she needs us," he said. "We'll just be across the hall in my room."

"After what went on in there, I'm afraid to leave her alone."

"We'll keep my door open and watch the room. Will that help? We won't be saying anything other tigers can't overhear. In fact, it might be better that everyone here knows where we stand."

"They wouldn't be able to hear us with the door closed?"

"There's some soundproofing on the guest rooms, but not enough to prevent a tiger from eavesdropping if he wants to. It's not like the meeting hall. That's designed to keep even tigers from hearing what's going on inside."

Zoe flopped into a new position, making a little grunt of irritation, and a frown creased her brow.

Rose whispered, "If I can watch the door, it should be okay. You'll hear her?"

"I'll listen closely. We can be back in here the instant she wakes."

Rose nodded and they moved across the hall. She stood in his doorway, staring at Zoe's closed door while he brought out two chairs from inside.

"That meeting was…" She sighed. "Those bastards can argue. I swear some of them kept playing devil's advocate just to be contrary. Most of them contradicted their own arguments at different points."

"They're all old enough to have seen a lot, and most of

them love the debate. They like fighting and discussing and one-upping each other."

"How the hell do they get anything done?"

"Eventually, they hold a vote and come to a consensus. I've been told the vote is usually a lot more straightforward than the debates preceding it. Most of them have made up their minds before the debates even start."

"Then why all the fuss?"

He shrugged. "Like I said, they like it." Vlad felt Elizaveta approaching, her scent reaching him well before she turned down the corridor.

Rose followed his gaze. "What?"

"Elizaveta is coming. Alone."

"That's…not normal?"

She turned the corner, all quiet, deadly grace as she approached. Vlad wouldn't have admitted it to his father, or anyone else for that matter, but he'd always found the female elder magnificent and terrifying. It was impossible to read her body language or her scent for clues to her state of mind. She was gruff and serious, her expression often set in severe lines, and she didn't pull punches when she spoke. She was probably the most outwardly undiplomatic of the elders—besides maybe Pavel—but she didn't have to be diplomatic because she was so damned powerful.

Yet, there was always a spark of mischief in her gaze. And he knew from his father that Elizaveta's machinations were deep and complex, impossible to fathom.

She was both intimidating and compelling in a way Vlad had never been able to define precisely.

She and his father had been at odds for years, so Vlad mostly avoided her, but now he needed her support.

"It's not normal," she said, answering Rose's question when she was near enough to talk comfortably. "In this place, my assistant and his aides are usually trotting at my heels, ushering me here and there. It is a nuisance."

Her Russian accent was still strong, despite the fact that she spent as much time in the US as she did in Russia these days, maybe more. The accent reminded Vlad of his father's mother, who'd passed away when Vlad was only eight.

"Why are you here alone, then?" Rose asked.

"I came to offer a personal apology. That nonsense about taking your baby from you was an abhorrent suggestion. You should know it was not a serious one. It was designed to provoke reaction and cause argument. As Vlad said, we like to argue. But some of us occasionally take things too far. Your daughter is not under threat here. And neither are you."

"I thank you for the apology, though you already gave one in the meeting hall, so this one isn't necessary."

"Yes, it is. My colleagues are a bunch of idiots. Pavel is not a father, so he doesn't fully understand what he said. If you had our sense of smell, you would have known that most of the tigers in that room were appalled by the suggestion. And they admired you for your threats. Like one of our tiger mothers. While the suggestion was poorly done, your reaction and the reaction it caused among our people were actually a good result. Things will go easier for you and your daughter among our kind if they believe you are strong. And dangerous."

"I am. When it comes to my daughter, I am."

Elizaveta smiled at her, closed lipped and tight, but a smile.

"I still feel under threat here," Rose said, "despite your assurances. And I'm not sure I like the idea that you elders think you can dictate Zoe's life."

Elizaveta gave a tiny shrug. "I understand. But she is a tiger—hybrid or no—and that makes her subject to our laws. It is important she is integrated into the community. For her own safety. Without the protection of tiger law, there is nothing to stop a desperate male from trying to take her."

"There's the rifle and handgun I intend to keep close by from now on."

"That would be wise. But having the protection of our laws will make the precaution less necessary. I promise you."

"So Vlad keeps telling me. You'll forgive me if I don't take that promise as gospel."

"I expected nothing less." Elizaveta finally looked at Vlad. "You've chosen a strong mate. I like her. She will do well in our community."

"The threats to her," Vlad said, "what of those?"

Elizaveta frowned. "You mean the debate over how she should choose a mate?"

He nodded.

Elizaveta waved a hand. "That is a debate we will have to take to the community at large for future reference. But she is fully human and outside our jurisdiction. As you said. We cannot demand a human adhere to our rules simply because she is capable of producing a hybrid. It's not practical or enforceable. Unfortunately, some of the other elders are not practical. So the debate will happen. But it will not affect Rose."

"Why not?"

"She is already mated. It is not an issue."

"The comment that I forfeited my claim when I left her?"

"Might have been a problem if you hadn't returned to her, and if she didn't want to keep you. If she doesn't keep you, then other tigers might attempt to woo her. She will have the choice. She could leave you for another human, too. That's the way with relationships, no? But she is not ours to order about."

"You think Zoe is, though," Rose put in.

"Ah. That is a different and more complicated issue. She is, in fact, one of ours. Her ability to shift makes her situation easier to fit into our current laws. She *is* a tiger shifter—unlike her aunt who is a human hybrid. But because she is a hybrid, the absolutes of her position are debatable."

Rose shook her head. "This is too much. I just wanted her out of pain. I didn't want to throw her into this…world."

"Such is the way of life. We must deal with situations we would rather not, and people we might not like."

Elizaveta opened her mouth to say something else, then paused, frowning. Vlad turned his full attention to Zoe's room just as Elizaveta glanced at the door. The sound of shuffling steps brought him to his feet. He could *sense* a tiger in that room.

He was across the hall, slamming through the door in a blink, Elizaveta just behind him.

The window was open. The room was empty.

Zoe was gone.

# CHAPTER FIFTEEN

Panic gripped Rose so tight she thought she might throw up. "Where is she? What's happened?"

Vlad glanced at Elizaveta, who was staring out the window. "A tiger was in here. He took her."

Rose's voice went to full screech. "How did this happen? Who was it? How did he get her so fast? Where have they gone? Was it one of your brothers?"

Elizaveta stormed into the hall past them, her voice booming down the corridor. "Trackers! Now!"

Vlad took Rose's hand. "Not one of my brothers. I don't recognize the scent. He moved at tiger speed, very fast to get in and out before we noticed."

"You did notice, though. You both felt something wrong."

"I heard shuffling and felt a tiger in here just before coming through the door."

A group of four large men stalked into the room and

began sniffing around. Behind them, an actual tiger walked in, going right to the window. The tiger looked about, sniffed at the sill, and then leapt out the open window.

Rose gasped. "That's a three-story drop."

"Not that difficult for us."

"How did the kidnapper get in? The window was bolted from the inside…" She paused. They'd locked it before the meeting. She hadn't checked it again when they'd put Zoe down to nap. But they were on the third floor. It should have been impossible to get in here that way.

"Three stories aren't beyond our ability to jump up to— even in human form. Someone obviously unlocked the window while we were in the meeting. The rest would have been easy."

"But Zoe can't make that jump. What if he hurt her getting back out?"

"She could survive that jump all on her own," Vlad said. "But she wasn't on her own. He would have had to hold her. So she wasn't hurt during the jump."

"We have to go after him. We have to get her back. Vlad." Panic made her so desperate she could barely think. She went to her closet and pulled down the borrowed hunting rifles she'd stored there. She stared at the 9mm pistol, then pulled it out as well. She needed everything she could get.

"If anything happens to her…" She couldn't think it. She couldn't even allow the idea to form. If she did, she'd fall apart. Zoe needed her strong now.

She was loading one of the rifles when Alexis and Victor came storming into the room.

"Victor got him on video," Alexis announced. "It was Nick Jameson." She looked at Rose. "He used to be a Tracker back when I was one. We had a…falling out. He's been retired for about fifteen years now. When he left the Trackers, he went to work for Elder Zhang Lei. Jameson doesn't come to the compound anymore, though, not in years. He's rarely even in the US. His scent would be difficult for most of the active Trackers here to identify. Though I can and so can Victor. He hasn't actually been inside the compound or Victor would have picked it up. They never really got along."

Victor signed something to Alexis. She nodded, and said, "He didn't know about the video surveillance on the window so we got him on tape. Victor hadn't told anyone outside a few trusted members of his team that he'd set that up in here. Obviously, whoever arranged this with Jameson didn't know either." She nodded to the window. "Lei's assistant unlocked it just after the meeting was adjourned, during the chaos of dismissal. None of the security team noticed at the time as they were watching too many corridors and monitoring too many possible problems in those seconds."

Victor made a few hard hand gestures, which Rose didn't understand, but from the look on his face, he was pissed about that breach.

"Lei," Elizaveta said, her voice low and without any sign of emotion. "Lei is responsible for this?"

Rose's voice was not so emotionless when she said, "Where is he?" She wasn't even sure which one Lei was, but that didn't matter. She was going to kill him.

"Trackers have gone to his apartment. He's not there. They're searching the compound now while Victor's team combs through the video feeds. We'll find something."

Rose was about to say more when a tiger leapt back into the room through the window. She spun to face it, rifle raised and poised to fire. Vlad put a hand on her arm. "That's the Tracker who just jumped out."

The tiger started to shift, a process Rose was still bothered by, but after days of watching Zoe shift, she didn't feel the need to look away. She waited with barely held patience and as soon as the man's head and mouth settled into human lines, she said, "What did you find? Where did they go?"

When he looked at her, his eyes were pinched at the corners and his brow creased. "They left through the west gate. A car was waiting." He looked at Alexis and Elizaveta. "I got a strong scent of Lei."

Elizaveta growled, a sound unlike anything Rose had heard a human make. The hair along her arms and on her nape rose in reaction to the threat in that growl.

"Which direction?" Alexis asked.

"They turned off the west road, heading toward the highway. Two from my unit are following. I came back to report."

"I'm going to kill him," Rose said, very quietly. Every tiger in the room turned to look at her. She was staring out the window. "He's a dead man."

"We need to concentrate on getting Zoe back first," Alexis said. "Then we can kill him."

"Not we. Me. I am going to destroy the men who took

her. And if she's hurt, in any way at all, I'm going to kill them slowly."

She barely recognized her own voice—deep, gravelly, harsh. She was so angry, so outraged, and so scared. Her every instinct screamed to follow the bastards and get her daughter back.

She returned to her dresser and pulled out her backpack, stuffing it with clothes, some things for Zoe, and a few of the snacks left over from their journey here. "I need water." She finished filling the backpack with all the ammunition she had for the three guns. She set her gear on her bed and went to the closet for her and Zoe's coats.

When she faced the room full of people again, she was mildly surprised to see bottles of water by her pack. And Vlad already in his coat, car keys in hand.

To Alexis, he said, "You have my cell number. Keep us updated. We'll take the same direction, but I'll need you to relay any changes the Trackers pick up."

She nodded. "You want me to send a few more with you?"

"Send whoever you can spare. No idea how many he's got with him." He glanced at Rose as she slipped on her coat and pulled the backpack over her shoulders, then asked Alexis, "Are my brothers involved? I just found out my people lost track of them earlier today. Do you still have them under surveillance?"

Alexis glanced away, frowning when she said, "They ditched the people we had tailing them, too. We haven't seen them since you arrived at the compound. We don't know where they are, or what they're doing right now."

Vlad cursed.

Rose wanted to curse as well, but somehow she couldn't summon any words. Too much anger and desperation clogged her throat. She tucked the unloaded 9mm into her coat pocket, then picked up both rifles, and without a word, she and Vlad headed to the parking lot and their rental car.

Alexis, Victor, and two Trackers followed them.

"We'll let you know as soon as we get information," Alexis said. "We uncovered who they were a lot quicker than they could have anticipated, so they aren't that far ahead of us. You'll get her back."

Rose swallowed hard but didn't comment. Her mind had gone quiet, only instinct and determination left.

And rage. A holy storm of rage.

They were on the highway heading southwest when Vlad's cell binged with a text. Since he was driving, Rose looked at it. "The Trackers just reported." She frowned. "The bastards who took Zoe have gone to 'the Mate Run area.' What does that mean?"

"Fuck," Vlad growled. "They've taken her deep into an area of the mountains where we hold Mate Runs on this coast. It's difficult to get back to, so there are almost never any humans in the area."

"Why take her there?" She swallowed as she imagined the worst and tried hard not to think about that possibility.

Vlad didn't answer but his hands flexed on the steering wheel, his knuckles going white as he gripped hard.

"Vlad, this isn't some...some perverse thing, is it? Please tell me we're not dealing with a pedophile?" That was almost as bad as the worst possible outcome—the outcome she didn't dare even think.

He shook his head. "Lei has never shown any taste for children."

"Then why are they taking her to the place you do Mate Runs?"

"I can only guess it's because it's isolated, no one around to see or interfere with...anything."

"Oh, God." She started praying harder than she'd ever prayed in her life. She promised God she'd go back to mass if He just got Zoe out of this alive. She promised to confess and do a thousand Hail Mary's. She promised she'd do anything if He just kept Zoe safe. She texted Alexis back, *Are the Trackers still following them?*

A minute passed. *Yes, but haven't caught up yet. Following their scent trail into the forest now.*

Rose told Vlad what Alexis said.

"Good. They'll know they're being followed and won't want to stop moving while the Trackers are so close. I don't think Lei planned on being found out. He'll be working out an excuse for his presence but won't want to get caught before he's in a position to make the story believable."

"Meaning?"

"He can't afford to be found with Zoe."

"That means he and his associate have to split up. That'll stretch the Trackers, maybe send them in the wrong direction. They can't feel Zoe. What if the men just...leave her somewhere and lead the Trackers off?"

"They can't feel her, but they'll be able to smell her. Besides, she's not going to just stay where her kidnappers leave her."

"She's just a baby. She doesn't have her coat or snow boots. It's freezing up here. If they let her go and she runs away, she'll be lost without food or warmth. Oh, Vlad." Panic tightened her throat again and her stomach churned with worry. She wanted to throw up, to scream, to move faster. She wanted to wake up from this nightmare.

"We'll get her back, Rose. I promise. We're not far behind them."

They climbed into the mountains, taking dirt roads that barely looked like tracks. When they couldn't risk taking the rental car any farther without it getting stuck, Vlad parked in the middle of the road. "Not likely to be any other cars up this way."

"I don't see signs of the car they took Zoe in."

"Probably had an off-road vehicle. See the tracks?"

She squinted to where the car's headlights reflected off the snow and realized there were tracks still visible.

"There's a place a few miles up from here where we leave our cars when we come in for a Run. They likely parked there."

"A few miles? Jesus. That puts us even farther behind. We'll never catch up."

"The Trackers are up there somewhere, too, remember."

Rose climbed out of the car and took a moment to get her bearings as she slipped on her gloves—tight leather ones that wouldn't interfere with her ability to fire the rifle.

Snow crunched gently beneath her boots, soft and ankle deep. The air was crisp, making her breath visible. The night filled in the area under the trees, though the snow gave a very faint glow thanks to the car's lights. When they got away from the car, they'd be hiking in complete darkness.

"I didn't bring a flashlight," she said as she pulled out her backpack. "I hope your night vision is as good as a real tiger's."

"It is. Maybe better. Stick close."

She slid the two hunting rifles out from under the back seat and handed one across to Vlad at the opposite door. Then she filled her coat pockets with additional bullets for her rifle and handed Vlad more ammunition for his. She left the handgun behind, under the front seat, because it would do her little good out here in the forest.

He looked at the weapon in his hands. "I'll be of more use as a tiger," he said. "I'm not the crack shot you are. But we won't be able to talk if I shift, so I'll wait until it becomes necessary. When I do, are you okay with both guns?"

She nodded.

"Let's get moving."

She settled her backpack over her shoulders. The pack was heavy with water, extra clothes, food, and ammunition, but nothing she hadn't hiked with before. She stared into the forest as Vlad led the way, her every nerve ending straining toward her daughter, somewhere in these trees.

*I'm coming, baby*, she thought, and then went back to praying as they started the climb.

.   .   .

Vlad's senses were stretched as far as he was able, looking for any sign of their quarry. He picked up the trail of a Tracker a half mile in and turned to follow. Rose was a silent presence at his back. Her comfort with hiking and her experience hunting made this a lot easier.

The scent of her fear and anger was so strong and pungent it was like a blaring red halo of light around her. A halo that smelled of forest fires and gasoline. His own fear and anger matched hers, creating a complicated mix of scents he had to force himself to ignore so he could focus on picking up signs of Zoe. She could be anywhere in this forest, and without being able to feel her like he would another tiger, he had to use his other senses.

After an hour, he picked up the presence of a tiger, roughly a quarter mile north of their position. He paused to scent to breeze. Another Tracker. Circling toward them.

He angled in the general direction the Tracker was coming from while still moving forward, hunting the area for signs of little footprints. When the Tracker caught up to them, he was in human form, but naked so he had obviously been hunting in tiger form. The man was vaguely familiar, his scent and his human form, and Vlad realized he was one of the Trackers who'd been guarding them on the way into the compound when they'd first arrived. That made things easier since they didn't need to waste time confirming identities.

"One of my guys has picked up Jameson's scent going farther east," the Tracker said, "but Lei has left the area. We lost him about an hour ago and haven't picked up his scent since."

"Zoe?"

"We keep catching hints of her, but not being able to sense her isn't helping."

"Which direction?"

"Last point we caught her scent was another quarter mile that way." He pointed the direction they were heading.

"Any…" Vlad glanced back at Rose. He didn't actually want to say this out loud, but he wanted to know if Zoe's scent indicated whether she was hurt or not.

The Tracker seemed to understand. "Pure scent. Nothing else."

He spoke vaguely, obviously equally reluctant to talk about the three-year-old being injured in front of her terrified mother.

"She was still with Jameson as far as we could tell," he finished. "I'll update you if I find anything."

Vlad nodded and continued forward as the Tracker started to shift back to tiger. Rose stayed with Vlad, not looking back.

"Zoe's not hurt?"

He grimaced. "You picked up on that?"

"I'm not stupid. And I know you care about her. I was about to ask that very question when you did."

"Sorry. Just didn't want to scare you."

"I'm already scared. Can't get any worse and there's nothing you can say that I'm not already imagining—or trying not to imagine."

He dropped back to put an arm around her waist and

hug her to his side for a brief moment. "She's okay so far—alive and uninjured. She's going to be fine."

Rose nodded but didn't look at him. Her gaze traveled over the trees and ground, looking for signs of her daughter in the darkness. She couldn't possibly see very well at this time of night. The moon was full overhead, so when they came out into clearings, the snow sparkled with enough light for human eyes. But under the trees, the ambient light was barely enough for him.

They trudged on, the night getting colder as they went. He couldn't help but think of Zoe without a coat or boots and only hoped the assholes who took her had seen fit to give her something warm to wear. Because they hadn't just killed her, Vlad had to assume they didn't want her dead. He couldn't think of any other reason to kidnap her.

They'd gone another mile when he caught a sound echoing from somewhere to the north—a hiss followed by a human yowl. Without thinking he took off through the trees, running in human form at top shifter speed. He realized too late that he'd left Rose in the dark without a guide, but he knew she'd have told him to get to Zoe fast and not worry about her.

He broke out of the trees at the edge of small stream, shallow and frozen solid. He hunted around. He could feel another tiger, and he caught the scent of blood. When he saw a crumpled form a few hundred yards away, he felt his heart stop. He raced to the body.

# CHAPTER SIXTEEN

Vlad reached the body in a flash, only to realize the writhing person on the ground was Nick Jameson.

The shock of relief was so profound, it took Vlad a moment to focus on the scene.

Jameson was groaning and holding his crotch. "Little bitch bit me." His voice was harsh and gravelly.

Vlad raised his brows, then snapped them down. "What were you doing that made her bite your dick?"

"Nothing," he gasped.

Vlad stepped on the hand that Jameson still held over his cock and pressed into the already injured area. Jameson screamed.

"What were you doing?" he asked again, his voice very quiet.

"No…not like that. She shifted suddenly. Then attacked me." He groaned again as Vlad dug his foot in. "Telling the truth. Stop."

"You kidnapped a three-year-old and took her into the forest. This isn't half the pain I want to cause you. Where did she go?" Even as he asked, he scented the air, hunting for her. He caught a faint whiff swirling around a few feet up the frozen stream.

"Don't know. Ah! Stop. I didn't see. I'm bleeding. Get the fuck off!"

Vlad felt another shifter approaching and turned to face the newcomer without actually moving his foot from Jameson's injured groin. To his surprise, he also picked up Rose's scent with the approaching tiger.

When the tiger cleared the trees, Vlad realized why he smelled Rose, too. She was riding the Tracker's back, her arms wrapped around his neck, her legs pulled up tight to his sides. She had the rifle pressed between her leg and arm and the tiger's body with the muzzle pointed backward.

She slipped from his back, dropped to her knees, and then climbed up, rolling the rifle into position. She approached Jameson with the barrel pointed at his head. Very purposefully, she pumped the lever. The sound was loud in the still darkness.

"Where's my daughter?" Her voice was a growl to rival any tiger's.

"Don't know."

She set the muzzle against his forehead. "Where is my daughter?" She enunciated each word slowly and carefully.

Vlad's heart thumped hard with so much love and fierce pride it almost pushed back the fear dogging him. He dug his foot in a little deeper. "She won't hesitate to shoot. Don't try her."

"She ran into the trees, okay," Jameson said.

"Why did you bring her here?" Rose asked.

Jameson had the bad sense to glower at her, a slight smirk pulling at his mouth. "She's unnatural, an abomination pretending to be a tiger. If she's a real shifter, she'll have no problem surviving in this forest."

Vlad dropped down, putting his knee in the man's groin, hard, and his nose in the man's face. Rose moved the rifle enough to give him room, but it still rested against Jameson's temple.

"You brought her out here to leave her?" Vlad growled.

"A test. Only a true tiger could pass."

"She's three years old," Rose said. "She's a baby. And you were going to abandon her in the woods." Her voice dropped to a vicious hiss on the last word.

Vlad's own outrage took hold and his tiger roared in his head. He gripped Jameson's head and snapped his neck in one swift move.

When he stepped off, Rose settled the rifle against Jameson's forehead and fired. The .44 Magnum bullet turned the top of his head into a bloody mess. She pumped the lever and fired again.

"Feel better?" he asked.

"Yes. Let's find our baby. Can you track her from here?" She nodded to a spot on the ice-covered river and said, "Looks like a cub print."

Vlad looked closer. She was right. "I love that you're a hunter, too." He glanced at the Tracker. "You go ahead, but if you find her come get us. She's scared and probably won't come out to you."

The tiger nodded its huge head and tore off into the trees, following the same scent drawing Vlad on.

"I've got her scent, but the snow makes it a little harder. Keep your eyes open for more signs of her trail."

"She's not used to hiding. She won't have thought to cover her tracks."

As they crossed the stream and headed up the opposite embankment, following the faint trail of cub imprints in the snow, Rose said, "Can you feel any other tigers? Besides the other Trackers?"

"Hard to tell because some of them are just at the edge of my ability to sense them, but I'm pretty sure the tigers left in the area are all Trackers. They're heading in this direction now."

They hunted through the underbrush, careful of their steps as they followed Zoe's trail. She could move as fast as any shifter cub, but she was scared and alone. Vlad didn't want to rush and miss signs that she'd doubled back or gone to ground to hide.

The other Trackers were in the area now. Vlad could sense them moving through the underbrush, careful and quiet so they wouldn't spook Zoe. Her scent got stronger as the breeze shifted. Vlad changed direction to follow it.

"You know," he said, "once she learns how to stalk and hide properly, she'll be really hard to find. Since tigers can't sense her, if she learns how to disguise her trail, she'll be able to outsmart any who come looking for her."

"Some comfort in that, I guess. If I call to her, will she hear me?"

"Probably. Her scent is getting stronger. She's close."

"Zoe," Rose shouted. "It's Mommy. Can you hear me? Come on back, baby. You're safe now. The bad men are gone."

In the distance, Vlad heard a rustling in the snow. He paused. "Keep calling. I think that's her."

"Zoe!"

One of the Trackers was closer to the location where Vlad had heard her. He waited, listening as the Tracker edged toward her. A moment later, the hiss and tiny roar of a tiger cub split the night, along with the growling whine of a hurt adult tiger.

Vlad tried not to laugh. "Hurry. This way. She's attacking the Tracker. We'd better go rescue him."

"That's my girl," Rose said as they took off at a trot toward to sounds of a scuffle.

When they found the source of the noise, Vlad released a breath and for the first time since Zoe had gone missing, he started to relax. The sight of his daughter in all her tiger cub glory hissing and swatting at an animal five times her size made him proud. The Tracker sat a few feet away, licking his front leg just above his paw. Little dots of blood colored the white and russet fur around his wound.

"Zoe," Rose called as she set her rifle on the ground.

The cub spun to face her, paused, then launched through the air with such speed Vlad couldn't react fast enough to catch her. To his amazement, though, Rose caught the white and orange blur securely and without being barreled over. He blinked. Damn, but her reflexes were quick for a human.

"Oof." She chuckled and cuddled Zoe close. "Oh, baby,

I'm so glad to see you. Are you okay? The bad men didn't hurt you, did they?"

Zoe licked her face, then settled her head on her mom's shoulder, hugging her as best she could in her tiger body.

Rose hugged her back. "I'm so sorry that happened, baby. Don't worry. Mommy and Daddy are taking care of the bad people. We'll make sure this never happens again. You're safe now. You did very good, going tiger and biting the bad man. That was very brave of you."

Vlad held perfectly still as Rose continued to coo reassurances to her daughter. She'd called him "Daddy" to Zoe. He was certain she'd done it by accident. And the slip would mean a lot of questions once Zoe returned to her human form. But the fact that Rose had referred to them as a family, as parents that would protect their daughter, made his heart pound hard.

He was so stunned and overwhelmed by the moment, he didn't realize the Tracker had shifted back to human form until he spoke.

"Feisty daughter you've got there," he said wryly. "She got me good."

Vlad laughed and leaned over to pick up Rose's abandoned rifle. "You okay?"

The man waved his previously wounded forearm. "All healed." He glanced around as the other Trackers—six in total—joined them, coming from different directions. "It's late and cold out here. We've gone too far from the cars to try and get you all back tonight. The Mate Run cabin is just a few minutes hike up that way." He nodded behind him, a direction a little farther west. "Stay there tonight and we'll head back out tomorrow morning." He motioned to the six surrounding tigers. "We'll sweep the area, make sure it's clear, and then keep watch. You'll be safe."

"Thanks," Vlad said. "Thanks for everything."

The Tracker glanced at Zoe and grinned. "No problem at all." He started to shift back to tiger as Vlad directed Rose and Zoe toward the cabin.

Rose carried Zoe the entire way, despite the fact that she was still in tiger form and weighed more as a cub than she did as a little girl.

Vlad didn't argue with her. If Zoe got too heavy for her, he'd take over carrying her. He completely understood Rose not wanting to let her go. They'd come so close to losing her, the reality of that was only just starting to sink in. He hadn't allowed himself time to even consider the worst-case scenario. But hearing Jameson admit they'd intended to leave Zoe in the wild to die… He saw red just thinking about it and panic made his gut clench, despite the fact she was safe.

When they reached the cabin, Vlad started a fire in the fireplace while Rose settled Zoe and waited for her to shift back to human. After she finished, Rose wrapped her up in the spare clothes they'd brought as well as a blanket from the huge bed which dominated the cabin's single room. Once Zoe was warm, Rose pulled her close and hugged her, murmuring quietly into her hair, soft words of reassurance. Zoe snuggled against her without speaking, staring at the fire as the flames flickered higher.

"Are you warm enough now, sweetie?" Vlad asked.

Zoe nodded. Her little face was set in serious lines, and she didn't look away from the fire.

Vlad frowned at Rose. She looked at him over Zoe's head and shrugged. "You tired, baby? It's been a scary night, huh?"

Zoe nodded again and buried her face against Rose's shoulder. "I scared, Mommy."

"Oh, baby, I'm so sorry. We've got you now. You're safe. I won't let anyone hurt you. I swear it. We won't let any other bad men get to you."

"Yes." Zoe waved a little hand in Vlad's direction. "Hug," she ordered.

He couldn't have resisted even if he'd wanted to. He dropped down onto the rug and wrapped his arms around them both, holding them tightly. His family. All the fear and worry of the last few hours drained away slowly and left him with a rush of overwhelming relief and love. He kissed Zoe's head, then kissed Rose on the lips.

They stayed that way, watching the fire, until Zoe drifted off to sleep.

# CHAPTER SEVENTEEN

After they'd settled Zoe on the bed, Rose went back to the fire and sat on the thick rug. Vlad followed.

She stared at the flames for a moment. Then she started to cry. Not a loud, sobbing cry, just the quiet drip of tears down her cheeks and a few gasping breaths.

"Rose." He pulled her into his arms.

She clung to him as her tears dampened his neck. For a long time, he just held her and let her cry, rubbing her back.

After a while, she took a stuttering breath. "Thanks, for this and for helping me tonight."

He lifted her chin. "She's my daughter, too, and I couldn't have done anything else. I've never been so terrified, or angry, in my life."

"It's tough, isn't it? The worry and fear. You love them so much, you know it'll cost you your soul if you lose them." She glanced at the bed and their sleeping daughter before facing him again.

"Worth it, though," he said, brushing her hair back from her face. "Worth every minute."

She stretched up and kissed him, a warm, comforting gesture that turned needy in an instant. All the anxiety and adrenaline of the night had left him both exhausted and desperate to assure himself those he loved were whole and well.

He hugged her closer, kissed her deeper, and poured all the love and relief he didn't know how to put into words into his kiss.

They kissed, and held each other close, and murmured soft reassurances, and for a time, Vlad's world was perfect.

"The Tracker called this the 'Mate Run cabin,'" Rose said, settling her head on his shoulder. "What does that mean?"

"We keep this place for couples to use once a female has been caught during her Run. Some couples never bother with it—they like being outside. But it's useful in the winter. And I'd guess a bed is a nice change of pace from the wilds of the forest."

"When was it last used?"

He chuckled. "Don't worry. The sheets are changed out regularly. The last Run was a few weeks ago."

"How do you know that?"

"We all know when Runs happen, which female is running, who she lets catch her. If she gets pregnant or not. Females are so rare, their every move is watched closely."

"That's a little creepy. Do any of them…I don't know, rebel against all that hovering and attention?"

He hadn't really considered it from that perspective

before. There were so very few females left, it seemed normal for them to be monitored. Since he'd grown up under the scrutiny of his own father, and later played cat-and-mouse games of spying on his brothers while they spied on him, he'd never actually considered there might be another way to live than under a microscope.

"I don't know," he admitted. "I've never talked with a tigress about the pressure they're under and the constant attention they receive."

"It'd drive me crazy."

"You're going to have to deal with it from now on, you know?"

"Because of Zoe or because they'll be watching me?"

"Both. Despite…what happened at the meeting, what I said, some tigers will still consider you available and try to court you. The entire community knows about you and Zoe by now, and the fact that you can have a baby with a tiger male is enough to make you a kind of celebrity, I guess."

"I'm not *available*," she grumbled.

He stopped breathing for just a moment, afraid to believe she was admitting what he hoped she was admitting. When she didn't say more, he said, "You called me 'Daddy' to Zoe tonight. Did you realize you did that?"

She winced. "Caught that, huh? I'm hoping she didn't notice. I'd still prefer to tell her in a calm moment when she can understand."

"But you do want her to know I'm her father?"

"Of course." She shrugged. "Okay, I wasn't sure at first, right after you came back. Not if you were just going to leave again. I didn't want her to be hurt."

"I'm not going anywhere, Rose. I'm here to stay. In whatever way you'll have me."

"And I'm starting to believe you, which is probably why I slipped up tonight. I guess my subconscious was already settled on telling her before my conscious mind acknowledged it."

"What will you…?" He paused, not sure how to phrase it. "Where will you tell her I've been? What reason will you give for not telling her about me earlier?"

She stared at his shirt, patting the flannel with one hand as if smoothing out a wrinkle that wasn't there. "I've been considering that. I think we tell her as much of the truth as she'll understand. When she's old enough, we can tell her the whole story. But I don't want to lie to her now just to make things easy. Especially after…"

She waved her hand toward the door, but he knew she meant the kidnapping.

"I want to be as honest with her as possible," she finished.

"What will you say?"

"I'll tell her you had to go away before she was born, and you came back when you realized we needed you. I'm not sure she'll understand much more than that now."

"She'll ask why I left."

"Probably. I don't know how to answer that one without fibbing."

"Would she understand if I told her I had to go off to school?"

"How is that not a lie?"

"Technically, I had to learn some lessons before I could be with you two. It's not a complete lie."

She frowned. "Semantics." She shrugged. "But probably a technicality we could get away with for the time being." She continued to stare at his chest, a crease between her brows.

He lifted her chin and made her look him in the eyes. "When she learns the full story, she'll understand. And I'll be there, Rose. I promise."

"I believe you. Because you were with me tonight."

She kissed him again, soft and full of emotions he was afraid to name.

When they pulled apart again, he cupped her cheek. "Are you hungry? Or ready to sleep? You take the bed with Zoe. I'll stretch out here."

"On the floor? That's not going to be very comfortable."

"I'll shift. Sleeping on the ground in tiger form is comfortable enough."

"What happens tomorrow? An elder tried to kill our baby. What do we do now?"

"Go back and make sure he's punished."

"We killed the one man who could actually verify Lei was responsible for all this. Will that make things more difficult?"

"The Tracker who was with us heard Jameson confess. Killing a female tiger is considered a heinous crime among my people. They'll want blood for that."

"You didn't answer my question. Will we have to prove Lei was involved? He can lie, make something up to explain his scent in the area, the reason it was his associate involved?"

He wanted to tell her Lei wouldn't be able to lie in front of other tigers because they'd smell it, but he knew that wasn't true. And so did she. Instead, he said, "Zoe might have witnessed something that will help."

"She's three. And she's in shock. She's not going to make a good witness. I don't want to put her through an interrogation anyway. She's been through enough."

"Agreed. It's possible Victor and Alexis will find something."

"But just as possible they won't."

"Elizaveta knows Lei is responsible for this. She'll make sure he's taken down."

"And in the meantime? If we bring Zoe back there, will he just try to take her again?"

"We have to go back. The elders haven't actually—" He stopped short when what he was about to say sank in. "Sonofabitch. *Sonofabitch*."

"What?" She frowned, glancing at Zoe who was still snoring quietly despite his hissed outburst.

"Zoe hasn't been formally claimed as a tiger shifter yet, which means, technically, she isn't covered by our laws. But because she's a tiger shifter, she's not covered under the 'don't kill humans' law either."

"Meaning?"

"Meaning Lei timed the kidnapping perfectly. At the moment, Zoe is in a legal no-man's-land—neither officially tiger nor human. And, technically, her kidnappers didn't even try to kill her. Lei just arranged to have her turned loose in the wild. While practically speaking that could have been a death sentence for her, he can argue she might have been fine if she went tiger and was able to hunt."

"She's a baby. How often do I have to say that? Even baby tiger cubs would have trouble surviving without their mothers. He can't possibly claim this was anything other than an attempt to kill her."

"You saw the way they argue. He can turn this from a murder attempt to a simple test—just like Jameson called it. Fuck me."

"So what are you telling me, Vlad? That he can't be punished? That no one can do anything about the fact that he kidnapped a child with the intent of leaving her in the forest to die?"

He knew she was upset when she didn't scold him for cursing while Zoe was in the room. That only made him want to curse more, but the truth was, legally, there wasn't a lot that could be done. "The kidnapping, by itself, is a crime that will require some form of punishment, but because she wasn't hurt and he's an elder, he'll get a slap on the wrist and a huge fine. Since he's extremely wealthy, he can afford the fine."

"He'll be able to remain an elder?"

"Possibly. It takes a lot to remove an elder. Short of death."

"So my daughter's future standing in the tiger community remains in the hands of someone who tried to kill her, and there's nothing that can be done about it? Are you serious?"

"I'm afraid so."

"I'm gonna kill him, then. Which one is he?"

"You can't kill him, Rose. He's protected by his position. Killing an elder is a death sentence."

"I'm not a tiger. Your people don't have any jurisdiction over me."

"They'll turn you over to human authorities."

"Will they? Do they want his body autopsied to prove murder?"

"They'll find a way around that."

"Vlad Dubrovsky, I am not letting that man get away with this. Do you understand me? I want my daughter to feel safe, and she won't so long as that man is allowed to remain in a position of power. Especially if that position gives him some say in her life. No. It's not going to happen. We find a way. You call in favors. We pay bribes. We doctor tapes. I don't care. Whatever it takes. Because if he's not taken care of any other way, I will shoot him between the eyes just like I did Jameson."

Vlad had no doubt whatsoever that she meant every word. And the part of him still seething from what had been done to Zoe was right behind her. He'd hold Lei down while Rose put that bullet into his brain.

But they couldn't simply kill an elder without bringing down a world of trouble on their heads—and that would leave Zoe vulnerable. He couldn't allow Rose or Zoe to get hurt that way.

"Give me some time to think about this. I'll figure out a way to make sure he's removed."

"In the meantime?"

"We get Zoe formally accepted into the community so

she's fully covered by our laws. We call for an immediate vote—no more debating—because we can't risk her remaining in this legal limbo. Since you're human, no one can hurt you without risking an automatic death sentence under our laws, but we also need to make sure they don't try to subject you to our mating laws."

"How do we do that?"

He sucked in a breath and took a huge leap off a cliff. "Marry me."

She stilled. Even her breathing paused for a heartbeat as she stared at him. He had to force his own breath in and out as he waited for her answer. A pang of fear moved through him—that she'd reject him, that she'd kick him out of her life forever. He had no intention of staying away from her and Zoe, even if he was only around to protect them from other tigers. But she could shatter his hopes for the future in that one moment.

And he wasn't sure he'd ever recover.

R ose's brain simply stopped working for the longest moment. Vlad had just asked her to marry him but not because he loved her. He asked as a way to protect her from his people, to ensure she wasn't sucked into their machinations.

The gesture was both incredibly sweet and heart-breaking all at once.

She'd waited a long time to hear those words from him. When they'd been together, she'd imagined him asking her in so many different, romantic ways. In those dreams, she'd always said yes immediately. Later, after he'd left them, she'd pictured him returning, begging forgiveness, and asking her to marry him. In those fantasies, she'd turn him down flat with a great deal of glee at his pain.

Now…

She loved him. She forgave him. She was about to tell Zoe he was her father. He'd said before he wanted their relationship to lead to marriage. She wanted to be with him. She *wanted* to marry him.

But she couldn't bring herself to say yes because he was asking for all the wrong reasons.

She didn't want to say no either, though, so she gripped his hand and said, "Marriage is a topic we'll have to discuss when things with Zoe are settled. I don't want you feeling pressured into it to protect me." She put her hand on his mouth when he opened it. "I'm not going to discuss it further now. When everything else settles down, when real life in all its perfectly ordinary chaos resumes, we'll come back to this conversation. But it's not something we can settle now."

He glanced away and swallowed visibly, but she couldn't read his expression. Was he hurt? Relieved? Reassured by her logic? Angry? He sucked in a deep breath and released it slowly. When he faced her again, she still couldn't tell what he was thinking.

He cupped her cheeks in his hands and said, "You've been through a lot. I understand. We'll talk about this again when you're ready. Now." He took her hands in his, rubbing them gently. "We have another complicated day ahead of us tomorrow. You need your rest."

He stood and held out his hands, helping her to her feet. She wasn't sure how to feel about his asking her to marry him or his reaction to her refusal to discuss it. For some reason, both things caused an ache in her chest that felt suspiciously like hurt feelings.

She sighed. He was right. She needed sleep. She was acting ridiculous. And no surprise, given the day she'd just been through. She climbed into bed next to Zoe without taking off her clothes. The fire had turned the chilly cabin into a warm oasis, but Rose wanted to be ready to jump into a fight if need be. She was too on edge to fully relax her guard.

Vlad gave her a kiss on the head and wished her a quiet goodnight before settling back on the rug near the fire.

"Are you going to shift?" she asked.

"I was going to wait until you fell asleep so you didn't have to watch."

"I've been watching humans turn into tigers and back for a week now. I can take it."

And she wanted to prove to herself, and to him, that they could be completely themselves with each other. She didn't want him to hide his shifts from her. If they had any hope of a future, they couldn't afford to keep secrets anymore.

She propped herself up on her elbow facing him, Zoe behind her and turned toward the opposite wall, still sleeping soundly.

He shrugged and stood, pulling his shirt off over his head. She tried not to react to the sight of him, all sexy muscles and gleaming skin, but watching him undress had never been something she could do without reacting. He was the sexiest man she'd ever known. She swallowed and tried to calm her suddenly racing pulse. It wasn't a moment when they could take advantage of the ever-present chemistry between them.

That knowledge didn't stop her from staring as he pushed off his jeans, or from imagining all the things she wanted to do to him when he wasn't wearing clothes. She bit her lip to keep from suggesting anything. They'd have to go outside to fool around and it was much too cold out there. It wouldn't be the first time they'd made love outdoors, but never in weather like this. And she just couldn't do that in the same room as her sleeping daughter.

From the look in his eyes, he wasn't unaffected by standing naked with her watching him. A glance at his now erect cock proved it. They hadn't been together since Arizona. Only a few days ago, but already it felt like they hadn't made love in ages. She clenched her blanket. What terrible timing. She should have looked away while he undressed.

She tried to tell herself to look away now. Nothing could happen and she was torturing herself, but her body didn't do what she told it to do. Her body wanted to take him to the porch, wrap her legs around his waist, and fuck him hard and fast, until all the fear of the last few hours was wiped away under raw, raging need.

She imagined her mouth on his skin, his thick cock buried deep in her body, his intoxicating scent enveloping her, his husky voice whispering wicked words into her ear… She was so close to braving the cold to be with him, she started to push the blanket down.

Finally, he took mercy on her and turned around. Except that wasn't much better because now she had an excellent view of his ass.

This wasn't going to work. She rolled over and faced her sleeping daughter. She'd just have to watch Vlad shift another time. But she would do it. If they got married, if they were going to be partners for the rest of their lives, she wanted no secrets between them.

As she closed her eyes, she realized she still held the biggest secret of all close to her heart. If she wanted full honesty, she'd have to admit how she felt about him. She'd have to take the risk and tell him she loved him.

And hope he returned the feelings.

## CHAPTER EIGHTEEN

The trip back to the elders' compound was infinitely more relaxed than the drive away had been. To give Zoe time to adjust and settle, they took their time, stopping for lunch at a fast-food restaurant, letting Zoe play in the snow at a rest stop. The drive up to the Mate Run territory had taken them a few hours. They took most of the day getting back to the compound, pulling into the parking lot at twilight.

Alexis met them at the door leading into the main building. "She's okay?"

Rose nodded. "She's still a little shaken up, but she was very strong and brave."

"The Trackers with you have reported in so I got the gist. What happened to Jameson has been deemed 'appropriate punishment under the law' so you're good on that count."

"There was ever a question?" Rose asked, a very slight

growl in her voice. This wasn't the human world where vigilante killing might be prosecuted. This was a deadly world that required brutal strength. She would have gone to war if they'd tried to hold her and Vlad accountable for what she considered justice. "Do they know what was intended?" She was vague because of Zoe, but she needed to know what the elders had heard.

"They do. The tiger who witnessed the exchange with Jameson reported everything that was said. Dev is one of the best and most experienced Trackers working. His word is above reproach."

"What does this mean for Lei?" Vlad asked.

They moved slowly down the corridors toward the guest wing as they talked. Zoe hugged Rose tight and refused to get down and walk, but Rose wasn't inclined to let her go either. She wanted to ask for different rooms as well, but she wanted Vlad's question answered first.

"That is…causing a dilemma," Alexis said.

"Because Zoe's not covered under our laws yet," Vlad said.

"You figured that out? Yes. Her position in the community is still unsettled so there's debate—"

Rose groaned loudly at that word.

Alexis flashed her a smile before continuing. "They can't decide whether to charge this as an attempt on a human or a tiger shifter female."

"What's the difference in punishment?" Rose asked.

"Attempts on tiger females carry a much more severe sentence than attempts on humans, even though success at…what was intended with either tiger or human carries the same ultimate penalty.”

Rose worked through that in her head. Since they were talking vaguely, because of Zoe, she wanted to make sure she understood. Vlad had told her killing a human was almost always a death sentence crime. So that must mean killing a tiger female was a death sentence crime as well. But attempting to kill a tiger female resulted in more severe punishment than attempting and failing to kill a human.

That didn’t make much sense to her. “Why the difference for attempts, when success carries the same punishment?”

Alexis shook her head. “Legal wrangling and complicated contingencies that aren’t really logical, but they are on the books. Basically, attempting on a tiger female is considered worse because they’re so rare and humans aren’t. If the attempt on a human isn’t successful, there’s no threat to the community—or at least very little threat compared to what would be posed by a human investigation into that ultimate result. The elders figure the punishment for completing that crime is enough to keep the community in line. Female tigers are so valuable, though, they don’t want even the attempts to look like a reasonable idea.”

“That still doesn’t make a lot of sense.”

“I know. But that’s the way the law stands.” She gave Rose a contemplative look as they turned down the corridor toward the guest rooms. “Actually, all those laws have to be reworked now. Humans like you are, in a very real way, as valuable to the community as any tiger female. Looks like more debates are in order."

"Oh, good," Rose said, her sarcasm clear.

Alexis chuckled. "I know. I'm glad I'm not an elder. I would have tossed half of them through a wall by now."

"We've gotten off track," Vlad said.

He stopped by the door to the room he'd previously occupied, but Alexis waved them on.

"We've given you different rooms," she said. "A suite this time. And for additional safety, the windows in the suite have had alarms added. The alarm is pitched to essentially disable any tiger nearby, which means it'll hurt Zoe. That's why we didn't use them before. But we thought you'd prefer her ears ringing to another…attempt."

"What will the sound do to me?" Rose asked.

"Nothing. You'll be good. So you can keep Zoe safe until backup gets there."

"Thanks," Rose said. She hugged her daughter a little closer. "I didn't want to be in the same room."

"Back to Lei," Vlad said as they continued to their new rooms.

"Outside of the argument over how to 'name' the crime, they're also debating if Lei can be charged, period. He has lots of good excuses for his scent being in Jameson's car, and plenty of 'evidence' that he didn't have anything to do with Jameson's decision or his own assistant's part in the kidnapping. He claims he's being framed." She rolled her eyes. "Everyone knows he's responsible, but proving it is… well, it's impossible. Unless Zoe saw something useful?"

Rose shook her head. "We asked. She saw Jameson and

a man with dark hair, but she never saw the second man's face. She said she smelled them both. Will that help?"

"Given the excuses Lei's come up with for his scent being there, and the fact that Zoe is so new to her shifter nature, I doubt it."

"What does Zoe being new to her shifter nature have to do with it? Her sense of smell is excellent."

"Lei will argue she doesn't have the ability to parse out scent subtleties the way a non-hybrid shifter would. And because we know so little of hybrid biology, others will agree with this excuse. Still, it might be enough for them to dig more. Maybe."

"You don't sound very hopeful."

Alexis shrugged. "Lei is smart and he set this up to protect himself from repercussions, creating enough plausible deniability to keep him safe."

"How the hell *did* he set this up in such a short period of time? Without leaving a trail?" Vlad growled. "We weren't even here a full day. He had to time it while Zoe's status was still undefined. He had to have all his people in place to work fast. How could he do all that and *still* have alibies?"

Alexis stopped at a new set of doors. She frowned as she held the door open for them to enter the suit. "We're wondering the same thing. The only possibility I can think of is that your brothers have something to do with it. We still don't know where they are. Maybe they've been working with Lei, knowing you'd eventually *have* to bring Zoe here."

Vlad stopped halfway into the room to stare at Alexis.

Then he cursed. He cursed low and colorfully. Rose winced and looked at Zoe. Her eyes were wide and her lips pressed together in what looked suspiciously like a suppressed grin. Since it was the closest she'd come to a smile in the last twenty-four hours, Rose decided not to scold Vlad for his language.

After a solid minute of cursing, Vlad went silent and stared at the floor, his hands on his hips. He took a deep breath and looked up. "I should have known. I should have expected this. My brothers turning up after we thought they'd left Phoenix? They probably did that to drive us to the elders quicker. Sonofabitch, I knew getting here was too easy."

"Vlad…" Rose wasn't sure what to say.

He ran his hands through his hair and faced her. The anguish in his expression tore at her heart.

"I'm so sorry, Rose. I should have seen this. I should have anticipated. I *know* what they're like, how they think." He shook his head. "I thought I did. When they didn't show up here after we did, I thought we were safe. I thought… It doesn't matter. I'm sorry."

"Don't. Just don't. You've done everything you could to keep her safe, to keep us safe. You aren't omnipotent or psychic."

"Guess I'm not as good a liar as I thought I was either. My brothers figured me out. Hell, my father might have known all along and told his favorite son. When I get my hands on Yuri, I'll be sure to ask."

The violence in his voice made Rose shiver with an

edge of excitement she'd be embarrassed to admit to anyone but Vlad.

"We can arrange to bring them in," Alexis said. "I'm sure the other elders would love to have an excuse to question them. But I have to tell you, Vlad, it's unlikely they'll be able to implicate Lei directly."

"Why?" Rose asked. "If they went to him with information on Zoe…"

Alexis glanced at Vlad. "If any of Vlad's brothers could directly implicate Lei in this crime, they'd be…" She trailed off as she looked at Zoe, resting her head on Rose's shoulder. "They wouldn't be walking around anymore."

Vlad's head came up. "Do we know if they are?"

"They haven't been found yet."

"Why do that?" Rose asked. "If they were working with Lei, why would he turn on them?"

"If they could directly implicate him, he wouldn't want to leave that kind of loose thread hanging, no matter what. Even if things with Zoe had gone as he'd intended, I wouldn't hold out much hope for them."

"Wouldn't *they* know that?" Rose said. "Why would they work with him, knowing he'd go after them?"

"If we get the chance to, we'll ask," Alexis said. "My guess…he worked with Petrov, Vlad's father, so the brothers might assume he held the same radical beliefs and would be supportive of their goals. They might not have realized he'd protect himself above any cause or ideology."

"My father was prepared to do anything for his cause," Vlad said. "He knew going after my sister would eventually earn him the ultimate punishment. He was a fanatic, and he indoctrinated my brothers with that same philosophy. Yuri in particular. It gives them tunnel vision. They probably thought Lei held the exact same convictions." Vlad closed his eyes for a brief moment, then looked at Alexis. "We need to find them. We need to know…"

When he didn't finish, Alexis just nodded. "I'll see it's taken care of. One way or another, we'll find them."

Rose kissed the top of Zoe's head. Though they'd tried to be vague, Zoe was hearing things Rose would have preferred she didn't. Too late now and not much she could do about it. Sadly, Zoe was going to have to know it all one day. They'd have to teach her how to protect herself against… God, against everyone.

Rose had hurt every minute of every day while Zoe went through more than a year of painful episodes. She'd prayed for the pain to go away and sworn anything else would be better. As she hugged Zoe, she was thrilled to know the pain would no longer be a part of her life but heartbroken that alleviating that pain meant Zoe had been dropped into this violent world, a world where she was in danger just for being born. It sucked.

Rose's every instinct screamed to fix it, to make things right and safe for her daughter. But the world wasn't safe and nothing was "fair." She'd just have to do the best she could. She looked at Vlad, knowing in her soul she wasn't going to be doing that on her own. He'd be there with her. No matter what happened between them personally, he was committed to protecting their daughter. Knowing this made her love him all the more.

Alexis broke into her thoughts. "I have to go, but the

elders will be voting on Zoe's status in the next hour. Lei has been removed from the vote because his current position is in question. While they might not be able to accumulate evidence to convict him of a crime, the fact that some of his employees were involved gives them the right to keep him from voting. Unfortunately, that means there's only eight of them, which leaves the possibility of a tie open. We'll have to wait and see what happens. In the meantime, relax and rest. We'll have some dinner brought up—with someone I trust. I'll be back later with an update."

She turned to leave, but Rose stopped her. "Thank you. For everything. This new world is…difficult. It's nice to know someone else in it who I can trust."

Alexis smiled. "I have your back. And hers." She grinned at Zoe. "Rest. I'll see you in a few hours."

Once the door closed behind her, Zoe finally let Rose put her down. "You want to explore the room?" Rose asked her.

She nodded, taking Rose's hand. They went through the two-bedroom suite, checking the huge en suite bathrooms, making sure everything was to Zoe's approval. She stayed well away from the windows, a move that made Rose's heart ache, but otherwise, she didn't seem nervous or scared. When Rose walked back out to the living room area, Zoe willingly stayed behind in their bedroom to go through her backpack, making sure her blanket had made the room transition.

Rose walked into Vlad's arms, hugging him tight. She didn't know what to say about his brothers, whether to hope they were alive or had been murdered by the bastard elder. Part of her didn't want the threat of their fanaticism hanging over Zoe, but without them, it didn't look like bringing Lei to justice would be possible. Both options seemed cold, though, when compared to what Vlad must be feeling. Like them or not, they were his brothers, his blood relations. She didn't have siblings of her own. She couldn't understand what it was like to lose one—even one you didn't get along with. Would he mourn them? Would he care?

"I'm not sure how to feel about my brothers right now," he said as if reading her thoughts.

She pulled back and frowned up at him. "Could you tell what I was thinking, or are we just thinking the same things?"

"Your scent is too full of complicated emotions right now for my tiger to separate them. And no, I can't exactly read your mind, even though your scent gives away your emotional state most of the time." He kissed the tip of her nose. "But it's an obvious topic. They may have set up our daughter to be kidnapped and..." He glanced to the bedroom and didn't finish the sentence. "Yet if they're alive, they could testify against Lei. If they're dead, they're no longer a threat but Lei likely goes free."

"And they're your family."

"That's... I wish I could say that matters less. I don't want it to matter. We've never been close. I've spent my life pretending around them and never letting them know the real me. The only family member I was close to was my mother. It makes my feelings for my brothers complicated."

"Will you be upset if they've been killed?" She asked quietly, not because of Zoe's excellent hearing, but because the topic seemed too somber for anything louder.

"Yes. And no." He shook his head. "I don't know. I'll know when we find out."

She cupped his cheek, failing to come up with words of comfort. So she kissed him instead.

"You kissing! Silly," Zoe said as she walked into the living room dragging her blanket.

The sound of her voice, sing-songy and happy, did Rose's heart good. Zoe had been through so much, Rose couldn't help but worry how this would affect her.

"Do you like when I kiss Vlad?" she asked her daughter.

"Ha! It's silly." She launched herself at them and hugged both their legs.

"Could have been a worse answer," Vlad commented dryly as he settled a hand on Zoe's head.

Rose chuckled. A knock on the door interrupted the moment. Vlad patted her back and went to answer. Rose pulled Zoe close.

Vlad stepped back to let Alexis in, and Rose frowned. "Is something wrong? You literally just left."

She motioned to the corridor. Rose looked around her to see a vaguely familiar man standing outside the door. It took a minute to place where she recognized him from—he was one of the elders' assistants, though she couldn't remember who he was or which elder he belonged to. Not Qiang's assistant, though. She remembered that much. Someone else's.

"What's going on?" Rose asked.

"They want to see you and Zoe. Alone."

"No," Vlad said flatly. "They don't go anywhere without me."

Alexis didn't even blink at his outburst. "Told you so," she said to the man in the corridor.

He edged to just inside the doorway, but when Vlad glared, didn't step any farther into the room. "The discussion is private, Ms. Callaghan. And you haven't…claimed Vladimir yet," he said. He glanced quickly at Zoe before pointedly looking away and keeping his gaze very obviously on Rose.

"I'm claiming him as my escort," she said. "He comes with us or Zoe and I stay here. What do they want anyway?"

"I am not at liberty to discuss such things."

Rose narrowed her eyes on the man. He shifted his gaze to the side, managing to look mildly embarrassed and annoyed at the same time.

"Fine. We'll go. But Vlad is coming with us. And I'm not going in there unarmed."

That got Alexis' attention. "They aren't going to let you bring a gun into the meeting hall, Rose. Not with just you and the elders in there."

"Will Lei be there?"

Alexis nodded.

"Then I'm not going into that room without a weapon. That's the deal. They don't think I'm fast enough to shoot them anyway. If they're so damned confident, this shouldn't bother them."

Alexis opened her mouth, then closed it. She pressed her lips together for a moment before saying, "Wait here. Give me a minute to see what I can work out."

When she stepped back into the corridor with the assistant, she closed the door behind her. As soon as they were alone again, Rose went to the room she and Zoe had been given. She pulled the handgun out of her backpack, where she'd stored it before coming back into the compound, loaded and checked it, ensuring the safety was on.

She wanted her daughter to feel safe again, and if it meant Rose had to walk around armed to the teeth to ensure the tigers stayed away from them, she'd do it.

When she returned to the living room, she said to Zoe, "Remember what Mommy and Grandpa and Granny taught you, Zoe? What do you do around guns?"

"Don't touch. Only for grownups."

"Good girl. I'm taking this with us to help keep us safe, but it's not a toy, so I don't want you grabbing at it, or messing with it in any way. Okay?"

She nodded, her expression solemn and wide-eyed again. The look of fear made Rose want to break her no-cursing rule.

Vlad said, "I'm not sure that'll help much in close confines."

"Better than nothing. Is Alexis still in the hall?"

Zoe answered. "They both there."

"You can sense them, baby?"

She nodded.

"She's on the phone," Vlad said. "A little ways up the corridor."

"Can you hear the conversation?"

"Only her side of it. She's talking to someone about your 'request' to come in armed." He paused, then smiled. "She's saying you're worried about being waylaid, and you want to protect the valuable child."

Rose scowled.

"She's saying what she needs to say to get you your way. Give her a break."

Rose let her annoyance drop. "There's no way Lei can possibly think I'd go into that room with my daughter alone, unarmed, and with no backup. Does he think I'm an idiot?"

"Likely he just thinks he's that smart and cunning, convinced he's gotten away with his crime."

"Maybe they shouldn't let me bring the weapon into the room," she said. "I might just walk in and put a bullet through his head and be done with it."

"Zoe will be there," Vlad said quietly.

Rose glanced down at her daughter, still clutching her blanket, looking scared and pale. "I'm sorry, baby, am I scaring you?"

Zoe nodded. "Don't wanna go there."

"I don't want to take you there, but I don't want to leave you alone either. You'll be safe with me and Vlad, though. I promise."

"We won't let anyone near you, Zoe," Vlad assured.

She nodded and hugged his leg. Seeing her so comfortable with him, knowing he made her feel safe, melted Rose inside. He really was an amazing father.

Would he be an equally amazing husband?

"Alexis is coming back," he said, breaking into her thoughts.

After a brief knock, the door opened. "Okay, you've got permission to come armed. They're breaking protocol, but I played up your 'vulnerability' as a human, and the fact that your daughter had just been kidnapped, so they acquiesced."

Rose pulled in a deep, fortifying breath. "Baby, you want to bring your blanket or leave it here?"

Zoe considered the yellow square in her hand for a moment, then she took it to the couch and threw it down. "Don't wanna get it hurted."

"Fair enough." Rose reached out for Zoe's hand with her free one.

Vlad took Zoe's other hand, keeping her safely bracketed between her parents. He gave Zoe's hand a reassuring squeeze and nodded at Rose over Zoe's head. Then they followed Alexis and the frowning assistant out of the suite.

CHAPTER NINETEEN

The corridors leading to the meeting hall were barren, as if the way had been cleared. When Rose asked, Alexis said, "It's actually meal time, so most people in the compound are at dinner. I suspect that's why the elders called you immediately. Most everyone else is busy." She gave Rose a small smile. "We tigers take our food very seriously."

Rose forced a smile, but her stomach was tumbling around in waves of anxiety. This was one of the few times in her life when she wasn't even a little excited by the adrenaline rush surging through her blood. She'd rather face down deadly white water or have a rope break while on a dangerous climb. In those situations, she wouldn't have her daughter with her and in danger.

When they were shown into the meeting hall through the main door, Alexis stopped just outside. "I'll stay here in case you need me. There are three Trackers here, too." She motioned toward the two side doors through which the elders and their assistants entered the hall. "And one behind each of those doors. The Trackers aren't usually on guard here, but given what's happened..." She shrugged. "Remember the room is soundproof, but just open the door and I'll be there to help."

Rose thanked her and went in, holding Zoe's hand tight.

The nine elders were already seated this time. No elaborate entrance to announce their presence. The main door closed as she, Zoe, and Vlad walked slowly to the center of the room, facing the council. There were seats set up before the dais, but Rose was in no mood to sit.

Vlad whispered in her ear and nodded to indicate which elder was Lei. He was the elder she'd been calling Seven. He was a beautiful man, almost unreal looking he was so gorgeous, but she no longer saw his stunning good looks when she faced him. All she saw was the spot on his forehead where she wanted to put a bullet.

She studied him, hunting for any signs that he regretted his actions or that he intended to threaten them more. His expression was neutral and impassive, as if nothing had happened and he'd had no part in Zoe's abduction.

Two assistants were still in the room, one standing at each of the two side doors through which only the elders and their assistants came and went. The two assistants were the only ones present beyond the elders and Rose, Zoe and Vlad. All the seating which had filled the shorter sides of the room was gone, leaving the space even more open and huge.

Rose kept her gun in one hand, resting casually

against her thigh, and held Zoe with her other hand. She stared down the elders and waited for one of them to start.

She didn't have to wait long.

Elizaveta spoke for the group. "We have voted unanimously to include Zoe in the community, with all the legal rights and responsibilities of a female tiger shifter. She will be protected by our laws, and any threat to her will be met by the full force of our displeasure and retribution." She glanced at Lei, but he didn't react outwardly to her gibe. "Additionally, because of the recent…difficulties, we have voted to award her an annuity in compensation for the trauma caused."

That startled Rose into dropping her scowl. "An annuity?"

Elizaveta smiled very slightly and her eyes glittered. "A substantial annuity. It will start at a million dollars per year and will go up to two million dollars a year when she reaches twenty-five."

Rose actually gasped. She opened her mouth but no sound came out. She closed her mouth, swallowed, and tried to force out sounds that would make sense. "Why?"

"In our community, under our laws, severe fines are often utilized to discourage illegal activities. Such a fine has been imposed for the abduction of your daughter. And rather than fold the proceeds into our own expenses, given the circumstances and the…conflict of interest that keeping the money would imply, we felt it would be best assigned to the injured party. You, of course, will be the executor of the funds until Zoe reaches maturity. And we will arrange to have the US taxes taken care of so you can enjoy the entire annuity amount."

Rose was so stunned she didn't know what to say or even how to feel. They'd basically set Zoe up for life financially. She'd never have to worry about money, ever. And because she was now officially covered under their laws, she was in significantly less danger from other tigers. Maybe. Would the fine imposed here be enough to discourage future attacks?

Given the amount, Rose had a feeling it would.

She was still trying to decide if she was happy for the compensation, or disgusted that Lei only had to pay a fine for his crime when Vlad spoke.

"What about Rose? What rules and laws will apply to her? How is she to be treated in the community?"

"Ah," Elizaveta said, leaning back in her seat. "There is our current conundrum. We are stuck at a four/four vote on whether she should be legally labeled a tiger female, a hybrid female, or a related human with no actual position in our community. Killing a human is a death sentence offense, so she would have that protection if the latter option is adopted."

Elizaveta's expression went strangely blank when she mentioned the death sentence for a human killer. Rose had enough functioning brain cells left to wonder about that, but not enough to mention it. She'd ask Vlad later. Right now, she was still in too much shock.

"However, if we adopt either of the former two options," Elizaveta continued, "she will have additional protections."

"She'll also have additional responsibilities," Elder Two said.

"Meaning?" Vlad asked.

"We will expect her to contribute," Two said.

"Contribute how, exactly?" Rose asked.

"You will be expected to mate with a tiger male and attempt to have more children. If they are females, they will be required to participate in the Mate Run when they reach maturity."

"Nila doesn't have to run," Vlad said.

Two shrugged. "Should Rose produce a human hybrid, the rules that govern Nila will govern that female. Any shifter females will be expected to take a tiger mate if they wish to benefit from the full protection of our laws."

"And if they don't?" Rose asked.

"They will be extremely vulnerable to our more desperate males," Elizaveta answered quietly, her voice softening in a way Rose hadn't heard before. "It is better if they are covered under our laws."

"Zoe will be expected to run?"

"She will."

"What happens if she refuses?"

The elders exchanged looks. "I told you this would happen," Elder Six said. "They are not *really* ours. They have no loyalty to our struggles. We should not—" He cut himself off and pressed his lips into a tight line. "But it is done," he muttered.

Next to him, Lei's expression tightened, just a little.

"Females don't refuse their responsibilities," Pavel said. "If she wishes to keep our protection, she will run."

"It won't be a problem," Vlad said. "I'll make sure she's ready for the Run."

Rose narrowed her eyes, ready to argue, but realized something in Vlad's voice sounded…off. It only took her a heartbeat to realize what was wrong.

He was lying, to the elders. She could hear it. She could tell.

She glanced back at the nine, studying their expressions. Six looked disgusted. Lei held his neutral expression. Elizaveta and Three looked approving. Pavel looked smug.

None of them seemed to realize Vlad had just blatantly misled them about ensuring Zoe would run. Rose forced her expression to remain neutral, but the realization that she'd recognized his lie when the others hadn't was startling.

And a huge relief.

She was about to speak, to play her part so the elders wouldn't recognize his deception through her reaction, when noise from behind one of the side doors drew everyone's attention.

Rose moved instinctively to put Zoe at her back and wasn't at all surprised when Vlad took up a position next to her, his body also blocking Zoe from the potential threat.

The noise went silent. Rose held her breath, though not entirely sure why.

Then the door flew open, crashing into the wall and throwing the assistant in front of it halfway across the room.

A tall blond man stood in the doorway, glaring and breathing hard.

"Yuri," Vlad said.

Rose had an instant to realize this was Vlad's youngest brother before the man stalked into the room. She clicked the safety off on her gun and put a hand on Zoe's arm to keep her close.

"I will not allow you to pollute our population," Yuri growled. "This is a travesty, an abomination, a crime against nature."

"And I won't allow you to hurt Rose or Zoe," Vlad said.

Rose was afraid to take her eyes off Yuri but took a chance and glanced at the elders and the assistant still standing, looking for help. Some of the elders had remained seated, others were standing but not making an effort to get to Yuri. The assistant held his spot, his gaze jumping back and forth between the elders and the door behind him as if he wasn't entirely sure what to do. Elizaveta took a step toward Yuri, but Two put a hand on her arm stopping her. Glares were exchanged.

Rose faced Yuri again, cursing inwardly. If she could get the damned main door open, she could let Alexis and the Trackers in—who wouldn't have heard the noise thanks to the room's soundproofing. Unfortunately, Yuri angled around to block them from getting to the main door even as he stalked closer.

"You're a traitor to your family and your people," Yuri said. "Father would have killed you with his bare hands."

"The way he murdered our mother?" Vlad said, turning with Yuri's progress while staying in front of Rose and Zoe.

"She killed herself."

"I was there. He murdered her. He was a monster."

"You're the monster." Yuri glanced at Rose and snarled. "You mated with a human and produced an abomination that will ruin us all. She must be destroyed."

"I won't allow that," Vlad said, taking a single step toward his brother.

"Then you'll die, too."

He charged them so fast Rose blinked and Vlad was no longer there. She spun, keeping Zoe behind her and a hand firmly on her daughter's arm as she circled to see where Vlad and his brother had landed. She spotted blurs of motion swirling toward the opposite wall, moving too fast for her to distinguish one brother from the other, despite their near opposite coloring.

The fight stopped suddenly with the two men facing each other in a crouch, eyes narrowed, Yuri panting and swearing, Vlad serious and focused.

Rose raised her gun toward Yuri, but the two swirled back together before she could get a shot off. Damn their speed.

Keeping Zoe behind her, she tracked them, gun raised, as she backed to the main door to let in help. Cursing and shouts from the elders echoed in the space, a fight she couldn't focus on because she didn't want to take her eyes off Vlad and Yuri. When she bumped against the door, she realized she'd have to either lower her gun or release Zoe to open the damned thing. She pushed Zoe even farther behind her back, boxing her against the wall, then reached for the knob as she stared at the blurs of Vlad and Yuri.

A whispered warning of instinct tightened in her gut just as she turned the knob.

Something big swept past her, knocking her to the floor. The door slammed shut behind her, and Zoe screamed.

"Zoe!" Rose searched the huge room.

To her horror, Lei had her daughter. He'd stopped a few yards from the damaged side door, the way now blocked by the assistant who'd been knocked out by Yuri's entrance. Lei had one arm around Zoe's body and another around her throat. One move and he could kill her. The room seemed frozen in that moment, no one daring to move or speak.

Panic broke Rose from her paralysis. She scrambled to her feet and started toward them as something heavy banged against the main door. Fear surged through her. Then a flash of movement swirled between her and Lei. Lei cursed. Rose blinked and realized his arms were empty. She scanned the room. Vlad seemed to materialize out of thin air at the far side of the hall, holding Zoe.

Rose took a shaky breath and turned toward them, keeping her gun aimed at Lei.

Two elders finally moved from behind the dais to take hold of him as he cursed and shouted at her. "She'll destroy us all. The hybrids will be our downfall! We can't allow them."

Another loud bang sounded from the main door, like a large body hitting it. Rose looked toward the noise and only realized in the chaos of the last few seconds that she'd lost track of Yuri when Vlad shouted her name.

She didn't pause to think or focus. She let her instincts

move her, the years of training taking over where her brain would have been too slow.

She stepped back and with her free hand reached across her chest to grab the hand moving toward her throat, then she pivoted and rolled his already rapidly moving body over her shoulder while keeping a grip on his wrist. The move slammed her attacker into the marble floor on his back, his head near her feet. She stepped to the side, pulled his arm up hard and twisted, dislocating his shoulder.

Then she pointed her gun at the center of his body and fired.

The gun clicked twice before she realized she'd spent her last bullet. Only then did she blink and focus on her surroundings, her brain slowly catching up to her actions.

She looked down at Yuri's prone body, his gut torn open by her tight circle of shots. Blood splattered darkly across the red rug, and when he tried to speak, it bubbled out of his mouth.

She swallowed hard and looked back at the gawking audience. To her relief, Vlad had Zoe's head tucked against his shoulder, her face safely angled away so she hadn't had to witness her mother's attack or the quick, brutal aftermath.

Vlad met her gaze, eyebrows raised.

For long moments, the only sound in the room was the wheezing gurgles of Yuri trying to breathe.

Qiang broke the stunned silence. "She will do well in our community."

Rose blinked. Elizaveta gave a brief bark of amusement.

Qiang motioned toward the meeting hall's main door and Rose spun to see Alexis and a silent line of six shifters just standing there staring at her. At Qiang's gesture, some of the tigers collected Yuri and carried him from the room while all the elders' assistants swarmed to the dais, hovering around their charges, their murmurs of concern finally filling the hall with noise again.

Alexis came up to Rose. "You okay?"

She nodded, though her limbs were shaking in reaction to the adrenaline rush.

Alexis motioned behind her to the main door. "Sorry. I had to break in. Something jammed it tight."

"Must have been Lei when he took Zoe. I was trying to let you in."

Alexis glared at the elder, now surrounded by tiger shifters. "There's supposed to be an alarm to let the security teams know there's a problem." She muttered this mostly to herself.

Rose didn't have the energy to think about that yet. She glanced at Qiang. "What happens now?"

"Now, we will see to *him*." He nodded at Lei without looking at him.

Lei was escorted from the room, his assistant following with his head bowed and his hands gripped tightly in front of him. Lei didn't even glance at her as he was taken away, but he continued to spew hateful vitriol about how hybrids would destroy their people.

Qiang continued, "We thank you for your assistance in this ugly incident."

Thanks? They were thanking her?

"A vote," Elizaveta said, her voice quieting the murmuring assistants. "Rose Callaghan's status in the community. We accept her under the new human hybrid laws. All in favor?"

One by one along the line of elders, each raised a hand in assent. Elder Six hesitated the longest before acquiescing with a slight snarl. When the vote finished, pro-hybrid Elder Three grinned smugly and nodded his approval.

"It is unanimous, then," Elizaveta said. "Rose Callaghan will be integrated into the community under hybrid laws and protected by such." She looked at Rose. "Welcome to the community." Then she rolled her eyes and looked at the other elders, motioning toward the bloody ground. "This was not the best of introductions."

Most of the elders had the grace to look embarrassed.

Rose shook her head. "What does this mean? Are we safe now?"

Elizaveta smiled just a little. "You are both completely safe now. There will be no more difficulties for you." She glanced through narrowed eyes at the other elders. No one argued her point.

"We will ensure the community knows this kind of attempt on you and your daughter will be met with vicious reprisal," Qiang added. "You may relax."

Rose actually did, then, letting her shoulders slump. She flashed a small smile at Alexis, tucked her now empty gun into the waistband of her jeans, and trotted to Vlad and Zoe, wrapping them up in a hug, her arms trembling. She buried her face against Zoe's neck and breathed her in, the terror of what might have happened bringing tears to her eyes.

"Thank you again, Ms. Callaghan," Qiang added, "for meting out the proper punishment to the criminal Yuri. The community will learn of this, too."

With that final comment, the remaining elders and their assistants filed out through the undamaged door.

Rose hugged Vlad and Zoe even tighter. Then leaned back and looked them over. "Are you hurt? Either of you?" She searched Vlad's face and body for signs of injury, rubbing a hand over Zoe's back as she hunted for sore spots. "Are you okay, baby? That man didn't hurt you, did he?"

Zoe shook her head, shifting positions so she could wrap an arm around Rose's neck while still keeping one arm around Vlad. She leaned close to Rose's face and said in a serious and intense tone, "Mommy, you a badass."

Rose choked on her surprised laugh. "Baby! Where did you even hear that word?"

"Daddy said it after you shot the bad man."

Rose glanced at Vlad, her brows raised.

He shrugged. "You are."

Zoe grinned, the seriousness falling from her expression. "Yes. You a badass, Mommy. Mommy badass!"

"Zoe," she tried to scold, but it came out more teasingly, which only made Zoe giggle and repeat "badass" a few more times.

Rose shook her head, laughing, afraid she might cry at the same time as her tension drained away. "My mother is going to make me do twelve rosaries if she finds out her granddaughter knows the word badass." She was about to say more when something else Zoe had said gave her pause. Slowly, the single word sank in and Rose realized… "Zoe, you called Vlad Daddy?"

Zoe tilted her head to one side and gave her mother a frown. "Is Daddy."

"You know that?"

"You said so."

"I did? When?"

"You said Daddy in woods."

"I didn't think you noticed…" She pulled in a breath and let it out slowly. "How do you feel about that, baby?"

Vlad went still at the question, but Rose kept her gaze on Zoe.

"'Bout what?"

"That Vlad is your daddy."

"Good. He smells like Daddy."

"He does?" Rose frowned at Vlad. "Do you understand that?"

He stared at Zoe a moment. "Have I always smelled that way to you, Zoe? Or just after you heard Mommy call me that?"

"Always, but didn't know I knew until woods. Where you been?"

He opened his mouth, closed it, and then sighed. "I had to go away and learn a few lessons before I could come back to you."

"Like college? Granny says I go to college, like Mommy did, or else I can't work for them. Was college fun?"

"Very. But I like being with you and Mommy better."

"Yay! I hungry."

Rose blinked several times at the change of subject, her already reeling brain having trouble keeping up with Zoe's train of thought. "Guess we'd better go get you food then," she said.

"I'll get you back to your suite without hassle," Alexis said.

Rose turned to face her. She was standing a few feet away, grinning.

"Vlad's right, by the way. You are a badass," she said, nodding toward the spot where Rose had taken Yuri down. "Humans can't usually defend themselves against shifter speed."

Zoe giggled when Alexis said "badass."

"Martial arts training," Rose muttered. "Years of it. Even went to Japan for a year before college."

"When things have settled down, I'd like to talk to you about a job. I've got these self-defense classes I give to the other female tigers. We could use another teacher."

"Huh?" It was the best Rose could do.

Alexis laughed. "Don't worry. We'll talk when you can focus again. In the meantime, let's get Zoe fed."

So much had happened in such a short period of time, Rose had no idea how to process it all. Rather than try, she hugged her family, then went back to their suite for dinner.

Thinking could wait.

# CHAPTER TWENTY

As soon as they entered their rooms, Zoe said, "I use the potty."

"You need any help, baby?"

"No. I big girl. I badass!" She charged into the bedroom, already pulling her pants down.

Rose shook her head. "My mother really is going to send me to confession for letting my three-year-old use 'badass' with abandon."

"You can blame me," Vlad said.

She turned to say something sarcastic, only to find herself in his arms, his mouth coming down hard on hers, his kiss full of such force and intensity, it swept her away and robbed her of thought.

He hugged her tight, almost too tight, and claimed her mouth with a fierceness that made her body and heart cry out in joy. The reality of what had just happened, of what they'd just done and survived, fed her need to feel and taste him. She ran her hands over his back and waist, down to his butt and back up his spine again, stroking and savoring.

"He didn't hurt you?" he said against her mouth, then kissed her again.

When he eased back enough for her to answer, she said, "No. You?"

"I had a heart attack when I saw him coming for you and knew I couldn't get there in time."

"You saved Zoe. That was the most important thing."

"No. Equally important. I couldn't get to both of you at the same time. I couldn't stop him."

"I'm okay." She kissed his cheeks, his chin. "We're all okay now." Then she dove back into another kiss, letting all the fear fall away for just a few moments.

Finally, he loosened his hold and reluctantly eased back. He glanced toward the bedroom. "She just flushed," he murmured. "We'd better stop or she'll learn other things your mother will send you to confession for."

Rose chuckled. She patted his chest, then cupped his face with her hands. "Thank you. For protecting her the way I would."

"She's my baby, too."

"Yes, she is." Rose scowled. "And she knows it. Little stink. I can't believe I've been worrying about how to tell her and she knew all along. Or at least suspected. Is that really possible? Can she really tell by the way you smell?"

"Family scents carry similar...tones. Flavors? It's a little hard to explain, but yes, it's entirely possible for her to tell from my scent that I'm related to her."

"Does that mean she could tell...about Yuri?"

"Hopefully that happened too fast."

He said this against her ear, so quietly she realized Zoe was on her way back into the living room. When she looked up, Zoe ambled in with one of her coloring books and a packet of crayons.

"When dinner time?"

"Soon, baby. Alexis is having something sent up."

"Room service! Love room service."

They spent the rest of the evening coloring, reading books, eating dinner, and generally just hanging out as a family. Rose savored the peace, and for the first time in a long while, she felt safe and relaxed.

* * *

Alexis knocked on the door less than five minutes after Zoe finally fell asleep.

Rose let loose a long sigh when Vlad let her in. "Don't tell me they want to see us again? Zoe just fell asleep. I'm not leaving her here alone. Besides, I thought everything was settled."

"It is. You and Zoe are part of the community and safe. The elders are done with the formal meetings for a few days anyway while that mess earlier is cleaned up." She glanced at Vlad. "Your brother survived—barely. He's lucky he was here with the medical wing on hand." To Rose, she said, "That was good shooting. We're exceptionally hard to kill, but you almost managed it."

"I should have aimed for his head," Rose grumbled. Then realized she was talking about Vlad's youngest brother. She grimaced. "I'm sorry. I shouldn't have said that."

"Don't," he said. "I was thinking the same thing."

She held his gaze, searching for clues to his feelings. She hadn't wanted to bring up the shooting in front of Zoe, so they hadn't had time to talk about it yet. She didn't think he was mad at her for it, but what he was feeling about the fact that she'd nearly killed his youngest brother had to be…difficult. But she didn't see any signs of recrimination, just a very small smile for her.

"Head would have worked," Alexis said matter-of-factly, as if there weren't more serious undercurrents to the conversation. She gestured to the couch. "We should sit down for this part."

Rose sat hesitantly, frowning as Vlad sat next to her and Alexis settled in a chair facing the couch.

"Lei killed himself not long after he went into confinement."

"What?" Vlad said. "How?"

"Arsenic. Huge dose. Would have killed two elephants. Guess he wanted to make sure."

"But…why?" Rose asked.

"Remember when I said he might not be as fanatical as Vlad's father and brothers? Well, apparently, I was wrong. He hated hybrids with the same blind passion that Vlad's father had. The Trackers are going through his records now with the help of his assistant. The assistant is talking and cooperating. He doesn't want to face a death sentence for being associated with Lei or helping him in Zoe's kidnapping. He's telling them everything. Lei has apparently been working on a plan to eliminate Nila, too."

"Fuck," Vlad muttered. "Have you told her?"

"I'll handle it, don't worry. Mitch would never let her get hurt anyway."

Vlad nodded and put an arm around Rose's shoulders, pulling her tightly to his side. She went willingly. She was glad Alexis had suggested they sit, because she wasn't entirely sure her legs would hold her up right then.

Alexis continued, "Lei started planning the kidnapping as soon as he got word from Yuri that Zoe was on her way here."

"So my brothers were working with him?" Vlad said.

"Yuri was, anyway. Lei's assistant confirms they were in contact through a few intermediaries."

"Bastards," Vlad muttered.

Rose squeezed his knee, not sure what to say.

"They'd originally planned to abandon her so they couldn't be held accountable for 'killing a human,'" Alexis said, "but when Lei found out she could shift, that pushed him over the edge. His assistant says the whole 'only a real shifter would survive' part of the plan started after the kidnapping. His assistant was actually surprised he didn't kill Zoe outright."

Rose squeezed her eyes shut for a moment as the full horror of what might have happened swamped her. She turned into Vlad's hug, knowing she'd have nightmares about this for years to come.

He rubbed a hand in comforting strokes up and down her spine while she regained her composure. "How did Yuri even get into the compound without being spotted? Even with Lei's help?" he asked Alexis quietly.

"There are still…questions about that."

"In the hall, you said something about an alarm?" Rose asked.

"Because the soundproofing on the meeting hall is so good, there are emergency buttons under the table for the elders to use if they need help. Those were disabled. Which is why I didn't know you were in serious trouble until you started to open the main door. Victor is raging about all the breaches. He's going to be ripping his security team apart after this."

"Were Anton and Andrey involved, too?" Vlad asked. "Or are they dead?"

"The twins turned themselves in," Alexis said.

"They're here? Now?"

"In confinement. They haven't actually committed a crime, not that we have evidence of, so they won't be held. They claim they came in to answer questions, and they're disavowing any knowledge of Yuri's plans."

"Did they know he was working with Lei?" Vlad asked.

"They say they didn't. Anton was surprised to learn Lei was as dedicated to the anti-hybrid cause as your father was. They were both visibly shocked to hear he'd attacked Zoe in the meeting hall."

"I'll want to talk to them later."

"That can be arranged. You might emphasize your woman shot Yuri and can kill them, too, despite being human."

"She won't have to because if they get anywhere near us, I'll rip them apart."

Alexis tilted her head in acknowledgment.

"Will Zoe's annuity continue?" Rose asked. "I assumed it came from Lei, but now that he's dead, does that still happen?"

"The elders have control of his fortune upon his death—a prerequisite to becoming an elder. Once you die, the council takes over distribution of your funds, outside of a few trusts set aside for family. So the annuity is still in effect. Elizaveta said he seemed more bothered by giving money to Zoe than by the possibility of a death sentence. Guess we know why now."

"I'm glad he's dead," Rose said. "Even if it meant Zoe lost the money. I would have happily killed him myself."

"And no one would've blamed you," Vlad said.

"By the way, Vlad," Alexis said, "any suspicion you were under because of your father? That's gone now. The Trackers won't be following you. No one is keeping track of your movements anymore. As far as the elders are concerned, you're back to being an upstanding member of the community."

He gave Alexis a tight-lipped smile. "Gee, thanks."

She laughed. "Hey, it's something, right? And it does mean you have the status and power to protect Rose and Zoe, beyond what the law can do."

"What about Zoe and the Mate Run..." Rose let that trail off. She wasn't sure at all about Zoe participating in that mating ritual.

Alexis looked away for a moment, then said, "There's

no telling whether or not it will even exist by the time Zoe reaches maturity. Don't worry about that for now."

"Something we should know about?" Vlad asked.

"Nothing certain. Nothing I can talk about because most of it I'm technically not supposed to know. But changes are in the wind."

Vlad nodded, looking thoughtful.

"What about the whole Mate Run for me?" Rose asked. "They made a lot of noise about me having to 'choose a tiger mate.' Now that they've wrapped me into the hybrid laws, do they expect me to follow the same rules as they expect from Zoe?"

Alexis glanced at Vlad, who was still deep in thought. "You won't have to worry about it. They'll hope you mate with a tiger and continue to produce tiger babies, but they finally argued themselves to the conclusion that they can't demand the same kind of community loyalty from hybrids that they do shifters, and certainly not from full humans. Elizaveta convinced them that they need to start taking a gentler approach, or the problems they already have with the young tigers are going to get exponentially worse with the introduction of reluctant hybrid and human females."

"What problems with the young tigers?"

"Long story." Alexis waved that away. "For now, just be assured, you're officially protected and safe under our laws. Zoe's annuity is guaranteed. And no one else will be coming after you."

Rose blew out a long breath. "After the last two weeks, this feels…strange. It's going to take some getting used to. We can just…go home now?"

"You can do anything you want now." Alexis stood. "Just let me know when you're ready to leave, and we'll set you up with flights back to Phoenix. Don't forget, there's a job offer waiting for you if you want it. Keep in touch. We'll talk." She glanced at her phone and smiled. "Now, if you'll excuse me, my daughter and youngest son just arrived. If I don't get to them before Victor, he'll put them to work trying to find the security breaches." She shook her head, waved goodbye, and closed the door on the way out.

Vlad was still staring at a wall, contemplating something.

Rose squeezed his knee to get his attention. "You okay?"

He pulled in a breath and looked down at her. "I'm good. I think we should run away to Alaska for a few weeks now, though. I need a vacation."

Rose laughed. She studied his face for a moment before saying, "You lied to the elders."

He narrowed his eyes in question, frowning slightly.

"About making sure Zoe would run. You lied to them. You have no intention of pushing that on her."

"Of course not. Our daughter will have choices."

"Then why did you lie?" There was no accusation in her question. She was genuinely curious. Her relief at knowing now that she'd recognize his lies probably helped her attitude.

He shrugged. "It was expedient. I didn't want to argue the point. Not yet anyway. We have years ahead of us to worry about it, and you heard Alexis, it might not even be a worry." He gave a rueful snort of a laugh. "I should have known you'd notice. I never could lie to you."

That surprised her. "You couldn't?"

He shook his head. "With you, I've always been an open book. Sometimes much to my dismay."

She chuckled, but raised a disbelieving brow when she said, "That's why I knew about the shifter thing all along?"

He made a face. "Okay, I kept a few secrets because I didn't want to scare you off. I would have told you eventually. I intended to before I let you marry me."

"Really?"

"Really. I only ever wanted honesty between us."

She smiled, and kissed him, and decided a vacation to Alaska sounded wonderful so long as she had Vlad and Zoe with her. She wrapped herself around him, as all the pent up emotions of the last few days exploded and the need to feel him, hot and naked and hers, overwhelmed everything else.

He stood with her still in his arms, a feat of strength that made her tremble, and carried her to his bedroom.

She kissed and nuzzled him, basking in his heat and the feeling of finally being safe, finally being able to relax and savor him.

He closed his bedroom door gently with a tap of his foot. Then he had her on the bed, sprawled beneath him and his hands were everywhere. They pushed and tugged at clothing until every stitch hit the floor. When she had him naked, Rose rolled him onto his back and kissed her way across his chest, down his abdomen to his erection, and took him in her mouth, needing his taste like she'd never needed anything before.

He arched up under her, his hands clenching in her hair. She sucked and licked, taking him to the very edge of his control. She loved the way he gave her so much power over his body. She loved the way he held nothing back. And she returned the favor, giving him everything she had to give.

When his muscles trembled and she was sure he wouldn't be able to take much more, she straddled him, positioned his cock and eased down, sighing as he stretched her, savoring the friction of his entrance. "I've missed this. It's only been a few days and I've missed this so much."

He reached up to cup her breasts, pinching her nipples as she started to move in a steady, even rhythm. "You're so beautiful," he murmured and then groaned when she tightened her inner muscles around him. "I'm never letting you go again, Rose. You're mine."

She was, completely and forever.

But then, she always had been.

As her pace increased, he moved one hand down and pressed his thumb against her clit, pushing her building orgasm over the edge. She strained against the pressure for a moment and then let go as everything burst apart.

By the time she settled, he'd rolled her onto her back. He nudged her knees up and hooked one arm under one of her legs, a position which tightened her entrance and started a surprising second orgasm building. She panted and clenched at his shoulders as he took control of her body and sent her reeling. He groaned her name as he pounded into her. The sound of his sexy, deep voice pushed her past any remaining restraint. This time they went together, leaping out over a chasm and flying free.

For long moments after, she couldn't manage more than holding him close and breathing in his familiar scent, savoring the peace.

He levered up onto one elbow and smiled down at her, the expression making her heart thump faster.

"So. Alaska, then?" he asked.

She laughed. "Absolutely. Though, my parents are going to want to see us before we go."

"Good. I need to ask your father a question."

"What?"

"I want to formally ask him for your hand."

"What?" she repeated, not sure she'd heard him correctly.

"That's what humans do, right? Suitors ask their prospective fathers-in-law for permission to ask for his daughter's hand?"

"Maybe some people do that. It's certainly not a requirement." She cupped his face. "Why are you looking for my parents' approval?"

"Because I know you're hesitant, and you don't believe I want to marry you because I love you. You think I'm just trying to keep you safe. But I've wanted to marry you since practically the first moment we met. I was planning on proposing long before Zoe entered our world. And now that you're back in my life, I don't intend to let you go. I know I might have to do some convincing, and we've got time. I'm not in a hurry. I just need you to know I'm serious about marrying you. I always have been."

She swallowed hard. "Did you just say you love me?"

"Rose, of course I love you. I never stopped."

"You haven't said it since you came back."

"I didn't think you'd believe me. I didn't think you were ready."

"I wouldn't have. And I wasn't."

He shifted positions so he was beside her, but pulled her close so they faced each other. "Now?"

"I love you, too. I never stopped."

His dark eyes sparkled and a very slight smile lifted his lips. "Does that mean you'll marry me?"

"Yes, Vlad. Yes."

His half smile broke into a full grin and he kissed her, tangling his hands in her hair and his leg over hers to tuck her tight against his body. She melted into him, taking all his heat and love, amazed and content to finally be with the man…the tiger of her dreams.

V lad settled into the simple metal folding seat across from his brother Anton's holding cell. The tiger-proof bars and thick plastic let them see each other and talk, but kept Anton securely confined. Vlad had checked. Both twins were being released in a few hours. They'd answered everyone's questions, been very cooperative and on their best behavior. The remaining hours in holding were strictly for paperwork.

But it gave Vlad a chance to face Anton without Andrey there to listen.

"Your daughter okay?" Anton asked. He sat on the small room's single cot, his back against the wall opposite Vlad.

"You coming after her? If you try, I won't hesitate to kill you. You heard what Rose did to Yuri? She's no typical human."

"I've no interest in killing your daughter or your mate, Vlad." He frowned. "But Andrey…"

"Tell him what I've told you. The fact that you're my brothers won't stop me."

"You still claiming us as family?"

"No."

He shrugged. "Yuri and Andrey have disowned you, too."

"You haven't?"

Anton stared at him for a silent moment before saying, "Our father really did kill Mother, didn't he?"

"He did. Why do you suddenly believe me?"

"Things Yuri said. He's as vicious as father was."

"If he gets out of confinement, you let him know I'll finish the job Rose started."

"I will. But I doubt he'll get out."

Vlad tended to agree. The elders didn't take well to having their inner sanctum violated—even if one of their own had helped Yuri break in. "Why are you here, Anton? Why did you turn yourself in?"

"Because of Zoe."

Vlad frowned at his brother. That made no sense. Anton's scent gave him very little to go on either, though there wasn't even a hint of deception in it.

Anton leaned forward, resting his elbows on his knees, his face suddenly full of something like excitement. "It's really possible? We can have children with the right human. And they'd be shifters. You did it. There have to be more women out there… It's really possible."

"I thought you believed it was disgusting and abhorrent. You don't even like human women."

"Not true." He leaned back and some of the excitement left his face. "Not entirely true. I want children. Thanks to father, no tigress will have me."

"You might find one who hates hybrids, too."

"That's not what I mean. He killed humans. He died in disgrace and left us all…tainted. We're no better than the Chernikov brothers now."

"Nikolai just got a tiger mate. Mikhail is going to marry our sister. That taint isn't as bad as you think."

"It's enough. We've little hope of a tigress."

Vlad relaxed into his seat. "The odds were always against us, Anton. A matter of numbers."

Anton waved that away, then ran a hand through his hair. "Doesn't matter. There are other options now. You going to marry Rose?"

He nodded. "Big Catholic wedding. Should be…interesting."

Anton smiled a little at that.

"Andrey will object to his twin looking for a human wife. You prepared to go against your twin, just for the possibility of having kids?"

Anton met his gaze squarely when he said, "Yes."

"Fair enough." He stood to leave.

Anton rose and raised a hand to stop him. "Before you go…" He looked around. There were cameras all over the holding area. This conversation was being recorded and watched, and they both knew it. Anton came close and pressed a hand to the plastic between the bars, then lowered his voice. "Vlad, be very careful around Kamal."

Vlad frowned. Kamal Ghosh was the one elder besides Elizaveta who was openly pro-hybrid and currently supported all Elizaveta's efforts to integrate them. He'd smiled when Rose was voted into the community. Kamal was the one elder besides Elizaveta Vlad didn't think he had to worry about. "Why?"

"Can't say." He glanced up toward an obvious camera. "Just, be careful."

Vlad nodded. "Thanks for the warning."

As he stared at Anton, he realized he was saying goodbye to his old family. He had a new one, a healthy one to replace it, with two people he loved more than life itself. And he intended to do everything in his not inconsiderable power to ensure his new family remained safe. Part of that meant giving up any hope of a relationship with his brothers.

But he'd always known it would come to this.

He put his hand against the thick plastic opposite Anton's. "Take care of yourself."

"You, too. Good luck."

Vlad left, knowing he wasn't likely to see any of his brothers again. A very small part of him mourned the loss. The rest of him rejoiced in the freedom.

As he left the confinement cells, he turned his full attention to the woman and little girl waiting for him upstairs, and the plans for his upcoming wedding.

Thank you very much for reading To Tempt A Tiger. I hope you enjoyed Rose, Vlad and Zoe's story. I'm sorry I had to put a three-year-old in jeopardy. That part was really really hard to write!

The Tiger Shifters world is getting more complicated, and I hope you're enjoying the journey. For an excerpt from Down Will Come Tiger, Tiger Shifters 6, please turn the page.

## CHAPTER ONE

The ambulance had driven away from the estate two hours ago. Joseph Bennett watched from his perch in a tree outside the massive security walls as the vehicle left silently. He hadn't been close enough to catch a scent, so he wasn't sure which of the estate's occupants had been inside, if any. Given the size of the staff in the mansion, it could have been anyone.

Now, hours later, he continued to study the distant lights of the main house, wondering.

He pulled in a deep breath, taking in the night scents, the green taste of the coming spring mixing with the cold remains of winter, manicured grass and damp soil, the distant chlorine tang from the estate's swimming pool, the even more distant fresh water bite of the river. He released his breath slowly, carefully.

He wasn't sure whether to hope Bradley Williams was still inside or not.

Rather than decide, he watched the estate and waited for a sign of the human man he wanted to kill more than he wanted anything else in the world.

He had tonight, tomorrow night, maybe the night after before Victor Romanov, his former boss and best friend, tracked him down and forced him away from Bradley. Again.

He was tempted, not for the first time, to kill Victor and get him out of the way. He wasn't sure why he never went through with it. Maybe the fact that Victor's wife Alexis might get to him before he could get to Bradley?

It was as good an explanation as any.

As he contemplated a way to get through the various security alarms and close to the house, a movement across the huge expanse of lawn caught his attention. The Williams didn't keep deer on their property and that figure was too large to be a dog. He scented the air, then lifted his eyebrows.

Paige Williams. Oldest daughter of Carmen Williams. Stepdaughter to Duke Williams. Half sister to Bradley Williams.

Years of stalking Bradley meant Joseph was well acquainted with who she was, at least in general. She was a weak human, always deferring to her father, avoiding eye contact in public, staying away from attention or notice. He'd seen the video of her attending her brother's trial for attempted kidnapping ten years ago—Joseph had been in confinement at the time or he'd have gone to the court-

house in person to murder the man. Paige had looked…
bland and timid.

Since then, he'd barely caught glimpses of her, as when
she did leave the estate it was usually in a limo with black
windows, going to her father's Philadelphia office where
she ran a charitable something-or-other. He'd never cared
enough to find out the details. He knew, in all the times
he'd sat in this very tree, watching this estate, he'd never
seen Paige Williams take a walk through the grounds.
Especially not at three in the morning.

Even from this distance, he could see she had her arms
wrapped tightly around her body, her head down. A dark
hat covered her pale blond hair. Her clothes were loose and
dark, too, not really hinting at a figure, and she wasn't
wearing a coat, though it was March and still too cold for a
human to be out without one.

Interesting.

She was heading right for him, and the small pedestrian
gate in the wall not far from his tree perch. He watched her
approach, her scent carried to him on the wind. His eyes
narrowed.

Paige Williams tightened her arms around her stomach,
hugging herself against the cold she didn't really feel. Her
body was numb even as her brain exploded with so much
chaos she couldn't think.

She reached the pedestrian gate in the northern part of
the wall near the main road without realizing she'd walked

that far. Keying in the alarm code, she pushed open the steel door and stepped out onto the grassy shoulder lining the road, making sure the door closed behind her out of habit more than conscious thought. Once beyond the walls of her prison, she just stood there, staring into the dark.

What now? What did she think this would do for her?

Pulling in a deep gulp of cold air, she let the night scents and sounds wash through her as she closed her eyes and tried with everything she had not to think.

She frowned when a slight shiver moved down her spine, an awareness of…something. Not like the feeling she got when she knew her brother was watching her, smirking at her, or when her stepfather was around. At those times, the hair on her nape rose and her shoulders hunched under the ever-looming sense of threat and judgment from the men in her life.

This was different. She didn't actually have any emotional response to the sensation, just a vague sort of awareness of… She didn't know how to explain it, though this wasn't the first time she'd felt it. If not for having experienced the sensation before, she might have wondered if it was her mother's ghost.

Did ghosts come back to haunt you only hours after dying?

She snorted at the idea. She couldn't imagine her mother pulling together the psychic strength to haunt anyone anyway.

Glancing around the quiet road, Paige wondered if maybe after all these years she really was going crazy, if the stress of her life, of hiding in plain sight from her family, had finally broken her. Shouldn't she feel some-thing about the death of her mother? Shouldn't she hurt?

Should relief really be the only sensation coursing through her blood?

She growled at nothing and started to walk. She'd only gone a few hundred yards before she turned back. She reached the pedestrian gate, put her hand to the alarm panel, cursed, and stalked away again. She didn't want to go back inside. She didn't want to be in that house, that prison, where her mother had died and her stepfather greeted the news with a raised brow and a snort of disgust. Where her half brother barely paused to hear the news before shrugging and continuing on to his wing of the house.

Paige had spent years, *years*, inside that mansion, playing a part, keeping everything she felt, everything she *knew* buried deep in her heart where no one could see. For her mother's sake.

Because despite everything, Carmen Williams had loved her children. Bradley didn't deserve it, but then their mother didn't really know the truth about the creature she'd given birth to, and given everything else Carmen had gone through in her sad life, Paige was grateful for that. She'd actively worked to keep her own knowledge of Bradley away from their mother.

It was one of the very few kindnesses she'd been able to give Carmen.

Now her mother was dead.

Paige stopped where the estate wall veered away from

the road and stared into the darkness. Her mother was gone. There was no longer a reason to hide.

She'd squirrelled away resources and money, things neither her brother nor stepfather knew about. She could just…go. Now. Leave everything behind and go.

The relief at that thought almost dropped her to her knees. She actually had to lean against a tree skirting the road to keep from falling. No more judgmental stepfather, no more psychotic brother. No more pretending to be as weak and malleable as her mother.

Enough. Done.

Her heart pounded hard as the chaos churning through her mind quieted and the clarity of a possible future descended. A vision of hope she hadn't dared consider, even as she'd planned for it.

She was so caught up in the thought of just…going, she didn't recognize when that awareness of something she could never pinpoint got stronger. But her instincts had been honed on the stone wheel of years of living as potential prey to the predatory men in her life. So she was already turning, preparing to scream and fight and run, when she heard the very slight sound of shoes shuffling over grass.

The scream building in her throat caught at the sight of the stranger. His features were impossible to discern in the darkness, though she had excellent night vision, but his face seemed full of shadows and sharp edges. He was considerably taller and wider than her. His hand were at his sides, loose and weaponless. He wore a black hoodie and jeans, dark enough that he blended with the background, and somewhat to her surprise, she lost sight of him once or twice even though he didn't move.

It was his stillness that really struck her. He didn't even seem to be breathing.

She swallowed to wet a dry throat and considered questioning him, but she was afraid to end the standoff, afraid if she said anything at all, it would break him out of his stillness. She was almost positive that once this man went into motion, there would be no stopping him.

And because she'd lived in the same house with a killer for most of her life, she recognized another one when she saw him.

He spoke, shattering the tense silence. "It's late. You shouldn't be out here alone."

His voice was husky and deep, rough like he didn't use it much, and completely emotionless. He might as well have asked what time it was or noted that the grass was green. She couldn't tell if he'd intended his comment to be a warning or a threat. Or simply a statement like the sky is blue.

She pulled herself up to her full height—which wasn't very impressive—and tried to put on the privileged, icy aura she adopted when all else failed. She infused prim frost into her tone, something her stepfather had forced her to learn, when she said, "And you would be?"

He tilted his head to one side as he considered her. "Roses," he murmured.

He said it so quietly she suspected she wasn't supposed to hear his comment. Or maybe he just didn't realize he'd spoken aloud.

"Are you going to answer my question or should I call the police?" she asked, still in that same clipped tone.

"You don't have a phone with you."

She blinked. He couldn't possibly know that. She had left her cell behind on purpose, but she was wearing loose clothing with pockets. She could easily have it.

To make her point, she reached into her pocket, pretending to grip a phone that wasn't there. "I will call the cops, whoever you are. I suggest you leave."

"Who was in the ambulance?"

Again, surprise made her blink. "You've been watching my home? Are you a paparazzi? I assure you, there's no story here."

His shoulders moved, just a little, not a threat but…a gesture she couldn't interpret.

"Who was in the ambulance?" he asked again.

She pursed her lips. He didn't have an obvious camera on him so he wasn't likely someone out for gossip. He felt too dangerous, too intense, for a paparazzo anyway. And there was that stillness, that emotionlessness in his voice.

For some reason, the mere fact that he didn't seem to care about this conversation much one way or the other made her feel better. She shrugged and answered honestly. "My mother."

"She's sick?"

"Dead."

His head moved just slightly, maybe a nod of acknowledgement at the news. She waited for him to offer the expected condolences. But the silence stretched on. He didn't say or do anything beyond that almost nod.

She held his intense stare, easier because she couldn't actually see his eyes, just the shadowed area where his eyes were on his face.

"Are you sad?" he finally asked.

"Of course," she snapped. "What a stupid question." She realized she'd dropped her guard and instantly put the wall back up.

But for the first time since confronting him, she saw something almost like an expression move across his face —one corner of his mouth lifted fractionally. It might have been a smile, though it could also just as easily have been a facial tic since in the next moment his mouth was flat and emotionless again.

"Is your father going to come looking for you?"

"Stepfather," she corrected almost without thought, a knee-jerk reaction to distance herself from the man who'd raised her. "And no." She paused. "At least, not yet."

"Are you going somewhere?"

There was the question. Was she? Tonight? She wanted to. More than she'd ever wanted anything in her life. But… "No." She needed her wallet first. "At least, not yet," she finished with a little smile.

The stranger's expression didn't change. "Where are you going?"

"None of your business."

"Will he come after you?"

She sucked in a breath, then tried to cover her reaction. "Who?"

"Your stepfather."

She didn't answer. She honestly wasn't sure if he would or not.

*If you report his beloved son, if you try to have Bradley arrested, he will come after you.* The voice sounded a little like her mother's, mixing with her own. And it was right. Her stepfather would come after her for turning Bradley in, maybe not to kill her but definitely to stop her. He'd have her discredited, perhaps even committed—just like he'd threatened her mother with through the years.

That was her best prospect. If her half brother got to her first, he'd kill her. And not in a quick, painless way she was sure.

She swallowed down the panic making her heart beat painfully hard and blinked a few times to clear away the darkness edging her vision.

She could just run away and not do the other thing she'd promised herself she'd do once her mother was gone —not go to the cops with what she knew, not give them the limited evidence she had. She could disappear and both her brother and stepfather would probably leave her alone, happy to be rid of her.

She'd be free for the first time in her life.

But could she live with herself if she ignored what she knew about Bradley?

She shook off the question. None of it was this stranger's business. "Why do you care what I do?"

"I don't."

She believed him. "What are you doing here?"

He'd been here for hours if he'd seen the ambulance leave. And he wasn't out for scandalous pictures. For the first time, it occurred to her that she might be facing something as scary as her brother. Oh, she'd known from the first he was dangerous, but she hadn't felt threatened, despite his frightening aura. She was just realizing that maybe she'd been mistaken in that idea.

Her stepfather had drilled into her the idea that she shouldn't go about alone; she was worth a fortune to anyone who wanted to kidnap her. Though she personally doubted her stepfather would bother paying a ransom for her, potential kidnappers didn't know that. Could this terrifyingly intense, emotionless man be here looking for a ready victim? Staking out the house, waiting for a chance to grab her and try to make some money?

It didn't seem logical given that she never came out in the middle of the night, and Gladwyne was an extremely safe area. But according to her stepfather, it was possible.

"Is your brother inside?" the man asked, not answering her question.

"Why? Do you know him?"

"He murdered my sister ten years ago."

Paige stopped breathing. For several long heartbeats, she simply couldn't pull in any air. He'd said it so bluntly, so matter-of-factly. So…emotionlessly.

And with absolutely no doubt whatsoever.

Still, she had to ask, "You're sure?" Her voice was faint even to her own ears and she realized she hadn't taken a full breath yet. She gulped a few times, trying to get enough oxygen to keep from passing out.

"Yes," he said.

She nodded. She believed him. She was positive her

brother had murdered many people over the years. Ten years ago… This man's sister must have been one of the first. At least, one of the first human victims. There'd been any number of poor defenseless animals before that.

She closed her eyes for a single beat, knowing it was a stupid thing to do around this man but not caring. He'd lost a sister to her psychotic brother. And she'd kept her knowledge of Bradley's crimes to herself all this time. Guilt rose over her and crashed onto her shoulders more powerful than any emotion she felt from losing her mother. She was still conflicted about that. But the guilt…oh, she felt the guilt.

"I'm so sorry," she said, then opened her eyes and looked right at him. "I'm very, very sorry."

"You know he's a killer?"

She nodded.

"Have you helped him?"

"No. At least…" She swallowed. Would he consider the fact that she'd never been strong enough to stop Bradley helping? "No, I never helped him."

"But you know."

"I know."

"Does your father?"

"Stepfather. Maybe. If he does, I'm not sure he cares."

The man was silent for long enough that Paige wanted to fidget. She didn't. She stood perfectly still, her hands clasped in front of her so she wouldn't play with her bracelet, her eyes slightly downcast. She hated this pose— the one she'd been forced into all her life—but it seemed necessary in that moment, a survival instinct she didn't dare ignore.

"I'm here to kill your brother," the man finally said. Just as emotionlessly as he'd said everything else.

The news didn't surprise her. What surprised her was that he'd waited ten years. "Where have you been?"

He actually frowned at her question, more reaction than she expected. "What do you mean?"

"You said your sister was murdered ten years ago. Why haven't you tried to kill Bradley before?"

"I have. My people keep stopping me."

"Your people?" What an odd way to phrase that. Before she even had time to ponder what he might mean, he answered her question.

"The tiger shifters."

**Look for Down Will Come Tiger**
**Book 6 in the Tiger Shifters Series**
**Out Now!**

ACKNOWLEDGMENTS

First and foremost, a huge thank you to all the readers who are traveling with me on this journey with the Tiger Shifters. I am beyond grateful to you for your support.

Thanks to the wonderful editors and betas I worked with on this book: to Jena at Practical Proofing for her always sharp observations, and Becky and the crew at Hot Tree Editing for their keen attention to detail and fantastic enthusiasm. Thanks all!

To the wonderful people on Facebook and from my newsletter who helped me pick a title for this book: Thank you! I would have had a terrible time trying to choose without you.

Special thanks to the fantastic woman who looks after my youngest for a few hours a week so I can get some work done. Estefania, you're a star! Thank you.

Thanks to all my mommy friends who bring me out of my fictional worlds to think about something else. And thanks to all my writer friends, who take me out of my mommy brain so I can think about storytelling.

And as always, I must thank my family. I love you guys! Thanks for the balance, for the fun, and for the super support.

# BOOKS BY KAT SIMONS

**TIGER SHIFTERS SERIES**

1 - Once Upon a Tiger

2 - Along Came a Tiger

3 - Here There Be Tigers

4 - Her Tiger To Take

5 - To Tempt a Tiger

6 - Down Will Come Tiger

7 - To Catch a Tiger

8 - What a Tiger Wants

9 - Taming Her Tiger

Tiger Shifters Series Vol 1 (Books 1 - 3)

Tiger Shifters Series Vol 2 (Books 4 - 6)

# ABOUT THE AUTHOR

Kat Simons earned her Ph.D in animal behavior, working with animals as diverse as dolphins and deer. She brought her experience and knowledge of biology to her paranormal romance fiction, where she delights in taking nature and turning it on its ear. After traveling the world, she now lives in New York City with her family. Kat is a stay-at-home mom and a full time writer.

For more on Kat and her future books:

Website: http://www.katsimons.com
Newsletter: http://eepurl.com/OxQQL